BATTLEFIELD OF LOVE

SOLDIERS AND THE ONES WHO LOVE THEM

Edited by Ron Hogan

Other books in this collection:

When Love Goes Bad
Falling In Love…Again
Forbidden Love
Losing It For Love
When Love Sizzles
Love In Strange Places
Bedroom Roulette
Women Undone
Mothers In Love

Second Acts Series– by Julia Dumont
Sleeping with Dogs and Other Lovers
Starstruck Romance and Other Hollywood Tails
Hearts Unleashed

Infinity Diaries – by Devin Morgan
Aris Returns, A Vampire Love Story
Aris Rising, The Court Of Vampires

Age of Eve: Return of the Nephilim – by D.M. Pratt

BATTLEFIELD OF LOVE

SOLDIERS AND THE ONES WHO LOVE THEM

By Anonymous*

*The stories presented here were first published as "true stories"... at a time when it was necessary to hide the true identities of the women associated with these tales to avoid scandal. We have chosen to maintain the veil of the authors' anonymity to protect the innocent... and the not so innocent.

The timeless love stories from
True Romance and True Love live on.

Edited by Ron Hogan

A BROADLIT BOOK

BroadLit

May 2013

Published by

BroadLit ®
14011 Ventura Blvd.
Suite 206 E
Sherman Oaks, CA 91423

Copyright © 1945, 1954, 1969, 1972, 1998, 2004, 2009, 2013
BroadLit, Inc.

ISBN 978-0-9890200-1-5

Produced in the United States of America.

Visit us online at www.TruLOVEstories.com

This collection is dedicated to all of you who are looking for true love or have already found it.

TABLE OF CONTENTS

INTRODUCTION by Ron Hogan 9

SERGEANT RYAN'S HOMECOMING
In the Arms of a U.S. Marine 11

SOLDIER'S LUCK 37

DISGRACED! I HAD TO RUN AWAY 59

I WENT ON A SINGLES WEEKEND
WHILE MY HUSBAND WAS IN VIETNAM 81

AM I A WIFE—OR A WIDOW? 101

DAUGHTER OF AN AIR FORCE MAN 117

MY SON WENT FROM MARINE—
TO BEAUTY QUEEN! 151

DEAREST SOLDIER The Story of a Gallant Wife 177

SERGEANT'S BRIDE 195

DAD, I'M A DRAFT DODGER 213

FAR FROM HOME: A Story of Love, War, and Recovery 233

INTRODUCTION

I enjoy all the *True Love* and *True Romance* anthologies I get to edit, but this one holds just a little more personal significance for me—because I'm the product of a military romance.

Both of my parents joined the U.S. Marine Corps in the late 1960s. My mother saw it as an opportunity to pay for her college education, while my father was a rebellious young man who was offered enlistment as an opportunity to straighten up—and found Marine discipline suited him perfectly. They met in a bar on base; before too long, they got married, and I was born just after my dad's 23rd birthday, a month before my mom turned 21. (Although, as I would hear the joke growing up later, her commanding officers had told her that if the Marines thought she needed a baby, they would've issued her one during basic training.)

I grew up in and around military bases for nearly the first decade of my life, along with my little brother, until my folks' divorce—and even after that, we'd spend our share of summers visiting our dad at various bases from California to New England. I've never felt like I was cut out for the Marines personally, but I was instilled with a healthy respect for the Corps... and, what the heck, for the other branches of the armed forces, too.

When I was editing *Bedroom Roulette*, an anthology centered on the early 1970s, I found a number of stories that dealt with soldiers coming home from Vietnam and the problems they and their wives faced readjusting to married life. I got to thinking about the decades of *True Love* and *True Romance* stories that we have archived, and I became curious about how the generations before and after Vietnam dealt with the disruptions of war and how they welcomed home their returning soldiers. We have stories that range from the last days of World War II to the most recent fighting in Iraq, offering a variety of perspectives—mostly from the women's point of view, but with a few men's voices making themselves heard as well.

I also found several stories that don't deal directly with combat or homecoming, but which reflect the military's deep influence in American life—from the generational split over the Vietnam war to a young girl grappling with her father's death on an Air Force mission in the first Gulf War. And then there's the Marine who found a very different type of uniform to wear once he got out of the service...

As always, I'm sure pulp romance fans will find this collection entertaining, but it's also a small reminder of how much we invest, emotionally and culturally, in the men and women who serve the United States in uniform—and how important it is for us to champion them when they return from the front the way we do when they set out to fight.

—Ron Hogan
February 2013

SERGEANT RYAN'S HOMECOMING
In the Arms Of a U.S. Marine

It isn't hard to guess where True Love came down in the debate over the war in Iraq and Afghanistan. The "Washington liberals" that Madison, the heroine of this story, meets are ridiculously overblown, like parodies of '60s hippies but with better fashion sense, and her own mother isn't much better. (A word of advice: When you learn that somebody has been visiting a military hospital that specializes in combat injuries, "I hope you haven't taken up with that Marine again" isn't your best conversation opener.)

Fortunately, they're just a sideshow to the real drama, which requires Madison to break out of her self-absorbed careerist bubble and pay proper attention to her boyfriend, Sgt. Connor Patrick Ryan (USMC), who's just come back from the front with serious injuries. She screws up pretty badly at first, and almost loses him to another woman, but she manages to get her head in the game just in time—leading to an explicit clinch that would probably have made previous generations of True Love readers blush.

Need. I never wanted to need or be needed. I am an independent, twenty-six-year-old, New York City-based single woman. Like Carrie in *Sex in the City*, I look after me, myself, and I. It's just the way I like it and the way it has to be.

All that changed when the phone rang in the middle of the night last May. I rolled over and reached for the receiver. There was always the possibility of a story brewing and I would throw on my clothes and run out into the city night to get the scoop.

"Madison? Madison."

I shook my head, trying to rattle away the sleepiness. The voice sounded familiar, however I couldn't place it.

"It's Gomez."

Gomez. I searched my brain index of informants, trying to remember someone named Gomez. Nothing surfaced. I sat up and rubbed my eyes. Gomez continued to talk at me. "Ryan's a casualty. RPG fire. The mother blew right through his leg."

I jumped out of bed. Now I knew who Gomez was. A Marine. A soldier in Ryan's squad.

Sergeant Connor Ryan of the U.S. Marines was either hurt or dead in Iraq.

I hate the word "casualty." It's so brutally ambiguous.

"Oh, my God. Is he dead?" I clutched my heart with my hand, trying to reach through my U.S.M.C. bulldog T-shirt to relieve the sharp pain that had suddenly settled in my chest.

"No, he's alive. Just banged up. They're trying to save the leg. Flew him in from Iraq via Germany last night."

The reporter in me kicked into automatic pilot. "Who're they. Where is he? When can I see him? Why did this happen?"

"He's at Walter Reed in Washington, D.C. They're operating on him. . . ." Bewildered, Gomez's voice trailed off as he tried to answer me.

Balancing the phone under my chin, I reached into my dresser drawers, pulling out jeans, T-shirts, and underwear and quickly throwing them into my backpack. Then I ran to the bathroom, found my toothbrush, lipstick, and a comb. Then I was ready to go.

"I'll be there in a few hours."

"Madison, he'll be pretty groggy when he wakes up. Why don't you wait a few days till he's more alert?"

"No, no—I have to be there."

I hung up the phone, grabbed my suede jacket, and glanced at the clock as I ran out the door. It was two o'clock in the morning. I would reach Washington by sunrise.

Tentatively, I stood in the doorway. The room smelled like bleach. Machines beeped and purred around Ryan's prone body. His plaster-wrapped leg was suspended above him; black-and-blue toes poked out from the end of the cast. The nurse at the desk had told me that the surgeons were able to save the leg. Nobody knew if he would walk again.

My heart thumped wildly as I stepped closer to the bed. Ryan's hazel eyes fluttered open; their cat's-eye color, usually so brilliant and penetrating, looked pale and washed-out, like a kid's watercolor set after too many uses. I clasped my hands in front of me and rocked nervously on my heels.

"Hi," he whispered huskily through dry, cracked lips.

"Hi. How are you?"

He reached for my hand, "Locked, loaded, and ready to go." He squeezed my knuckles as I forced a smile.

I sank into the metal chair next to his bed and searched his battered face, trying to identify the man I knew amongst the cuts and bruises. His right eye was swollen shut from a blow to the head. A long row of neatly spaced stitches held the brow together.

My heart sank. Where were the dimples that made me melt? The strong lantern jaw and square, white, devilish smile?

A nurse strode purposefully into the room. "Hello, Sergeant Ryan. Looks like you're back with the living."

Ryan tried to lift the corners of his mouth in a weak smile, but the effort was too much for him. My stomach rolled as I fidgeted with his fingers in my clammy hand. He wore a *SpongeBob SquarePants* band-aid on his right thumb. Finally—something I recognized.

The nurse adjusted the traction, checked the monitors, and reached for a Styrofoam cup filled with ice chips. "I bet you want something to drink. Your friend here can help." She passed me the cup.

I furrowed my brow and stared at it.

She checked his blood pressure, wrapping the cuff around his barbed wire tattoo. "You can feed him," she said, her voice laced with authority.

I stood and put the cup next to his lips, gently placing my other hand behind his head. The ice avalanched down his chin and piled around his ear. Ryan sputtered an obscenity. "Haven't you ever cared for anyone? One piece at a time."

Nurse Ratched grabbed the cup from my hand, staring at me like I was the village idiot, and demonstrated the technique. I followed her lead when she shoved the cup back into my hands.

Just to set the record strait: No, I have never cared for anyone. Except for that time when my friend, Josh, got six stitches in his forehead after a particularly rowdy party during our freshman year of college. I took him to the emergency room, held his hand while they sewed him up, and put him to bed when we got tack to the dorm. By the following afternoon, he was fine. So, needless to say, considering my lack of experience with sick people, I didn't have the foggiest notion about how to help Ryan, and the whole situation was making me pretty darn uncomfortable.

Nurse Ratched shook her head at me and strode out of the room. I stuck my tongue out at her retreating back before returning my attention to Ryan.

There had to be a part of him that I could recognize. I laced my fingers between his and studied the bruises on his arm. The tan skin, muscular curves, and sun-bleached hairs made me think of the cocky, swaggering Texan I knew back in Iraq. "Madison."

I leaned over the bed. "Connor, don't talk." I put my index finger over his split lips.

"Madison. Listen to me." His voice was breathless, urgent.

"Connor, please--don't talk. Save your strength."

"I need you."

My head jerked back and I dropped his hand. Those three little words skyrocketed my sense of unease one hundred percent. I glanced around the sterile, white room and felt a headache coming on because of that awful, antiseptic smell.

I grabbed his forearm, my fingers digging into his flesh. "You'll be fine, Connor. In no time at all, you'll be walking out of this hospital like nothing ever happened."

He grimaced as his eyes fluttered shut. I realized then that the nurse must've given him something for the excruciating pain.

I waited a few minutes to ensure he was asleep before standing. I glanced at my watch: seven-thirty. If I put it into high gear, I figured I could get an eight-twenty train back to New York and be at my desk by eleven.

Did I ever hightail it out of there. I screamed at my cabdriver in Washington. Ran through Union Station hurdling luggage like Gail Devers. And once I was back in New York, I sprinted the twenty blocks from Penn Station to my office.

There, I sat down at my desk with a huff and flicked on my computer. My screensaver materialized as the machine warmed up; a picture of Connor Ryan in the desert flashed before me: full combat gear, M-16 rifle, muscles, tattoos, and a crap-kicking grin.

My warrior.

My hero.

One guilt-ridden week later I was back at Penn Station, pacing in front of the train leaving for Washington. A grande skim latte clutched in my fist, I jumped on just as the doors closed. Hopefully, Ryan had been too groggy to notice my fly-by-night visit the week before. I figured it was time for a fresh start. A new beginning.

On the Metroliner, I lectured myself about being the supportive girlfriend. I had gone to Barnes & Noble during my lunch hour and read up on traumatic injuries and the roll of the caretaker.

Yes, *caretaker*. The word made me nervous; however, I was more than willing to try. If Ryan wanted a pillow, I would get it for him. If he wanted ice chips, I would know without him even having to ask. I would get extra blankets if he was cold or turn on the AC if he was warm. I was ready to "be there" for him.

At Walter Reed, when I walked into the room, I found Ryan and Gomez sitting in wheelchairs in front of the TV, watching football. Men always seem to find that annoying game on some channel—even when it's not football season.

Neither of them noticed me. I stepped closer to the TV; Ryan wore the New York Yankees baseball cap I'd sent him a few months back. His dark hair curled around the edges of the frayed hat. He was a Texas Rangers fan and we'd hogged a lot of ether sending emails back and forth, arguing about which team is better.

A Budweiser commercial came on and both men looked up. Ryan's relaxed face immediately closed; his jaw clenched. He leaned back in his wheelchair and said, "Hey, Gomez—look who the cat dragged in."

Okay, so he was mad. I can accept that. Obviously, he had *not* been too groggy to remember my last visit.

This will be harder than I thought. I should've looked at a relationship book when I was at Barnes & Noble.

Gomez nodded at me, smiling as he wheeled himself toward the door. "I'm going down the hall. A double amputee came in last night. He needs some cheering up."

Once we were alone, I studied Ryan. "You look good," I said, nodding. I meant it. He looked much better than he had the last time I saw him. The swelling had gone down on his face; I could see this as I watched the muscles in his jaw clench. His beautiful, hazel eyes were wide open and glaring at me skeptically; a thin, pinkish scar lined the crease above his eyebrows.

"I heal fast. Not that you stuck around long enough to find out."

I sank into the chair next to him. "Work's been crazy. And you know what a slave driver my boss is. I've been up day and night finishing stories."

He looked down his lean nose at me, nodded dismissively, and returned his attention to the game on TV. My fingers clenched into fists. This was the first time we'd seen each other with both of us conscious in more than eleven months and he was watching football!

I stood and placed myself directly in front of the TV. Fists on my hips, I asked, "Are you gonna talk to me?"

"What's there to say? I've been home a week and you're two hours away and you don't find the time to visit."

"We agreed to respect each other's careers."

He snorted, throwing his hands up in the air. "Next time I'll plan on getting hurt around your work schedule. I'll tell the bad guys in Fallujah, 'Hey—not a good day for you to launch that RPG, my friend. My girlfriend's real busy at work and she can't help me out when I'm in the hospital.'" His tone grew harsher with each word uttered. The voices in the corridor outside his room went silent.

I turned and flicked off the TV, breathing hard through my nose. "I said I was sorry. What more do you want from me?"

"I don't want squat from you." He picked up the remote and turned the TV back on. Somebody scored and he pumped his fist with gusto.

I grabbed the remote out of his hand and turned the TV off again. "What do you mean? I'm here now. I took a few days off from work and I'll have you know they were damn hard to get."

He shrugged his muscular shoulders and looked up at the ceiling. "Madison, I don't need your help. I'm fine. Really frickin' fine. Now get out of the way."

"Well, I'm glad you're 'frickin' fine.' Don't let me disturb your stupid football game, then." I threw the remote at his head and groaned when he reached up and casually caught it midair.

I stomped out into the corridor and found Gomez lingering with a few other wounded soldiers. Disgust was written all over their battered faces.

"He's impossible!" I spat, violently pointing at the room I'd just left. Inside, the football game blared from the TV. Ryan had turned up the volume. "I'll come back tomorrow."

Before I turned away in a huff, I looked at Gomez sitting in a wheelchair and suddenly thought to ask him, "Why have you been here so long? I thought you would've healed and gone home by now." Last year at the start of the war, back when I was an embedded reporter, I'd helped save Gomez's life when RPG shrapnel nearly decapitated him.

Gomez tipped his head toward his feet. "Yeah. I've got frequent flyer miles in this place."

My eyes followed his gaze to the empty cuff at the bottom of his sweatpants. His right foot was gone.

Completely gone.

I gasped, "Oh, Gomez. What happened?"

"Some scumbag tossed a grenade at me. I can't seem to stay away from those mothers."

Thinking Ryan would need me, I'd taken a few days off from work and asked my friend, Josh, if I could sleep on his couch. Josh works for a Washington, D.C.-based liberal think tank and since he spends his days with opinionated intellectuals, he thinks of himself as one.

I met him and his new girlfriend at an Ethiopian restaurant in Adams-Morgan, a hip neighborhood in the District. I settled into a cushion on the floor and introduced myself to Karina. Moments later, the intensely aromatic food came on a huge platter and everyone used their fingers to dig in, as is the custom.

"So, how's your Marine?" Josh asked, breaking off some spongy bread and scooping up lentil stew.

I leaned back against the mural-painted wall. "He's not *my*

Marine." Karina wrinkled her nose. "You're dating a *Marine?*"

Josh ignored her. "What do you mean he's not yours? You've been writing him love letters for the past *year*. I figured wedding bells would be ringing by now."

I shook my head and stared at the food in front of me. "Let's just say we have a very bumpy relationship and we just hit a huge rut in the road."

Karina interrupted again. I was really starting to not like her. "Did he go to Iraq? Did he kill people?"

Once more, Josh ignored her. I figured their relationship was probably working out quite nicely—since neither of them listened to a word the other one said. Maybe Ryan and I should follow their lead.

"Seriously, Madison—you're the best thing a guy like him is ever gonna get. I mean, women love Rambo, but they marry the nerd. Right, Karina?"

She nodded obediently. "Does he feel any moral outrage to know that he was part of a foreign invading army—an army that kills civilians?"

Both of them had been living *way* too long in the Beltway. I tipped up my wineglass and drank it down.

My eyes scanned the restaurant. A conversation about the relative merits of both the Yale and Harvard law schools grew heated to my right. A shouting match between two navy blue-suited Capitol Hill aides about whose senator was more brilliant erupted in the corner.

With a stewed onion hanging part way out of his mouth, Josh snickered sardonically. "The last laugh is certainly on him, huh?"

I squinted my eyes and studied my friends for a moment. They were both starting to annoy me: Karina with her Kate Spade messenger bag and righteous attitude; Josh with his wire-rimmed glasses and hipster ponytail.

"What do you mean by that?" I asked.

He shoveled more food into his mouth. "Duh. They didn't find weapons of mass destruction, so he almost got his leg blown off for nothing."

I shook my head adamantly. "Josh. He had a duty to do. He was called to war by the people of this country."

Josh rolled his eyes and threw his hands up. "I didn't ask him to go to war. *You* didn't ask him to go. *Karina* didn't ask him to go."

I stood, feeling my blood boil as my face burned crimson. "That's not the point, *Josh.*"

All other conversations in the restaurant abruptly halted.

"Madison, it's a volunteer army. He didn't have to go. Would you please sit down?"

Instead, I threw my napkin down. "*Josh.* It's a volunteer army for the rich. The rich get to decide whether or not they want to enlist. Many young people from lower income backgrounds have no choice because there aren't any jobs and if they want to go to college, the only way they're going to get there is if the military pays for it!"

Josh stood and scanned the room, his face flushed. He put his hands on my shoulders. "Madison, I know a lot of people in here. Can you please keep it down? We're on the same side." He gently nudged me toward my pillow. The tone of his voice reminded me a lot of my mother when she was particularly disappointed in my behavior.

"Screw you, Josh." My eyes scanned the shocked faces in the restaurant. The only person smiling was the cocoa-colored waitress carrying a tray of drinks in from the kitchen. "And screw all the rest of you, too. I hope you choke on your silver spoons."

I turned on my heel and stomped out. I could hear Karina's whiney voice as I pushed open the door and breathed in deeply of the night air: "I don't understand how she could even touch that killing machine."

After leaving the restaurant, I walked the neighborhood for

about an hour, fuming. I needed a reality check and I knew exactly where to get it. Visiting hours ended at oh-twenty-one-hundred hours; I had time.

When I arrived, Ryan's room was bathed in moonlight and an old *Rolling Stones* song about not getting what you want hummed softly in the background. The smell of incense tickled my nose. At least he'd turned off the TV; maybe we could have a civilized conversation. I took a step into the room, my eyes adjusting to the darkness.

A muffled groan came from somewhere near the window. I stopped dead in my tracks and stared into the shadows, my spine stiff.

The moan sounded again—more urgent, demanding—a woman's moan. I squinted to see more clearly.

She sat on his lap, balanced precariously on his good knee. Her head was tipped back; waves of glossy, red hair fell down her back. His hand was up under her shirt, on her breast. Mick Jagger moaned about getting what you need.

Ryan made a trail of kisses down her long, pale neck. She shuddered. I shuddered.

My movement caught his attention. He pushed the girl off his lap. She squeaked as she scampered to her feet.

Dumbfounded, I stared at him. He stared at me.

The thought of fleeing occurred to me. Unfortunately, my feet were glued to the floor. Probably because my heart had dropped there with a thud.

I opened my mouth; no words came out. Ryan rolled over, slightly abashed, but ready to take control of the situation.

"Madison, this is Ashley. A friend from Texas."

I shook my head. The only word that came out of my clenched throat was, "Why?"

"My mother had a stroke last month. My sister needs to stay home to care for her. Ashley came to lend a hand."

My lower lip trembled. Along with a hand, Ashley was apparently lending a breast—and probably a few more body parts. *Why couldn't he find a nurse like Nurse Retched?*

The thoughts ran through my head; however, none of the words flew from my lips. No, instead of speaking, I turned and ran—and bumped right into Selena Gomez, Gomez's wife, in the corridor outside.

"What's up, girl? You look like you just saw a ghost!"

I shook my head and sprinted past her.

"You're gonna cripple someone running like that," she called after me. "And these guys have already been through enough hell—they don't need any more of that crap!"

I was already out the door before she could berate me further.

After a few days of wandering around D.C. visiting war memorials, I decided Gomez needed me. Maybe I couldn't do the ice chip thing or fluff pillows, but I could certainly tell a story, and there were men in Walter Reed who needed their stories told.

Ryan, I knew, would never let me interview him. But Gomez was always ready to talk. He liked being in the spotlight. So, with tape recorder and laptop in hand, I headed back to Walter Reed Army Medical Center.

When I arrived, the TV was on with a group gathered around it watching baseball. There were a number of women in the room and Selena Gomez came over to greet me. I wondered where Ryan and his ladylove were hiding.

Selena was a small Latina with a beautiful face and a killer body. Behind her appealing facade lay a heart of gold and a will of steel. She grabbed me by the elbow and pulled me out into the corridor.

"I thought you were gonna look nice—you know—dress up a bit," she whispered urgently, frowning her disapproval. When I'd called to make the appointment with Gomez, Selena had come on the line and told me that I needed to "fight" for my "soldier."

"I put on a clean pair of jeans."

She crossed her arms over her chest as her eyes roved disapprovingly up and down my frame. "Ripped jeans. Tie-dyed T-shirt and Doc Martens. I don't think so, Madison."

A razor commercial appeared on the TV and Gomez yelled, "Hey, Madison, you gonna make me famous or what?"

We stepped back into the room. "What's up with the hair?" Selena muttered under her breath.

I pushed a loose strand of hair from my mouth and waved to Gomez as my eyes scanned the crowd. I spotted Ryan seated in his wheelchair in a corner of the room with "the appendage" still in his lap. Her hair fell across his face as she whispered something in his ear. They both laughed.

He nodded tersely at me, eyes smoldering.

I looked away.

I breathed deeply and reminded myself, you *are* a *professional*. Using a voice of authority, I said to Gomez, "Let's get cracking."

Gomez wheeled over and Selena got me a chair. She pushed on my shoulder as I sat down. "The braid has *got* to go."

Gomez scowled at her, rolling his eyes. "Selena, we're not talking about friggin' hair, baby. We're talking about the war. This is important."

Selena squeezed his shoulder. "You're right, baby. You tell Madison what happened."

Laughter drifted over from the other side of the room. A few "Oh, Connors" reached my ears. The bimbo sounded like a stripper putting in an appearance on *Howard Stern*. I focused my attention on Gomez, reminding myself once again that I was a professional journalist with a successful career back in New York. I crossed my legs, stiffened my spine, and lifted my chin.

"Gomez, do you feel that the war was worth getting injured for?"

Gomez nodded once, his face a study in steely resolve. "I was asked to do a job and I did it. I'm proud of the job I did."

"Has getting injured changed your feelings about the war?"

"What kind of dumb-ass question is that? Of course it changes his feelings. He doesn't have a frickin' foot, in case you haven't noticed," a familiar voice snarled from the other side of the room. Ryan always lost his drawl when he was fuming.

At least finally, I had Ryan's attention. Maybe not the way I wanted it, but I had his attention. "Do you blame the leaders of this country for your wounds?" I asked Gomez.

Ryan pushed the girl off his lap and wheeled himself over to where Gomez, Selena, and I sat. His leg looked better, pinker—the muscle tone was coming back. Less like a dead fish, more like a spawning salmon.

"Every damn politician in Congress voted for this war. Even Hillary Clinton and John Kerry," Ryan said sternly.

The room grew silent. Someone turned off the TV. Everyone's attention was on Ryan; they were all waiting for him to speak the unspeakable. Selena muttered an amen. Gomez breathed heavily to my left. Ashley studied the dirt under her pink fingernails.

"We trusted the leaders of this country to make the right decisions."

"So, was it the right decision?" I asked him.

"It was at the time."

"And what about now?"

He wouldn't answer me, but his eyes never left mine.

Then everyone started talking at once. The floodgates had opened. Furiously, I took notes as the questions flew around me.

Then Ryan reached for my hand and I stopped writing. I studied his proud, angular face. All the voices in the room faded into the background as I looked at the truth in those deep, bottomless, hazel eyes. Then he smiled, dimples dancing in his cheeks. It was the grin I knew and loved; the old Connor Ryan was back and ready for the fight.

It was damn good to see him again.

I fluttered my lashes at him and asked, "Can I quote you on that?"

"Sure—as long as it's anonymous. I don't want to give my mother another stroke."

I nodded; I could live with that.

"Yo, Sarge—this is my fifteen minutes of fame. Madison came to talk to me, remember?" Gomez said, laughing.

"Sorry, man." Ryan bowed his head and rolled himself to the doorway where Ashley stood, waiting for him and sulking.

"Come on, Connor—let's go outside."

I stood. The sound of my chair sliding back caught his attention. "I know this doesn't help," I began, clearing my throat and biting my lower lip, "but I just wanted to say—I'm sorry, Ryan."

He shrugged. Ashley blew a lock of hair off her forehead, sighed, and rolled her eyes at me obnoxiously.

"Yeah, I am, too, Bradbury. See you around." With that said, Ryan promptly turned his strong, proud back on me and wheeled himself out of the room.

"Good luck with everything," I whispered as he disappeared around the corner and out of my life.

Selena walked up behind me, her breath hot on my neck. "What's this good luck and good-bye crap, huh? I thought you were gonna *fight* for the man!"

"He said good-bye, first. Not me." I dropped my eyes to the floor and clenched my hands into fists at my sides, shaking my head miserably. "He doesn't want me."

"He wants *her* because you keep disappearing and then reappearing dressed like some don't-screw-with-me, hippie feminist!"

Feebly, I tried to defend myself. "He was the one with his hand up her shirt."

Selena shook her head in disgust. "Your man needed comfort and *your* warm body was long gone, girl."

I pounded my fist against my chest. "I had to *work,* damn him."

Selena put one hand on her hip and waved her index finger in my face. "Well, let me just tell you then about what Connor was doing while *you* creeps ambushed my man. Connor stood in the middle of a dusty alley, laying down fire so they could Medivac Gomez out. That RPG bounced off Connor's knee before it exploded. He saved my Ricky."

I felt like my jaw dropped to the floor. "He did all that?"

"Look—I like you, Madison, but you've got to cut it out. Either stay and show some interest and help the guy, or go home and find yourself a nice, clean white boy who doesn't get his hands dirty."

So I went home.

Back in New York, I wrote a tribute to those men lying in their hospital beds at Walter Reed, fighting demons that no late-teen or twenty-something should have to fight. When I wasn't writing, I was crying. I felt like Diane Keaton in *Something's Gotta Give.* The waterworks wouldn't stop.

Weeks went by, and my story about the wounded warriors appeared on the newsstand and the phone rang.

It was my mother.

"Madison, what were you doing at Walter Reed? I hope you haven't taken up with that Marine again."

I sighed. "No, Mother. I tried, but he dumped me."

Her voice perked up. "Oh, well, it's probably for the best, sweetie. Men are never right in the head after war. Thank God it took your father six years to get through college; Vietnam would've *destroyed* him."

How just like my mother to offer little sympathy—and loads of stereotypes. I hung up the phone feeling even worse.

After that call I didn't dare get excited when the phone rang. I felt like I'd had enough disappointment in one year to last a lifetime. I decided to embrace the bitter attitude of my single, fifty-year old, studio-apartment-living neighbor down the hall:

Men *suck*.

One afternoon, I sat at my desk contemplating my navel and attempting to write a story about how much men suck when the phone rang. I didn't recognize the number; however, I was hoping to get a call from a woman in the East Village who shellacs pictures of her ex-boyfriends to the inside of her toilet bowl, so eagerly, I picked up the receiver.

"I need you." I pressed the receiver closer to my ear as the caller continued talking: "But not in the way I. thought I needed you."

I gasped. I'd recognize that deep, sexy, Texan twang anytime, anyplace.

"You're my conscience, my heart. I need you to keep it real and to fight me every step of the way."

My heart leaped. No, I think it actually jumped out of my chest and danced across my desk. I couldn't speak; I just breathed heavily into the mouthpiece.

"Is this Madison Bradbury I've got on the line—or just really good steamy phone sex?"

I giggled and dropped my voice a few octaves. "It's whatever you need."

Ryan laughed—a deep, low rumble that warmed my ears and slid right through my body, right down to my lonely toes.

"I take it you read my article."

"Yeah, I did."

"You liked it. You really liked it." I sounded like Sally Field receiving the Academy Award.

"Heck, yeah."

That evening when I arrived at the hospital, Ryan met me at the door, standing. There wasn't a wheelchair in sight. He wore tan cargo shorts, flip-flops, a U.S.M.C. T-shirt, and a smug grin. I unzipped my coat and his eyebrows popped up to his hairline. "A short denim skirt. Is that for me?"

I shook my head. "No, it's for Selena Gomez. She told me she'd kill me if I didn't wear it."

He grinned. "I've always liked Selena."

Then he limped toward me and opened his arms. I flung myself at him. He fell against the wall behind him with a *thump*.

"Whoa, whoa—take it easy, darlin'. I'm still a hurt man." He steadied himself, then me, before pulling me up hard against his rock-solid chest. I wrapped my arms around his neck as he ran his fingers through my loose hair.

He pulled on the collar of my coat, I slipped out of the sleeves, and it fell to the floor.

An old vet wearing a vest covered in metals hobbled by, calling out, "I sure do like them homecomings! You treat your soldier well, girlie!"

Ryan grabbed my ass and saluted the man with his other hand. "I'm sure she will, sir."

I rubbed my body against his and nestled my ear to his chest I was so immensely relieved that he was alive and healthy and in my arms. "You're walking," I whispered as the tears formed in the corners of my eyes and rolled down my cheeks.

He took my face into his large, battered hands. "It's all because of you. I was so frickin' mad and I couldn't do a damn thing about it except lift weights. Everybody thought I'd popped a screw. They kept sending me to the shrink."

I laughed and waved a finger in his face while pressing my hips against his. "You see? I serve a purpose in your life, Connor Ryan. You just won't always know what it is."

He pushed himself off the wall and put his arm around my shoulders. "I know what it is right now."

Together, we limped into a nearby, empty sitting room. Hungrily, his eyes roved up and down my body.

"Is that strategically ripped Texas Rangers T-shirt for Selena, or me?"

I threw back my shoulders, making the word "Texas" stretch across my breasts. "Sorry. It's for Selena."

He rubbed his fingers across the stubble on his chin. "Hmmmm, and what about those breasts? Are they for me?"

I crossed my arms over my chest and studied his beguiling, hazel eyes. I realized we had to set a few things straight before moving on to second base. "Is the 'Beauty Pageant Runner-up' still here?"

He shook his head. "She left a month ago. Take a moment to process that piece of intelligence in your Ivy League-educated brain."

I beamed and unfolded my arms. "Heck, yeah. These breasts are for you."

He grinned all dimples and cuteness and fell onto the sofa, pulling me down with him. Our lips met when we landed. I closed my eyes and felt the familiar warmth of his mouth, savored his taste. Wanting more, I laced my fingers in his hair, deepening the kiss.

He pulled away.

Placing his hands on my shoulders, he held me at arm's length. I groaned in frustration, digging my fingers into his forearms.

"Madison, as much as I can't stand emotional crap, we've got to have a gut spilling." He pushed a loose strand of hair behind my ear and pressed his lips together. "About Ashley . . . I needed help and—"

I waved my hand dismissively in the air. "And I totally freaked. I understand. I'm sorry I couldn't be here for you."

"I'm sorry you saw me with her."

I snuggled against him, infinitely pleased. "Some women would think I'm letting you off the hook too easily, but the truth is we both screwed up. Royally."

He put his injured leg on the coffee table and reached for a pillow to prop beneath it. "Yeah, we sure did." I grabbed the pillow from him; this was my chance to shine. "Can I fluff it for you?"

He laughed and lightly hit me over the head with it. "Hell, no; you're gonna hurt me!"

I feigned dejection.

"Okay, okay. Don't get your panties in a wad. Just be gentle." He passed me the pillow.

With many theatrics, I hit the pillow over the side of the couch and then threw it up in the air, followed by clapping it between my hands. "Now for my final act, I will carefully place this *expertly* fluffed pillow very GENTLY under your knee."

When I reached for his leg he cried out in pain, moaning and groaning like a sideshow at a haunted house.

"Oh, gosh—I hurt you." I grabbed his rock-solid shoulder.

A devilish grin broke out across his rugged features.

"You jerk." I hit him upside the head with the pillow, and then carefully placed it under his knee. The scar was fading; golden hairs dusted the skin, outlining the powerful contours of muscle.

I stood and put my hands on my hips. "Can I get you some ice chips?"

He grinned and winked at me. "As long as you feed them to me."

When I came back, I kneeled next to him on the couch. My breasts pressed against his shoulder. He wrapped a big, muscular arm around my waist. He must've been totally pissed at me; the man was *buff*.

I smiled and placed a large chip of ice between his full, kissable lips. He sucked it into his mouth, licking my fingers as he pulled me onto his lap. He found my lips with his own.

I opened my mouth and nibbled on the tip of his tongue as he pressed himself into me. My hands slipped up under his T-shirt, feeling the springy hairs on his chest and the muscular ridge of his pecs.

"Why don't you get yourselves a room? This is indecent."

We broke off our kiss to find Selena and Gomez before us with their arms crossed over their chests.

"Gomez, I told you that T-shirt would work. Stop looking at her breasts—you're a married man!" Selena scolded playfully.

I coughed and pulled on the front of my shirt, trying to make the words readable.

Ryan took his hand off my upper thigh, but kept the other one wrapped possessively around my waist. "Hey, Selena—you done good."

Selena shrugged. "The girl's got the goods."

Ryan smiled. "It works for me."

For a moment, all four of us grinned at each other like fools. Finally, inspired to say something meaningful, I expounded, "You know what I like about all of you?"

Gomez shook his head. Ryan's fingers gripped tighter around my waist. Selena snorted, "Girlfriend, don't go getting all sentimental on us now."

"I like your brutal honesty. Most of the people I know—"

Interrupting me, Selena grabbed Gomez's arm. "Oh, my gosh, Gomez—this is like Goldie Hawn in *Overboard*. She hangs with the poor people and learns life's valuable lessons!"

"No, Selena, she's Madonna in *Swept Away*. The poor cabin boy teaches her how to properly love a man."

They high-fived each other while Ryan chuckled next to me. I shook my head and raised my voice. "I didn't mean it like that."

Ryan stood and stuck his hands into the pockets of his cargo shorts. "If I'm the man to teach her how to love, I better start my mission."

Gomez grinned. "The roof. That's probably the best place to go. I disarmed the alarm."

Ryan grabbed my hand and a blanket off a nurse's cart. We headed toward the elevators. Selena and Gomez made lewd comments at our retreating backs.

The sun was setting when we arrived up top, giving us a

spectacularly exclusive view of the Capitol Building and the Washington Monument reflected in red, gold, and burnt orange.

Ryan laid the blanket out and eased himself down onto it. I pulled two bottles of Sam Adams from my purse. "Will these help ease your pain?"

"Heck yeah."

I grinned at him as I gently ran my fingers down his forearm. "We aim to please." With my other hand, I passed him the bottle opener.

He popped open the beers and leaned back on his elbows. He looked down the length of his lean body and tipped his chin toward me. "Come here."

I straddled his hips, my hind end resting on his loins, feeling the contours of bone and muscle. Even hurt, he was a powerfully built man. He rubbed his large, callused hands up and down my arms. In my excitement, I tipped my beer bottle up too quickly and the foam spilled down my neck and chest.

"Ugh." I reached for a napkin.

Ryan sat up, took the napkin from me, and pressed his mouth to my neck. Little, wet licks of his warm tongue sent shivers down my spine and heat pooled in intimate places as he worked his way to the top of my T-shirt. I shuddered with pleasure.

He looked up at me, his hazel eyes demanding more. "Mmmmm, there's still some beer to be cleaned up."

I panted, "It got down as far as my belly button."

"Consider the job done." With practiced ease he flipped me onto my back.

I held onto his shoulders, shaking my head. "Be careful of your knee." Ignoring my warning, he pushed my T-shirt up and sucked the beer out of my bellybutton. "I've always liked a good, strong stout."

I giggled. Then he dipped his tongue into the crevice. I moaned and dug my fingers into his hair. Next, he blew the skin dry. I bucked upward, wrapping my legs around his waist, pressing my hips into him.

Grasping the ends of my T-shirt, he easily pulled it up and over my head. I tugged my arms out of the sleeves and threw it, having no idea where it landed—most likely in a bush down below on the ground.

"Black lace. I didn't know you had it in you."

I was panting too much to answer. Instead, I pressed his head down to my breast. He pushed the lace away and took my nipple into his mouth. His warm hand covered my other breast as my hips rocked against his. He sighed, stopped, lifted his chin, and took my head between his hands.

"Madison. I'm horny as hell. It's been too long." He rolled his hips against me to prove his point.

"What about your knee?"

"At this moment, I'm feeling no pain."

He popped the clasp on my bra, pulling the garment from my arms. His index fingers circled my nipples as he studied my face.

"Madison, I don't know what the future holds. I may be going back to Iraq. I may be dead in a year. But for tonight—" He looked away and bit his lower lip. "Tonight, I want you real bad."

I nodded earnestly. "I want you, too."

He groaned and reached up under my skirt. I opened my legs as his fingers found my wet, hot core. He slipped my panties down over my hips and dropped his shorts.

"Wait, wait!" I cried, diving for my purse. I dumped out my cell phone, Blackberry, wallet and notepad, not finding what I needed and cursing under my breath. Connor ran the tips of his fingers gently through the mess and, picking up a condom, he held it between his index finger and thumb.

"Always prepared, huh? Just like a good Marine."

I grabbed it from him and straddled his hips. "My type A personality turns you on, I see," I said, ripping open the condom packet.

Moments later, he guided my hips into position and entered me with an urgency and intensity that will forever be branded on my flesh, the purest sense memory of all.

Sated, I buried my head in his chest, feeling the warm, springy chest hairs against my cheek. Color caught my eye suddenly, and I lifted my chin.

"A new tattoo." I ran my index finger over it, studying the pattern in the dim light. "A bulldog."

"Yeah, I figure after all the shit we've been through, I needed to mark myself in some way. You like it?"

I nodded and traced it delicately with my fingertips. "I just hope my mother doesn't see you with your shirt off."

He chuckled and ran his fingers through my hair, gently tracing the contours of my ear. I curled against him like a contented cat. Then his movement stopped and I lifted my head to look at him.

He studied my face for a moment. I nudged him with my knee and asked softly, "What?"

He sighed and released me. Rubbing his face with his hands, he said, "Madison, I still look at rooftops for snipers. A car backfires pulling out of the parking lot and I jump for cover. That crap over there has messed me up."

I gripped his shoulders, gently forcing him to meet my gaze. "I understand, Connor."

His chest heaved as he shook his head slowly, thinking. "I don't know if you want me like this." Slowly, he took his hands away from his face.

I sat up on my knees and pulled his T-shirt over my head. Choosing my words carefully, I said, "My mother told me to stay away from you." I looked down at my lap. "She says men are never the same after war."

He chuckled. It wasn't a happy chuckle, just a painfully real chuckle. Then he reached up and traced my chin with his knuckle.

"Your mother is a smart woman."

"Yes, but what she doesn't understand is that I saw the war, too, and I'm not the same anymore, either." I shook my head. "Every night before I go to sleep now, I lay in bed thinking about all that blood after Gomez was hit. I think about the dead, burnt Iraqis along the road. I think about you and you getting hurt."

He sat up and pulled me into his arms. "They should have debriefed the embedded reporters for reentry into civilian life."

"Connor. I didn't see a tenth of what you saw. But what I'm trying to say, in a small way, is that I understand."

He looked up at the sky for a moment. A plane passed over. Then a mischievous grin broke his seriousness.

"It sucks, doesn't it? Needing each other?"

I smiled and snuggled closer to him. "Yeah. It does."

He laced his fingers with mine and whispered, "We'll get through this somehow—together. Semper Fi."

"Semper Fi," I whispered back, planting little kisses along his shoulders and neck. THE END

SOLDIER'S LUCK

Male narrators aren't a common occurrence in True Love *and* True
Romance, *but they do show up occasionally—and soldiers can make
for excellent romantic heroes. Take Dick: He's on an American military
base, waiting to be shipped overseas, and he's fallen in love with a local
girl named Fay. The problem is, he's convinced himself that he's not
good enough for her and her family, and if he's not careful, he's going to
convince Fay, too.*

*One of my favorite things about this story is the way it almost seems
to go for the downbeat ending, with Dick learning a tough but important
lesson about not taking girlfriends for granted. But then her parents help
turn everything right side up so the marriage proposal can go forward—
although maybe not quite as planned.*

**It seemed as if he had been offered the sun and the moon
and a thousand stars—as if he had been offered the world with a
white picket fence around it. That's the way it seems to a soldier
who's lucky in love.**

When I fell in love with Fay, I didn't stop to remember how little I
had to offer her—I was too amazed, and thankful that I'd found her.
I'd gone to camp with my mind fixed on the war, and then, right
there in the next town, I'd met Fay. And the way I felt about her,
of course I wanted to marry her before I went overseas.

It hadn't taken me long to love her, and the more I saw her
the more I was crazy about her. Sure, she was good-looking, with

a mass of curly light hair, and the kind of enchanting smile that could lift my heart right over, and the kind of figure that would stop a bunch of GI's short in their tracks. But I loved her for a lot of things more than that—I loved her for a sort of generous warmth she had, the way she listened to people and cared about how they ticked. I loved her because she could be gay and light-hearted and the best kind of fun. And I loved her for the serious times, when we talked about the war, and she changed swiftly from a girl to a woman I could trust with my deepest carings. She could change like that, laughing and care-free one moment, and soberly earnest the next minute—and whatever she did and said, I loved her, loved her achingly, desperately yet—I didn't tell her how I felt about her.

You see, I'd met her family, and the better I knew them, the more I began to worry about asking her to marry me. It was like asking a girl who's living in a beautiful home to go and live in a cold one-room flat—a fellow wonders if he's got the right even to ask her. It wasn't the house she lived in, you understand; it was the swell people in the house—and the kind of happiness they had together, happiness and warmth and security. It did things to me—meeting them.

I was walking on top of the world, that evening when I first met them. I was taking Fay home from the Saturday dance, and I believed she was beginning to care about me, and the way I felt I could have reached up and brushed off a star. We'd had dates, half a dozen dates besides the dances, but I'd always met her in the little park in the center of town. Now I was taking her home, and that proved she liked me, didn't it? Besides, I could tell—the way she looked at me when we danced together, the way her fingers answered when I took her hand. And I could tell from the electricity that sparked between us, the way everything we said and did together had a bright glow.

"You're the most amazing girl I ever met," I told her, as we walked along the village street.

"Why?" Fay wanted to know.

"Well. I can take a drink of plain water, and look at you, and feel as if I were drinking champagne. You go to my head—"

"You're just dizzy from waltzing," Fay told me, laughing.

"I'm dizzy. Period," I said. "From looking at you and not drinking any water, either."

"You can't see me in the dark," Fay protested.

"Oh yes I can," I told her. "I can see you in the dark. I can see you any time, whenever I close my eyes."

Fay was silent a moment, and when she spoke her voice was lower. "Maybe you'll forget what I look like when you go away."

"I'll never forget," I said, and my voice rang out with sudden force in the quiet night. I reached for her hand, and felt her fingers tighten in mine, and the sudden drumming of my heart was loud in my ears.

"Fay—" I said, and perhaps I would have told her then that I loved her.

But she was turning in at a gateway set in a high hedge, and I could see a path stretching up to many lighted windows. The light stretched out to meet us, welcomingly, and the big front door of the house stood open. There was no time to say anything more to Fay, and ruefully I let her hand slip away.

"We're home," Fay said. "There's just my mother and father and little brother here now. My sister is married and lives down the hill."

We'd left the dance early, and I could hear voices inside the house as we crossed the porch. Then a woman came to the door, and I'd have known it was Fay's mother anywhere, because she had the same deep dark eyes and the same warming smile.

"This is Dick, Mother," Fay was saying. Her mother drew me in as she greeted me. "I'm glad Fay brought you in," she said, and she made me feel she meant it. I liked Fay's father, too, a tall spare man with a good handshake and a dry twinkle, who had me settled in a big chair with a glass of beer and a cigarette before I'd said half a dozen words. And Bud, the fifteen-year-old, looked like a good kid.

Fay was telling them about the dance, and I took a look around—and that was the swellest room I'd ever been in. Not swell swanky, because the furniture was worn and the rug showed signs of plenty of sliding around by Bud. But swell because, somehow, it was a room where people lived and were happy. Maybe it was the personal things scattered around, the walky-talky Bud was putting together, and the cribbage board, and books and magazines lying open. Maybe it was the comfortable old chairs, or all the family photographs on the walls. Maybe it was just the nice comfortable feel of the place, with the white curtains blowing a little at the windows, and the radio playing softly, and a man-sized plate of cookies on the table with a hunk of cheese on the side.

Anyway, I eased down in my chair and relaxed, and pretty soon I found myself telling about the girls' stag line at the dance, and how the girls had cut in on the fellows—as if I'd known Fay's family for years. And I ate molasses cookies and cheese, which is a fine combination in case you haven't tried it, and nobody asked me to tell all about the Army, and Fay sat across from me smiling at me and—oh heck, I felt as if I were where I belonged.

Pretty soon Fay's sister, Sally, and her husband dropped in to say good-night on their way home. He was on the late shift at the munitions plant, and she'd walked to meet him coming home. They were a cute team.

And the whole gang of them began talking as if they hadn't seen each other for years, and I had the time of my life and listened till my ears nearly fell off. I guess one reason I liked the setup so much was because I'd never had a family of my own. I'd been brought up by an aunt who was pretty much vinegar-mouth and whalebone-corset stiffness. And this family—this was the nicest family I'd ever come across.

I said something like that to Fay's mother, when she sat down beside me and started talking to me.

"You're a fine gang—your whole family," I told her. "I didn't know they grew families like yours."

Fay's mother laughed, sort of pleased-like. "We stick together," she said. "I guess we've always been a pretty chummy bunch. Look at the way I pick up slang from Bud. I told the cook the other night to 'sock a little more water on the beans', and she was certainly surprised."

"I bet she liked it," I said.

"Well, maybe she did. She's been cooking for us here in this house for thirty years, so she must be used to us by this time."

"Thirty years—right here in this house. That's wonderful," I said. "I've sort of roamed around. The aunt I lived with kept moving, she never liked any place so she kept on going."

"More than thirty years in this house," she told me. "I grew up here, and Ben—that's my husband—Ben joined Dad's law firm and moved in here, and I married him and we just kept on living here. When my parents' died, well, our children were here and they loved the place. You'll have to see it by daylight, there's a brook and a honey-suckle tangle as high as the trees, and a long meadow where the boys play baseball."

"That's the way to live," I said, wishing I belonged to any one place, that way. Living in camp, you hear a lot about the other guys' homes.

"Cookies?" said Fay, coming over to me with the big plate.

"Thanks," I said, and then forgot to take one for a minute, looking at Fay. I felt as if I knew her better, in her own home—funny, how much closer she seemed. And she had that little quirk at the corner of her mouth that always made me wild to kiss her.

"Thanks, no cookies?" she said.

"Oh—no, I mean yes," I said, and took three.

Her mother went to the door with the couple from the other

house and I said to Fay, "Are you going to stay across the room the rest of the evening?"

She laughed and shook her head, and we were all busy saying good-night for a minute, and then her mother came back and the room settled down. Bud went back to tinkering with his walky-talky, and the cribbage game went on again, and Fay sat down by me.

"I like your folks," I told her.

And she lighted up as if she had candles inside her. "I'm glad you do, Dick. Come on over, whenever you like. Somebody's most always here."

"I'll try to make it when you're here—" I told her.

"That'll be nice," she said demurely, but her eyes sparked at me. It's a wonder I didn't grab her and kiss her right there, in front of her family. Anyhow, I fixed it up for a date the next night, and she asked me to come to dinner.

So I went walking back to camp, feeling all warm and happy inside, remembering how her dad had told me to come early and we'd walk around the place before dinner, and her mother had made me feel at home, and Bud had grinned at me—remembering most of all the feel of Fay's hand in mine as she said good-night.

And the next night—well, that was swell all over again. And it wasn't the fried chicken and apple pie, though they were tops. That wasn't why I had such a fine time. It was watching that family, how they managed to have a good time just by being together, and how they let me share it, too. I liked the comfortable wide fields back of the house, and the high-ceilinged rooms inside, and the feeling of security I got from the big old house and the people that lived there.

But there was one thing—I never got a chance to talk to Fay alone for more than two minutes the whole blamed evening, and no matter how fine a time I was having, that didn't stop me wanting to have Fay for a while all to myself.

She'd walk by me—and I tell you, I'd just stop breathing for a minute, wanting to reach out to her. She'd smile at me, with that little turn-in of her mouth, and I couldn't see anything but her face.

"I've got trouble ahead," I told her one time when I'd caught her briefly by herself.

"Trouble?" said Fay, looking to see if I were serious.

"I won't be able to see you for five days," I explained. "That's trouble—"

"What happens for five days, Dick?"

"Manoeuvers. In the field." I said. "So next Saturday, if I can get an all-day pass, will you save the time for me?"

"We could go on a picnic," Fay said.

"Just the two of us?" I inquired.

Fay laughed. "Just the two of us."

"Swell," I said. "I never had that many hours with you, all at once—"

And then Bud came along, and wanted a man-to-man talk about how soon he could get into the Service, because he looked a lot older than fifteen, he said. And I didn't get any more time alone with Fay, except when I said good-night.

She walked to the gate with me, and after she'd held it open for me she stood there, looking up at me, with the light from the windows shining through her hair. I kissed her without any figuring about it—nothing could have stopped me.

Kissing Fay—that was madness and safety all mixed together, it was excitement and it was coming-home right. I couldn't let her go, pulled her tighter.

"You're adorable—" I said huskily, bending to kiss her again.

And she wasn't stopping me—not a bit—and her hands were tight around my head.

When we pulled apart, breathless, half-dazed, I couldn't speak for a minute. So this was what it was like when you really loved a girl.

"You're—Wonderful—" I tried to tell her. Words were so bare, how could I put glory into words? She was the end of dreaming, and I had found her.

"Dick—" she said softly.

I started to pull her close again, and I knew my controls were slipping. I was heading straight for a spin—and this was the girl I wanted to marry. And it took all I had to let go of her.

"I'll—see you Saturday.'" I managed to say. "I've got a lot—of things to tell you—"

"All right, Dick," she answered, and her voice sang with gladness. She must care something about me—I was sure of that—and if I never did anything else I was going to win her. I loved her so someday she'd love me enough to marry me. She had to belong to me. Maybe I hadn't known her very long, but when I loved her so terribly, couldn't she learn to love me that way, too?

"Good-night," I said, touching her bright hair. "Till Saturday—"

"Till Saturday," she repeated, and ran back to the house. She waved from the steps and went on in. Just for an instant, I had a streak of worry—of dismay—but I didn't know why. Something about Fay, going home, into that house, where warmth and affection and security were waiting for her—and me walking off down a dark road to camp. But why should that bother me, I asked myself. She'd kissed me, hadn't she? What more did I want for that night till the next time—and the next time, I would ask her to marry me. A whole long day alone with her, a whole day to tell her how I loved her—

So I shrugged off the crazy chilly feeling, and remembered back to Fay's hands behind my head, Fay's lips on mine. What more did I want? Plenty. I wanted Fay for my own, as long as I lived. I was crazy about her, and I went back to camp singing out loud, and the next five days looked like forever, but Saturday would have to come sometime.

Well, we had a busy five days of it on manoeuvers, getting toughened up the hard way, and I got callouses on my knees from crawling, and dust on me two inches thick. But believe it or not, Saturday finally came along, and I was back at camp and starting out for town and Fay.

I guessed I'd better not buy any food, till I found what she wanted me to get. Fay was waiting out on her front steps, in a blue and white dress, with her hair tied back with a blue ribbon. She came down the path to meet me, with a lunch basket on her arm, and I just stood there by the gate looking at her.

"Now how could I forget?" I asked her.

"Forget what?"

"How lovely you are—"

She laughed and gave me the basket, and we walked away, Fay keeping step with me.

"I missed you like everything," I told her.

"We've got all day—" she said, and her voice sparkled and her eyes sparkled. "All day to go adventuring."

"Where?"

"The only hill in thirty miles," she told me.

"Hey—I want to buy something for the picnic, Fay."

"You can get some fruit," she told me.

So we picked up pears and big purple grapes at a little store, and set off down the road.

Walking the curving path up the hill, she told me what she'd been doing that week and I told her high spots about the manoeuvers, as if we wanted to bridge the time we'd been apart. But when we came out on top of the hill, we stopped talking, and stood a while looking out over the valleys. Fay and me, high up there together, looking out over the tree-tops—as if we stood together looking out over our future, all the years ahead.

"It all belongs to us, down there," Fay said at last softly. "And the sky belongs to us, and the hill is ours. Do you feel like that,

Dick?"

"Uh-huh, just like that," I said. "And there's nobody in the world but us, for a little."

"Just us," she said in that lovely low voice.

After a while, we walked around a little. We climbed the fire-patrol platform on its stilts, and found a flat stone and unpacked the lunch. Funny—Fay had talked about adventuring. Well I'd never imagined a picnic on a hill could be adventuring. But when it's with the girl you love—then every new tilt of her head, every curve of her throat is exciting. And when you aren't sure just how she feels about you but you're dead set on wooing her and winning her, well—that may not be adventuring the way the old pirates did it, but it can send your blood racing.

"That was a swell lunch," I told her when we'd finished. "You'd make a wonderful wife, Fay. Or didn't you make that cake?"

"Yes I did," she said, grinning across at me. "But I didn't make the olives."

"Oh well, don't feel bad about the olives. So you really don't mind being domestic?"

"Nope," she answered, "do I look the playgirl type?"

"You look like a picture, you look like a cover girl," I said with sudden fervor.

Fay leaned back against a big tree trunk, watching me, and I couldn't read the expression in her eyes.

"You always look happy," I said suddenly. "I guess I never knew a girl before—who looked happy all the time."

"I guess—I'm lucky," Fay said. "I guess I always have been happy. Oh, I've had my bumps and disappointments, but—there was always the family to go home to."

"Yes, you've got some family," I said. "That must be a secure sort of a feeling. I didn't have a family, but I can guess."

She nodded. "I go in the house and—suddenly everything's all right. And we're fond of each other, specially. Like Sally."

"What about Sally?" I asked. Sally was her sister, the one who lived down the hill.

"Well, when Sally got married, Dad gave her the north section, and helped them plan their house—and they're right close by, sort of an annex to the family. And Dad is going to give me the south section, that's the lot where the brook is, when—" She stopped, flushing faintly. "I mean, if I get married someday. So we'll all be close together."

"That's a nice way to be," I said, and I spoke calmly, but I didn't feel calm inside.

I suddenly had caught a glimpse of the way Fay dreamed about her marriage. She expected to marry a guy who had money enough to build a house for her, the way Sally's guy did for Sally. Fay expected to live there with her husband, near her family, but not "too near." She probably had other plans and dreams, just as clear as that one, just as bright. But—how could I give her that kind of marriage? I hadn't been working long before I went into the Army, and I had about a hundred and fifty dollars in the bank. I couldn't buy Fay a house—on that land where the brook ran. I was going off to fight in a war—I couldn't settle down.

Another kind of girl would be different. Lots of girls, and nice girls, too, would marry a soldier and never think about the future. But Fay brought up in a home like hers—how could I ask her to walk out of that home and marry me, and live on a GI's pay? And how could I ask her to marry me and go on living at home, when I'd be asking her to marry uncertainty and worry and fear, along with me?

I sat there, realization striking home, hard and cold. I didn't have anything to offer Fay. Fay had happiness and security already. I didn't have the right to ask her to take on a load—the responsibility of being a soldier's wife. Not my happy, safe Fay. I couldn't be selfish enough to do that to her.

Sleepless nights I'd be giving her, and loneliness, when I wanted to give her everything good in life. I was licked before I really started, and this was the day when I was going to tell Fay how much I loved her.

"You're so quiet suddenly," Fay said.

I had a sharp, fierce struggle for a minute. All of me cried out to tell her how much I needed her, how I adored her. I wanted fiercely to try to wake her to loving me. But if I succeeded—once again I pulled myself back. If I succeeded, I would be tearing apart her safe, happy life. All I could offer her was love—and insecurity and loneliness. Maybe after the war, maybe someday I could come back, hoping desperately that some lucky guy hadn't come along who could take care of her the way she deserved. But I couldn't do it now, and suddenly it seemed as if Fay's family stood between me and her, holding her safely away from me, ringing her around with loving arms, so I couldn't hurt her. Her family had given her happiness and security—I couldn't snatch them both away from her.

"What is it, Dick?" Fay said once again.

"I was just thinking—how insecure my future is," I told her slowly.

"Think about today," said Fay. "Just today." She straightened up, leaning toward me a little, and her bright hair blew across her face.

I wanted to reach across and smooth that hair back, and I didn't even have the right to do that. What kind of blind fool had I been—caring only about what I wanted—never seeing how unfair it would be to Fay to try to make her love me?

"You deserve the best," I tried to tell her. "You rate—nothing but the best."

Her eyes were puzzled, as if she were trying to understand my change of mood. "It'll be a lucky guy—who can give you the kind of life you deserve," I tried again.

"I don't know what you're trying to say, Dick," she said slowly.

It was what I was trying not to say, that mattered—it was all the love I was crushing back that mattered. But I couldn't tell her that. I stood up abruptly, not trusting myself to keep silent, staying so close to her. "Let's walk—" I said.

Fay packed away the lunch things, not looking up at me. "Shall we go?" she said at last, and her voice was strangely formal.

She knew something was wrong, but I couldn't explain. Because if I tried to explain. I knew too darned well I'd forget everything but how much I loved her; I'd forget everything but the need to marry her and make her mine forever. I had to keep it all dammed up, because that was the only way I could take care of her.

"Yeah, let's go," I said.

It was different—going down that hill, with a new kind of aloof silence between us. And none of the little things we said brought us back to the natural, happy companionship we'd had before. Well—maybe it was better this way, maybe it was safer. Her hand brushed mine, and my heart jerked—and I made myself look straight ahead.

"Thanks for going with me, Fay," I said when we reached her gate at last. "Thanks for a lot of things, Fay."

"You sound as if you were going away," she told me. "Dick—you're not going overseas—right away?"

"Oh, no, not yet a while," I answered. "I'll be seeing you, Fay."

"Good-bye, Dick," she said, and her smile was different. "We'll be looking for you."

"I'll be over," I said, but I didn't say when.

The walk back to camp was gray, for all the sun was shining. So this was the end of the day I'd counted on so much—the day when I was going to take Fay by storm. Crazy, selfish fool I'd been—but that didn't stop the ache in me, that didn't stop my loving her. It was going to be bad, without her—without the hope of winning her.

I didn't know the half of it that Saturday. I didn't know how I'd keep on wanting to see her, no matter how busy I was, day-after-day; no matter what I did, policing the company street, practicing on the rifle range, slogging along the obstacle course with its walls to scale and ditches to leap—no matter what I did, I kept on thinking about Fay. And the nights, staring into the dark.

I stuck it out for a week, and I didn't see her or phone her. I wasn't any good for that girl, I told myself. I'd better stay out of her life. But the way I felt didn't get any better, and I couldn't stop thinking of her.

It was partly not caring what I did, and partly a dim idea that maybe seeing another girl would dull the sharp edge of remembering Fay that made me agree to go along on a double date with a pal of mine. We took the girls over to a carnival tent that had come to town, and I tried to throw myself into the evening and not look back.

The girl I was with was a nice gal, pretty and friendly, and I took her around to all the booths, and showed her how to shoot the pop-gun rifles, and she shot two oranges off a shelf and won a red plate: I bought her taffy and I took her on the flying boats. She was an all-right girl—nothing wrong with her—she just wasn't Fay, that was all. And I wanted Fay worse than ever, for being with the wrong girl. This was one thing I wouldn't try anymore; if I couldn't have my own girl, I wouldn't date anybody. But I set myself to be decent.

One thing never occurred to me—I was so blamed busy trying to shove Fay out of my mind, and failing too miserably, it never occurred to me that naturally Fay'd be coming to the carnival, too.

And when I rounded a corner, my little red-haired date by my side, and found myself facing Fay and Bud—I was knocked speechless. Fay gave me one look and my date one look, and she spoke to me nice and polite, the way you'd speak to a neighbor.

"Hello, Dick," she said, as casually as if she merely met me once or twice—as if I hadn't kissed her—as if we hadn't stood on top of a hill and owned the world together.

"Hello, Fay; hello, Bud," I managed to say, and then they were past.

What did Fay think of me, dating another girl when I hadn't seen her or called her for a week? Did she believe I hadn't really cared about her?

That was one thing I couldn't stand. I couldn't let her think I'd kissed her lightly, carelessly—and now I was running after another girl. Not the way I loved Fay, not the way I set her up high and fairly worshipped her.

Somehow I got through the rest of the evening and the night. And next day, the first break I got, I phoned Fay.

"Fay, can I see you tonight—please?" I asked her urgently.

"You're quite a surprise, so sudden," she said, and her voice was cool.

"Please, Fay, I've got to see you, I've got to talk to you," I said.

"All right, come over after dinner," she said finally.

So I got a pass, and as early as I figured she'd be through dinner, I was walking through the gate and up her path. She must have been watching for me, she came out the front door as I came to the steps.

"Dad's got a client calling," she told me. "We can go for a walk, if you like."

She was pleasant to me, very pleasant, but all the old personal warmth was gone. That was better for her, I tried to tell myself, I was the wrong sort of guy for her to care about, I couldn't look after her and keep her happy. But I was bleak and cold lonesome, walking along beside Fay—with her so endlessly far away.

It was heavy dusk, and as we walked along, we could smell the fresh-cut grass and the flowers, in the yards we passed. We could hear the friendly voices, in the comfortable little houses. A safe little town, and I was going away to fight to keep it safe, that was my job. I'd he fighting for Fay, even if she didn't know it.

We reached the park, where I used to meet her, where we used to walk. I led her over to the bench by the little pond.

"Fay—I want to tell you something—"

"Yes?" she said in that cool sweet voice.

"I was double-dating with a friend of mine last night," I blurted out. "I never saw that girl before, I don't ever expect to see her again. That's what I wanted to tell you."

Fay said, "Why are you telling me this, Dick? Why did you want to tell me this?"

And before I knew, it all broke out of me, in answer.

"Because I love you!" I said passionately. "Because I wanted you to know I love you." The words hung in the darkness, eager and glad to be said. And Fay's hand was suddenly in mine, and I hung on to it tightly.

"But why didn't you tell me—" she asked bewilderedly. "Why have you stayed away? Dick—"

And I told her quick to get it done. "I didn't want you to care too much about me," I said, stumbling along. "I didn't want you to get thinking about marriage, and get hurt—."

That was the truth—and sticking to it had me plenty. Why did it make her change so swiftly?

Her hand was pulled away in a flash, and said in the queerest voice, "But what made you flatter yourself that I'd cared too much about you?"

"I didn't mean that," I exclaimed. "Fay—"

But she was going on— "How dare you take it for granted that I'd fall in your arms, when you weren't interested in marrying me? I admit you aren't the kind of man I thought you were. But what ever made you so conceitedly sure of me?"

"I wasn't sure of you! For heaven's sake, Fay, what's the matter?"

"Nothing," she said furiously. "Do you expect all the girls you meet to fall in love with you?"

"Fay—listen, Fay—"

But she'd stood up, she was already moving away from the bench. "I'm not interested in any more of your romantic ideas," she told me. "You'll find plenty of girls to amuse you. Just don't worry about anything foolish—" her voice snapped and went again harder—"anything so crazy as my caring about you."

Well, that was telling me. I'd wanted to take myself out of her life, and it seemed that I didn't belong there anyhow. And as for fixing up whatever mess we'd got into now, it was beyond me. I'd made her sore, but she wouldn't listen to me.

I walked beside her silently, too miserable to talk. And when we reached the main street, she turned to me.

"Don't bother to walk home with me," she said crisply. "Goodnight. Dick. And you're quite right, I'm not interested in your kind of love-making."

I watched her walk off in the dimness of the street lights, I watched her out of sight. She was walking out of my life, and I didn't have the right to raise a finger to stop her.

Well, you can figure out I wasn't precisely happy, from then on. Whatever I'd felt before, it was worse, now. But there a was little job of being in the Army, and I plugged at that, and tried to get used to living with so much hurt.

I didn't go to town for a couple of weeks, didn't go anywhere where I might meet Fay. And it was plain, miserable, hell.

Then the rumor ran around my unit that we'd get alerted for overseas any day now and it was one of those rumors that sounded like business. And knowing that, I suddenly realized that I couldn't go overseas and leave such a miserable tangle with Fay behind me. I'd hurt her that night in the park with my stupid talk, somehow or other. Maybe I'd made her feel I'd been attracted to her some light easy way—and I hated that idea.

Now I was sure she didn't really care for me, the way she'd

lashed at me in the park—well, now I could tell her just once the way I felt about her. I wouldn't be asking for anything, I wouldn't be expecting anything. I wanted her to know how I felt about her before I went away.

And her family had been swell to me, they'd taken me in and made me feel as if I had a warm place in their home. I wanted to say good-bye to them, and try to tell them what it meant to me—just knowing them. Oh, heck, I couldn't say it like that, but maybe I'd get it across to them.

And once I'd decided to go—then I knew I had to see Fay once more, then I was all afire to get to her, and all the locks I'd set around myself were burned away.

So one more time I found myself walking up the path to Fay's house, and one more time I stopped for an instant in the friendly light of their windows. That house—those people—how had they come to mean so much to me in such a little while? It wasn't just because they belonged to Fay, though that was part of it.

I rang the bell, and Bud came running, and let out a yip of pleasure when he saw me. "Well look who's here," said Bud. "C'mon in."

When I stood in the doorway of the living room, all I saw for a moment was Fay. Her startled face—her bright hair—all the dearness of her—

Then her mother came to me, smiling, and her father had a strong hand on my shoulder.

"Glad to see you, Dick," her father said, with that nice grin of his, as if I'd never been away—as if he'd expected me to come walking in.

"You've not been getting enough sleep," said Fay's mother. "Come and sit down, Dick."

The peacefulness of the room settled around me, the warmth of the welcome filled emptiness inside me. But I had to get things straight with Fay, first. I looked right at her, across the room where she sat very straight in a big chair.

"I've come to say good-by," I said, and I said it to all of them, but I looked at Fay. "I'll be leaving one of these days, and when that happens they won't give us any notice. I wanted to be sure—to say good-by—"

They were all saying things, and Bud was exclaiming loudly, but it was only Fay I really heard.

"That was thoughtful of you," Fay said in her new cool voice, and her face was a mask I couldn't read. Her hands were in her lap, clinched tightly, but there was no anger in her eyes. She had no smile for me—and somehow, I couldn't find that happiness I'd always seen in her face.

Fay had me licked, because I couldn't ask her for anything. But I looked at her mother and father, at the friendly warmth for me—for me—in their eyes. And I knew suddenly that I wanted to tell Fay's parents the truth, so everything would be straight between us, at least. I sort of pulled my courage together, and kicked myself into saying what I had to say.

"Look, I want to tell you something—" I said.

"Sit down and tell us," said Fay's father.

"No. Let me say my piece," I said.

Fay's mother studied me. "Bud" she said suddenly, "will you run down to the corner and get some ice cream?"

"Okay, I'll get out of your hair," Bud said, his kid voice tolerant. He left the room with a flourish.

"It's this," I said, my voice too loud in the quiet room. "It's like this. I just want you to know—I'll never forget how swell you've been to me. And I want to get it on the record, before I go overseas—that I'll never want to marry anyone but Fay, as long as I live."

There was a startled silence in the room for a moment, and Fay's father cleared his throat. I couldn't look at Fay. I looked at him instead. And he had that dry twinkle of his in his eyes.

"Well, Dick—I'm glad you wanted us to know that," he said in an odd sort of voice.

"You see, I can't ask her to marry me," I stumbled on. "But I wanted to say it once—and you've sort of been a family to me—and well, I guess that's all."

Fay's mother spoke swiftly. "Why do you mean—that you can't ask Fay to marry you?"

"Marry me—on a hundred and fifty dollars in the bank?" I exclaimed, and bitterness sharpened my voice. "Marry me—and have nothing? You've given her everything, and all I have to give her is loneliness."

Fay spoke, and her voice startled me. Her eyes were stormy. "Why didn't you tell me this the other night?"

"I did—I started to, and you blew up—" I said. "I can't ask you to marry me, and go away and leave you—worse than before, the worse for knowing me. But I can tell you that I'll love you as long as I live." It was queer, to be telling her that, in front of her family. But it was right, too.

Fay's mouth trembled suddenly, and I wanted to stride across the room to her.

"That last night in the park, Dick—" she said. "You talked—you talked as if you didn't want to marry me. As if you were afraid I'd take you seriously."

"Are you crazy?" I exclaimed, and I was half across the room to her before I stopped myself. A little more, and I'd have hold of her—a little more, and I'd never let her go. I had to get out of there, I had to get out—

"So anyhow, I've told you," I said, looking at all three of them. "So I'd better be going, now."

"Hold on—" said Fay's dad forcefully.

And her mother laid a hand on my arm. "Dick," she said, "Dick, you said something wrong. You made a mistake."

"What?" I asked.

"You said that all you had to give Fay was loneliness, Dick. Do you think that your love is nothing?"

And my knees were shaking now, and the room blurred a little. They were being too kind. How could I go on being decent, when they were kind? Because it took hardness to force myself out of that room, away from Fay.

"I'd take her away—from security," I tried to explain. This was the craziest thing, to be explaining to Fay's family why I wasn't good enough for her.

Fay's mother said clearly, "Dick, we give up some kinds of security, gladly, when we love someone. You are in Fay's life now, Dick, my dear. Love can't turn back."

"What do you mean?" I said stupidly.

"You're doing the fighting," Fay's dad was saying. "It's our job to look after Fay while you fight for us. You'll be coming back, with a lifetime to take your turn taking care of her. This is your home, Dick."

"Wait—" I said dazedly, staring at Fay. And her mother's words were beating inside my head—"You are in Fay's life now."

But it was no use hoping that they could mean—that Fay loved me. Not while Fay was leaping to her feet, her eyes blazing.

"Will you all stop trying to arrange my life?" she cried furiously. "Will you all stop talking as if I weren't in the room?"

"Fay—" I said, and I took three steps and I was near enough to touch her. "Fay—your folks don't seem to feel it would be wrong, if we got married."

"Well, nobody's consulted me," she exclaimed.

"It would be just a few days—and then I'll be gone," I said. "I don't know if you'd want to marry me—but I'll love you wherever I am."

"I haven't even been proposed to," Fay said, and behind her smile I saw something else that set me wild with happiness.

"Will you marry me, Fay?"

She looked at me for one long, close moment. Then she turned to her mother and father. "Much as I'm fond of you," she told them, "I don't want an audience when I'm going to accept a man."

They tiptoed out of the room, the two of them, and Fay turned back to me.

"What did you ask me?" she demanded, and the little quirk was back at the side of her mouth.

"Will you marry me, Fay?"

"Yes, with all my heart—" she said. THE END

I was a spoiled kid, always ready for fun.
When I joined the WACs, I still got a kick out
of breaking rules ... until that day I hitched
a plane ride. Too late I learned I couldn't buck
Army regulations — and get away with it.

DISGRACED! I HAD TO RUN AWAY

I don't mean to throw the "true" part of True Love *into doubt, but I question whether this story is an accurate reflection of military discipline between male and female soldiers. And Kathy, the spoiled young woman who's determined to slack her way through the army on her own terms, is a bit of a mess as a character. How does somebody with such an obvious lack of respect for authority decide to voluntarily enlist in the WACs? And how does she get away with kissing her sergeant in the middle of getting a dressing-down without repercussions?*

But it's all worth it for the part where Kathy's drifting off to sleep and, she confides, "all my dreams were mixed up with Daddy and Sgt. Rankin, and somehow they were the same person. Funny, the things you dream!"

Somebody was having fun writing this story, you can tell.

While the M.P. stood next to my seat in the bus I searched through my purse, carefully at first, and then as if I were really anxious. I was conscious of the whole busload of soldiers and WACs watching me.

Darn it, why did the M.P. keep standing there? The last time I'd been on the bus back from town he hadn't even bothered to check passes. Now that I didn't have one he was double-checking everybody. Had they missed me at the detachment, I wondered. Kelly, my best friend, had promised she would cover up for me. Oh, for Pete's sake, how much longer could I stall him?

I looked up and widened my eyes. "I guess I must have lost it. I was sure I had it in my wallet." I tried to look worried, and it wasn't hard. I wondered feverishly what my First Sergeant would say if I was caught without a pass again. I smiled up at the M.P., a tentative, apologetic smile.

But he stared back at me coldly. "I'm sorry—I can't let you through without your pass. You'll have to get off the bus and wait till I call through."

I was beginning to feel worried now. "But I had one. I just can't find it!" Suddenly I began to realize that what had started out as a big joke wasn't so funny. I had boasted to the girls that I could sneak out without a pass. I had done it before. But if I was caught, it would be a charge of AWOL, and I had a bad enough reputation as it was. Kathy Williams, goldbrick, first-class! My Company Officer had threatened to put me on K.P. for a month if I got into another jam, and she wasn't kidding.

I stood up reluctantly and started out of the bus, when suddenly a tall Technical Sergeant near the front stood up and put his hand on the M.P.'s arm. I looked up at him and my heart dropped into my shoes. It was Sgt. Rankin, the non-com in charge of the laboratory where I worked. I had never seen him in anything but hospital whites before, and somehow in his uniform with the stripes on his sleeve he looked as formidable as any officer on the post. I swallowed and nodded when I met his eye, but he looked right through me. Now I was really in a jam!

Then to my amazement I heard him say to the M.P., "She's got a pass, Corporal. I called her C.O. and checked this afternoon."

The M.P. looked doubtful. "We'll step off the bus and settle it."

We waited near the M.P. booth while the bus went through the gate and down the road to camp, then the M.P. turned to Sgt. Rankin. "Can I see your credentials, Sergeant?"

He looked at Sgt. Rankin's pass and identity card, then at mine while I stood there stiffly. "Okay." He handed back our papers. "You say she works for you?"

"Private Williams is one of my technicians. She's very reliable and I can vouch for her. You can call her detachment in the morning and check."

The M.P. relaxed. "I'm sorry about this, but you know how tough regulations are. You'll have an hour wait for the next bus, or you can walk. It's only a mile to the detachment."

"We'll walk," I said quickly, and Sgt. Rankin nodded. When we were out of earshot of the M.P. booth I wiped my forehead. "Wow, that was close. Gee, thanks a million, sarge."

"Don't thank me, Private Williams," he said coolly. "I'll get it out of you in detail work at the lab. Look, I did this so the laboratory won't get a bad name. I'll call your C.O. in the morning and fix things up."

I swallowed. "That won't do me much good . . . she's really after me. I've been in dutch before."

He looked down at me and I saw the edge of a smile on his lips. "I'll tell her I gave you a pass in the lab and forgot to notify your First Sergeant. She'll square it. Your C.O. owes me a few favors anyway—but you'd better toe the line from here on in."

I looked up at his face as we walked. He wasn't handsome, but there was a rugged quality to him that had often frightened me a little in the lab. He was a regular Army man, I knew, and he had seen action in the last war.

Hard and tough—I felt a quick rush of resentment towards him. What right did he have to tell me to toe the line? Just because he was my boss in the lab and he had done me a favor tonight? But he hadn't done that for me. He had made that pretty clear.

We didn't say much for the rest of that walk, but by the time we had reached the WAC detachment some of the anger had left me. No matter how you looked at it, he had done me a big favor. I said, "Thanks Sergeant." And then I added, "I'll try and mend my ways." And as I said it a little devil rose up in me.

Sgt. Rankin stood there, looking down at me. With a little start of surprise I realized that he was at a loss for words. He wasn't used to dealing with anyone like me. He could bark at the men, but I wasn't a man. At that moment I couldn't help myself. The devil in me made me stand up on tiptoes and kiss him full on the mouth.

I grinned at his stunned look, and I turned and ran into the barracks. Let him figure that one out! At least I had discovered the Sergeant was human. But somehow the joke was on me. And that night I lay awake in my bunk, listening to the soft breathing of the girls and thought of Sgt. Bill Rankin and his dark eyes and grim face.

He wasn't my type. I had never dated anyone that serious and— and deep, I guess. Back home in Allenton High I had a reputation for being a crazy kid. Kathy Williams, always in trouble, always running away from rules. Racing through town on a motorcycle with some guy, caught necking in the school tower, dragged up in front of the principal for smoking in the locker room—but none of it was serious. I was young and I had to rebel. Daddy used to laugh it off.

"For a girl with no mother you've done pretty well, baby. I trust you and I'll stick by you." And he had even when I asked for his permission to enlist in the WACs. "If it's what you want—" he told me, and signed.

Dad wrote every day, and came down to see me often. I didn't go home on my first furlough. The girls and I went to New York instead, but Dad didn't mind. "Anything that makes you happy, baby. Write if you need money."

There was only one father like mine in a million, I decided, as

I dropped off to sleep that night. But all my dreams were mixed up with Daddy and Sgt. Rankin, and somehow they were the same person. Funny, the things you dream!

The next morning I came to work at the laboratory a few minutes late, and I was just slipping into my white coat when Bill came in from one of the wards. "You're late, Kathy," he said quietly.

I tried to look serious. "Sorry, Sarge. I had a heavy date last night." I thought I was being cute, but I grew red when he gave me a long stare and then turned away. I went over to the work bench and started running through some blood chemistry that was waiting, but I couldn't concentrate on my work. Something about Sgt. Rankin's attitude bothered me. I remembered how I had deliberately teased him last night with that kiss, and I realized what a dopey thing it was. He must have me figured for a real goon!

I went through my work automatically. I wondered what it would have been like if he had kissed me back last night, and for just a moment I closed my eyes. Then I came back to reality with a bang. While I'd been daydreaming I had turned back to the bench and brushed the edge of the Colorimeter with my hand. It went crashing to the floor!

I cried out, "Oh no!" and then there was a shocked silence. The other technicians turned from their work and stared at me, and I stared down at the smashed glass and broken metal.

Sgt. Rankin came over and he was just bending to pick up the shattered instrument when the Major walked in. The major's mouth dropped. "What happened to the Colorimeter?"

I edged back against the table as his face reddened. I knew how hard he had fought to get this new equipment. "Do you men think everything is expendable?" he thundered. "Let me tell you—soldiers are a lot easier to replace than this precision stuff. Who dropped it?"

My heart was pounding and my mouth was dry. I swallowed and

started to speak, but Sgt. Rankin stepped in front of me. "It was an accident, Sir." His voice was very quiet and the Major stared at him.

"I realize it was an accident." He said acidly. "But who did it?"

"I—I—" I stepped forward and tried to speak. But before I could say anything Sgt. Rankin broke in, "I did it, Sir. I'm sorry. I was showing Private Williams how to operate it."

There was a long silence, then the Major touched the broken casing and shook his head. "Well, we'll have to order another. I'll see you in my office when you clean this up, Sergeant." He turned and left.

"Sergeant, you're a darling!" Relief washed over me. If I had taken the blame it would've been awful. I was in so much hot water anyway. I had been gigged at the last inspection and had goofed off on K.P. twice. "Thanks a million," I said gratefully. "I'm so sorry I did it."

But Sgt. Rankin's face was dark and angry. "Don't bother to thank me, Williams. You ought to be ashamed of yourself!" His voice lashed at me like a whip. "You handle your equipment like a baby. Look at your table—it's a mess! The accident was pure carelessness. I saw it."

His voice was hard as he went on. "I took the blame because I wanted to give you another chance. We need technicians even when they're as sloppy as you. I'm giving you another week to get on the ball!"

"I said I was sorry!" I was terribly hurt and humiliated, and angered too. What right did he have talking to me like that and in front of the whole lab? I didn't have to stand for that!

"Being sorry doesn't replace the Colorimeter." Sgt. Rankin turned away.

"What do you want me to do?" I cried. "Get down on my knees and thank you for taking the blame?" I could feel the tears start behind my eyelids. "I hate you, you big bully!" I turned and started running from the room, but Sgt. Rankin caught my arm, turning me around, his eyes blazing.

"Tears are a cheap trick, and using them is no credit to the WAC! You joined the Army. You took on the job of a soldier, and a part of that job is taking your punishment like a man—or a woman soldier."

I looked up at his angry face, and forced back the tears. "All right," I said. "I'm sorry, Sergeant."

"And I'm sorry too, Private Williams. You're a good technician when you want to be, and as long as you do your job I'll go out on a limb for you. Now let's forget it. Get back to work." He turned abruptly and I watched him walk into bacteriology. I turned back to my bench and did my work that afternoon, but I was so ashamed of myself that I couldn't look anyone in the eye. When I got back to the detachment I discovered that all the girls had heard the story. That made me furious, and all I wanted to do was get even with Sgt. Rankin for the embarrassment he had caused me. I knew deep down it was childish, but I didn't care. I'd show him!

He spoke to me several times after the incident as if nothing had happened, but I answered him coldly, retreating behind a mask of military language. Purposely, I addressed him as "Sir," even though he was a non-commissioned officer. I knew that annoyed him.

Finally, on Friday as I was leaving the lab he took me aside. "Kathy, I want to talk to you." I lifted my eyebrows and waited. "Look," he went on awkwardly, "I know you're mad about the dressing down I gave you, but that's over. I want to get along with you. It's important that everyone in the lab work together. Personal grudges affect our work."

I looked up at him and for just a moment I wanted to reach up and touch his cheek. What would it be like to be friends with Bill Rankin? To be more than friends? What was he like deep inside?

I knew what he was like on the outside —how lean and tall

and strong he was. I had seen him bend metal equipment into shape with his bare hands, watched the muscles flex in his arms. How would it feel to have those arms around me, those lips against mine?

I felt eager at the thought, but pushed it aside. The guy was a square, just not my type! I made my voice flat. "I have no personal grudge against you, Sir."

"You can drop that Sir stuff. You know I'm a non-com." He took my arm. "You're a little child trying to get even. What's in back of it?"

I pulled away furiously. "I'm not a child! And as for getting even, you're way off the beam. I don't care about you that much."

"Okay. We understand each other." He turned abruptly and walked away, and I felt a quick disappointment well up inside me. I wanted him to apologize for bawling me out, and I wanted him to treat me like a woman, not a soldier. And yet, I resented the fact that I wanted that! Oh—I was too mixed up to know how I felt.

That Friday night I went out with some of the girls and on my way back to the post, at the terminal in town, one of the Lieutenants who worked in Supply started kidding around with us. When he asked me to have a beer before the bus to camp left I said yes, though I knew that enlisted women weren't allowed to date officers at our post. But I had seen Sgt. Rankin at the Terminal Bar, and I wanted him to know I was out with another man. I guess it was a kid thing, but at the time it seemed like fun.

I stepped into the bar with the Lieutenant and the only empty stool was next to Bill. I gave him a frosty smile and introduced him to the Lieutenant. Bill nodded coldly. You could see he was boiling inside, but whether it was because I was dating an officer or another man I didn't know.

And then of all the G.I. luck in the world, in walked my First Sergeant. She frowned when she saw me and her eyes went from Bill to the Lieutenant. She came over finally and nodded at Bill and said, "Hello, Williams. I don't like to interrupt, but are you with the Lieutenant?"

I wished the floor would open up and swallow me, and I saw the Lieutenant look uncomfortable. It would mean a reprimand to both of us from our C.O.s.

I looked at Bill Rankin appealingly, but he just stood up and said, "Well, I'll be running along." And he walked away as carelessly as that. My First Sergeant nodded and fixed the Lieutenant with a fishy stare. "I'm sorry, Sir, but you know the rules at this post."

"Well, at every other post I've been at—" he began. And then he shrugged and turning left the bar, leaving me alone with my First Sergeant.

"And now you listen to me, Williams—" I tensed up and listened for five minutes of the sharpest tongue lashing I had ever gotten—and I didn't dare say a word.

The next day the C.O., Captain Jane Ellis, called me into her office. "You're leaving next week on the first shipment to California and Camp Stoneman. You may be sent to Japan from there."

I felt my face grow pale. "I—I didn't put in for transfer," I said weakly.

"But we're giving you one. I'm sorry, Private Williams. I just don't think you belong here. Your silly escapades and utter lack of responsibility have been no credit to the Woman's Army Corps."

I looked down, ashamed, as she went on. "Being in the Army isn't an easy job. It isn't a lark or an adventure. You should be proud to wear the uniform of your country, instead of breaking rules and treating it as a joke. What you've done at this post has been a reflection on every girl in the Army. They're fighting for equality and a chance to prove their value as citizens, and you're out for nothing but a good time. I won't have it. That's why you're going to Stoneman."

She paused and looked at my papers on the desk. When she spoke again her voice softened a little. "I don't want you to think of this as disciplinary action, so much as a new chance. None of this will go on your record. You have a chance to start clean. Now, good luck."

I couldn't meet her eyes. I just stood there at attention and fought to keep from crying. I knew how well I deserved what she'd done. Finally, I saluted and turning smartly, I left the office.

I decided that from then till I left I would do my best to obey rules and behave like a good soldier. I'd been deeply impressed by the Captain's words, shamed too. I wanted to show everyone that I was more than a dumb goldbrick—most of all, Sgt. Rankin. Now that I was leaving, I wanted him to approve of me.

But no matter how hard I tried everything seemed to go wrong. I mixed the agar plates incorrectly, and at inspection on Friday I caused the whole lab to be gigged because I forgot to clean behind the bottles in Serology. Afterwards Bill Rankin bawled me out and I blew my top and walked out.

Everything I did was wrong, so I decided it was no use. If I was leaving the post I might just as well do as I pleased, and have a good time while I could.

I was taken out of the lab and put into overseas training for two weeks. It was awful, worse than basic training had ever been, and worst of all was our being restricted to quarters for a whole weekend. I couldn't take it. I was always being called down for something, and finally I started goofing off.

I reported to sick call and got out of a five-mile hike. During the lectures I sneaked out and went to the PX for malts. I tried to convince myself that I was pulling a fast one on the Army, but actually I was miserable!

Finally I felt I couldn't take it any longer, and decided to go AWOL. I would go to see Daddy. Maybe he could get me out of the Army, or at least see that I didn't get shipped out. I knew he had some influence in local politics. I left camp Saturday night, cutting through the empty field behind the lab to the back gate. I took a little road into town, and was at the station getting ready to buy my ticket when someone took my arm. I gasped and turned to see Sgt. Rankin.

"What are you doing here?"

"Gosh, you scared me!"

"You're restricted to quarters, aren't you?" he said slowly.

I tried to laugh. "No one restricts me." Only it didn't sound tough. It sounded silly.

"Are you crazy, Kathy? Going off like this. You're AWOL and on a shipment. You could be court-martialed."

"A lot you'd care!" I flared up. "Besides, what are you doing here, checking on me?"

"As a matter of fact, I am." His voice was tight. He led me out of the station to a small bench near the tracks. "Kelly told me you were out. She was worried and I don't blame her. I figured you might try and go home. That's why I'm here."

"I *am* going home." I turned away. "I don't belong in the army. I'm a misfit. That's why they're shipping me out, to get rid of me."

"Kathy, if they do ship you overseas, you should be proud. It's an honor. They don't send misfits where guys are giving their lives." He touched my shoulders. "There's a lot I want to say to you, and I don't know where to begin. I like you, or I'd let you take your medicine. You're a smart girl and pretty too. You're good in lab work and the Army's trained you. Then why this clowning, why this breaking rules? You're not a kid any more. Is growing up so hard—now stop crying!"

"I know, it's a woman's trick." My face twisted and suddenly I couldn't hold back the tears: "And you hate me. You think I'm a real dope."

"Kathy, Kathy!" He pulled me to him, my head against his shoulder, and stroked my back while I cried.

"I don't hate you. You know that. I love you, Kathy. I've been in love with you from the moment I first saw you. Why do you think

I stuck my neck out for you so often?"

I drew back and looked up at him wonderingly. "When that Lieutenant was buying me a beer—" I began.

He put his finger on my lips. "There are some things I wouldn't do, and you deserved that." He looked at me, and then slowly smiled. "I owe you something. You know what it is, don't you, Kathy?"

"What, Bill?" My heart began pounding.

"That kiss you gave me. . . ." He bent down and his lips touched mine, and it was as if every second I had ever lived I'd been waiting breathlessly for this.

"Oh, Kathy baby, I've been wanting to kiss you for so long!"

"Why didn't you then?" I whispered, and I pushed back the dark, curling hair from his forehead. "I think I've been in love with you ever since that night on the bus."

He laughed. "You were a spoiled brat. Still are, probably."

"But you love me anyway?"

He tipped up my chin. "Always, Kathy."

"Bill," I said earnestly, and I meant what I said. "I'm going to change. You wait and see. I'll make you proud of me!"

"I know you will. But just to be on the safe side, I'm going along to Camp Stoneman to keep an eye on you."

"What?" I stared at him. "You're on the shipment too? But why—how?"

He smiled. "They need a Tech Sergeant for a station hospital in Japan. That's me."

"Bill—then we'll be together." I felt as if nothing could go wrong now.

"For a while at least. Now let's get you back to camp before you're missed. Come on."

That last week we spent at camp was absolutely perfect. I did my best at training and surprisingly enough it wasn't hard. The evenings were free and Bill and I spent them dancing at the service club, or at the post movie. Sometimes we'd sit down by the lake, kissing, talking, making up for all the time we'd lost without knowing each other.

I told him about Allenton and high school, the dull, meaningless life of a small town. I told him about Dad and all the trouble I used to get into, and he shook his head.

"What a kid—always breaking rules. You haven't changed, Kathy."

I pouted. "Isn't that what you like about me?"

He was silent a while. "Not really, Kathy," he answered slowly. "I like the person you are deep down inside. That's the Kathy I've fallen in love with, and I'm willing to sweat it out till she takes over."

I didn't answer him. I didn't quite know what to say. I felt all choked up and ashamed of myself, and yet still a little defiant. I loved Bill and wanted him to approve of me. And yet I felt hurt that he didn't completely.

At the end of the week we received our travel orders and discovered that we both had to report to Camp Stoneman on the same day. We'd both gotten separate travel allotments, and were left to ourselves to meet the shipment in California. We had one week.

"We can spend the whole week in New York, Bill," I said excitedly. "And then fly out. That way we don't have to spend all that time traveling."

He seemed uncertain. "I don't know, Kathy. I hate to chance being late."

"But Bill, it's no chance. We'll just spend less time traveling than if we went by train. Please Bill, please!"

In the end he gave in and I wrote Daddy an apologetic letter explaining why I couldn't see him and telling him all about Bill. I knew he'd understand.

How can I describe those days with Bill in New York. We tried to do everything, see all the shows, eat at all the fancy restaurants and even visit the museums and art galleries.

The first day in the city Bill booked passage for both of us on a through flight to San Francisco. I talked him into waiting till the last possible moment before leaving the city.

"I hate to do it, Kathy. We ought to give ourselves a day of leeway just in case anything happens to delay the flight."

"Oh Bill, you know it's perfectly all right."

He smiled. "Okay pumpkin. Let's not waste time arguing. Come over here and kiss me."

But when we got to LaGuardia Airport the night we were to leave, we discovered that the flight had been postponed indefinitely because of bad weather over the Rockies.

Bill spent a worried half hour at the desk, and then came away with a long face. "I got two reservations as far as Chicago for tonight, but from there on we're on our own. We just can't afford to get to camp late."

We got into Chicago in the early hours of the morning, held up by the weather, and the clerk at the desk told us we had just missed the San Francisco flight. There was another plane scheduled in a few hours, but there was only one seat available.

We took the reservation. "It's going to mean trouble for one of us," Bill said. "You take the seat and I will follow."

"No, Bill," I said. "The whole mess was my fault to begin with. Let me stay for the next flight. I couldn't get into any more trouble."

"That's silly. I'll get out of it. I'm still a non-com."

"Yes," I snapped back, "and they can bust you for this!"

Still arguing we went into the terminal to have coffee, and while we were sitting there talking I noticed two Air Force men at the next table. Somehow we got to talking and they asked where we were heading.

"Stoneman," Bill answered gloomily. "We thought we could get a plane out in time to make our orders, but it turns out there's only room for one."

The Captain, a young, dark-haired man, grinned. "Too bad you don't have Air Force orders or we could take you both tonight."

"You mean you're going there now?" I asked excitedly.

He glanced at his watch. "In about half-an-hour."

"But can't you take us anyway?"

He looked over at his buddies. "It's against regulations."

"Rules and regulations!" I shook my head disgustedly. "I thought you fly-boys were above all that sort of stuff." I smiled appealingly. "Who'd know we were on the plane. Come on, Captain, let us bum a ride!"

"Cut it out, Kathy." Bill put his hand on my arm, but I ignored him.

"Bill and I may be shipped overseas. We want to be together, even if it's only for a few hours on the plane. Gee, Captain, haven't you got a girl yourself somewhere?"

I could see both of them weakening, and I kept on coaxing till they finally gave in. I didn't dare look at Bill when we left to pick up our luggage. I knew he was annoyed, but I was pretty sure I could talk him out of that. And now the whole thing began to seem like one of my old larks. What fun I'd have telling the girls about it later!

Bill was quiet and withdrawn during the flight to Denver, and afterwards on the last lap. It was a C-47 plane, and besides the Captain and co-pilot, there was a seven-man crew. We had a lot of fun during the ride, laughing and joking. They teased me about the WACs and I kidded them about the Air Force. Only Bill seemed glum.

When I tried to tell him I was sorry about the whole thing, he just shrugged and said it was all right.

Finally I got a little angry and I whispered, "Relax, Bill, and have some fun. You act as if this was an ordeal instead of an adventure!"

He looked at me strangely. "That's what it is to you, Kathy. Just an adventure. You don't care about the fact that we're doing something illegal, that if we're caught we'll be in one hell of a jam, that these planes aren't as protected as civilian ones—oh, what's the use. Everything is one big joke to you, maybe our being in love is just an adventure too!"

I was hurt by that and I turned away. I loved Bill, and he knew it. Why was he deliberately mean?

We were over the Sierra Nevadas when the plane engine began to sound labored, and I could tell that one of them was skipping. One of the men let out a low whistle, "Hey, look out the window. It's snowing!"

"Snowing!" I stared at Bill, and then out the window. We were in the middle of a snow storm that'd come up so quickly we hadn't had time to notice. One of the men muttered, "I don't like it. Snow at this altitude is no joke."

"It's a freak," someone answered, and then the left engine missed and stopped, and a sudden tenseness ran through the cabin. I felt a sinking feeling in the pit of my stomach and I reached out to take Bill's hand. He drew me to him and put his arm around me.

The Captain stepped out of the pilot's cabin and said, "Listen men. We're having a little engine trouble. I think we'll get through all right, but the snow is piling up on the left wing and the defroster—"

He never finished the sentence. The plane seemed to swerve, and I felt as if I were on a fast down elevator. I saw the Captain dash back to the pilot's cabin and I heard him yell something. There was silence for a moment, and then someone whispered, "Oh, my God!"

The lights went off in the plane and I clung to Bill . . . I remember the crash. As long as I live I'll remember that! It was a flame of twisted motion and tortured metal. I felt myself flung about like a rag, slammed violently to the floor, and after that there was blackness, an eternity of blackness.

I came back to consciousness with the sound of a scream ringing in my ears. I forced my eyes open, and then I closed them again. There was an unbearable throbbing in my head and my leg hurt. Again there was the scream, and somewhere I heard someone sobbing. When I opened my eyes it was dark, and I moved my hand away from my body cautiously till it hit metal. I was still in the plane. Realization flowed back, and with it terror, for myself and Bill. I cried out, "Bill—where are you?"

Somewhere in the darkness someone cried out, pleading for help. I pulled myself up and there was a blaze of light, and one of the men stood there holding a torch in his hands, his face a mask of blood.

He stood there, trying to wipe the blood from his face with one hand, his mouth working with pain. I went to him, hobbling along, and I propped up the torch, staring frantically around the cabin. Where was Bill? Dear God, where was he?

The men had been flung around the plane by the crash, some of them in twisted, unnatural positions, some struggling to sit up, others too injured to move.

"Can you help me with the door?" The soldier who had held the torch was fumbling with the clasp, and I realized he couldn't see. I joined him at the door, both of us struggling to get it open.

Somehow we managed and I helped him out. Fighting an impulse to run back and search for Bill. It had stopped snowing, but the sky was cloudy and there was a cold, biting wind. We had crashed into a clump of trees, but the belly of the plane was on a line with the ground. Both wings had been shorn off!

I found a clearing and helped the soldier to sit down, then I stumbled back to the wreck, each step sending a lance of pain through me. One of my legs was cut at the ankle and sprained and my clothes were half-torn off me, but other than that I wasn't hurt.

I found Bill, and at first I thought he was dead. He lay there so still and white. Then I saw that he was breathing and I dropped to my knees and caught him to me, sobbing softly.

The only other soldier who was able to move was the one that had been blinded. I washed his face and bandaged it, and together we worked through the rest of that long and horrible night, getting the men off the plane and into the clearing. Three of the men were dead, and another died before morning while I stood there helpless and desperate!

Bill regained consciousness, but one of his legs was broken and I could tell he was in agony. His medical training helped, however, and he directed me as much as he could.

By the time morning had come I was thoroughly exhausted, but I knew that our troubles had just begun. We were in an isolated part of the Sierra Nevadas. Our radio was smashed and there was little chance of the plane being found for days. We couldn't hold out. The men needed medical aid, and soon.

"I'm going to try and get down to help," I told Bill as I wrapped a bandage around my sprained ankle.

"You can't go, Kathy." He was breathing heavily. "You're hurt and you'll get lost in the woods. Stay and maybe they'll find us today."

"They may not report us missing for hours yet," I said. "And even then it may be days before they find us. None of the men can wait that long, and none of them is able to go for help. I've got to, Bill." I put my hand on his forehead. "It's my fault that you and I are here. I got us into it."

"Kathy, don't talk like that."

I kissed him and then made the others comfortable. The pilot was conscious and he told me where he thought we were. "Maybe ten miles," he pointed east. "There should be a road, but don't try it. If you get lost—"

"I'll find it," I said, with more confidence than I felt. I limped off and one of the men called out, "Good luck!" Boy, I'd sure need it!

I could feel my eyes fill up. With all the pain they suffered not one of them had complained. And now I was leaving them, and if I couldn't find the road—if I were to get lost in the woods, what would happen then?

I paused at the edge of the clearing and I looked back, and it seemed to me that a breathless sort of hush had fallen over the snow-covered ground.

These men would die, unless I reached help at once. And there was little chance of my finding my way out of this white wilderness. No—I couldn't desert these men on the very slim chance of reaching help.

"This is one time you can't goldbrick or goof off," I said grimly, as I limped back to the wreck.

I'll never forget the light in Bill's eyes when I told him I was staying, nor the expression on the pilot's face. I had to mark the spot of the wreck. If a plane came over, it mustn't miss us. But how could I do it? It seemed practically impossible. I stared at the wreckage-littered ground and I realized the answer. I had to make some sign out of the broken and battered gear of the plane. It would be a tremendous job to move enough gear to make any visible mark, but I had to do it!

Piece by piece I dragged the wreckage out into the snow and arranged it in the form of a huge cross. No plane flying overhead could miss that.

I worked for hours, pulling and tugging. My injured leg grew steadily worse, throbbing and sending a fire of pain through my whole body—but I kept on. I had to build the cross—the marker!

Somehow, during that nightmare struggle to build the cross, I grew up. The scatter-brained girl who broke rules for fun died. She became a woman, resolute and strong, with only one thought, to help the men who needed help, so desperately.

And then, when the shadows were beginning to lengthen, and I had all but given up hope—when Bill and the pilot had lost consciousness and the blind soldier was almost delirious, then I heard the roar of a plane.

I stumbled out to the cross and I stood there, waving frantically. The planecircled twice and then turned and roared back into the sky.

They picked us up by helicopter an hour later, and I was kneeling next to Bill's unconscious body crying softly when they came. "Dear God, let it not be too late!"

It wasn't. The ride back was confused in my mind. I think I fainted before we were unloaded. And then I slept—forever, it seemed.

I remember the day Bill came to see me for the first time. I was sitting up, sipping orange juice when the door opened and he hobbled in on crutches wearing maroon hospital pajamas. "Hi, Goldbrick, still taking it easy?"

Tears came to my eyes and I couldn't answer. I just held out my arms and he came to them. Then I found my voice.

"Oh, darling—darling! I'm so glad you're all right. Bill, I've been such a stupid, crazy kid—breaking rules that were made for good reasons. I got us into that whole mess."

"Hey, cut out that talk. You're speaking about the woman I love. No, seriously baby, you'll probably get a medal for heroism for what you did."

"But look what I might have done," I said, shaking my head. "I might have caused you to—to--"

"Only you didn't," Bill cut in. "And it was my fault too, this time. Now look, forget what's been. You've learned your lesson, haven't you?"

"I have, Bill, oh I have! And I've learned how much you mean to me. I grew up out there on that mountain, Bill, and I could never go back to being the hare-brained girl I was!"

"Then everything is going to be all right." He kissed me gently. "I spoke to the post commander at Stoneman by phone. There's some trouble and we may miss our shipment, but I think they'll overlook that. We did try to get there, and what you did—well, Kathy, I've never been as proud of anyone as I was of you." He drew back and smiled. "There must be some way I can keep you in line though."

"What way, Bill?" I asked softly.

"I'm going to marry you before we get out of here—that's how. Now get some rest. I'll see you later, baby."

I watched him go out the door and my heart was singing. Whatever trouble there was ahead because of what I'd done, I knew I had the strength now to face it. I had grown up—learned that rules are set up for good purpose—and I had Bill's love. I closed my eyes then, and dropped off to sleep. THE END

I WENT ON A SINGLES WEEKEND WHILE MY HUSBAND WAS IN VIETNAM

Two months after Jim and Rita started dating, he got his draft notice. When she finds out that he would like to marry her, she suggests they go ahead and do it before he ships out to Vietnam, but once he's gone, she realizes that she misses the carefree life of a young single woman, gossiping with her coworkers about their dates.

Then a friend tells her about a resort that caters to "swinging singles" on the weekends. "You know—you go up and just let yourself go all weekend," her friend explains. "And from what I hear, most people go pretty far."

The sexual revolution was in full swing (ahem) when this story was published, and it would've been silly for True Love to pretend otherwise, or to act as if many of the women reading the magazine hadn't already done a little sexual experimentation of their own. That didn't mean they had to like the new morality, though, and Rita's psychological punishment for going to that resort is swift, although not quite merciless—this way, she gets to learn from her mistake.

For whatever his reasons, he looked forward to weekends, but I dreaded them. For me there was no fun or no family to hurry home to—just the same loneliness I felt during the week, and more time to think about it. The flow of people from the building tapered off, and I closed my eyes. In my mind I could picture Jim running out and coming toward the car.

I smiled and opened the door for him, and before he even said hello, he put his arms around me and kissed me. Neither of us cared how many people saw us.

"Do you feel like going out tonight, Rita?" he asked me as we sat in the car.

"Let's not," I answered, leaning against his shoulder. "Let's just stay home and 'be married'." We laughed, and he kissed me again.

"That's fine with me, honey," he said softly. "Just fine."

I opened my eyes, and the image of Jim was gone. Instead I looked around the parking lot, empty now except for a few cars belonging to the maintenance crew. I couldn't put it off any longer, I knew. I had to go home.

In a strange way, it was funny, I thought as I drove home. If things hadn't worked out so badly for Jim and me, the scene I had pictured in the parking lot would have happened today, instead of more than a year ago. By now he would probably be manager of his department, and after work we'd meet in the parking lot and drive home together.

Or maybe I wouldn't be working at all. Maybe by now I'd have a baby, or be expecting one, and Jim would drive home alone. In either case our apartment would be warm and friendly, and I wouldn't think of it as a prison I dreaded going back to each night.

Thinking about what might have happened didn't do me much good—I had to face the facts. Everything had happened so quickly that I often found it hard to believe, and even harder to sort out all of the details, day by day.

Instead I remembered mostly the feelings. I remembered the happiness I felt when I first met Jim. I had been working at National Insurance for two months as a typist, and I was beginning to think that my mother was right when she told me that I would be sorry I had left Augusta.

I shared an apartment with Claire Michaels, a girl from back home, and although we both went out a lot, I was beginning to wonder if I would ever meet a guy I really cared about. Then, one day at work, a tall good-looking man was sitting at the table Helen and I usually shared in the employees cafeteria.

"I'm sorry if I'm sitting in your seats," he said when we walked over. He began to pick up his tray, and to my surprise I found myself blurting out that there was more than enough room for all of us. "Thanks," he said, and got me a chair from an empty table nearby.

He told us that his name was Jim Mitchell, and that he had just been transferred from the Chicago office.

"How do you like Hartford?" Helen asked.

"Well, it seems nice, but you know how it is when you're a stranger. You don't know where anything is."

"I'd be glad to show you around," I found myself saying. "I've only been here a couple of months, but maybe I can help." As soon as I spoke I was surprised at myself, and I was afraid that I had been too forward. But Jim smiled and looked at me with a warm and friendly gleam in his eyes.

"That's very nice of you," he said. "Say, you wouldn't be free tonight, would you?"

I had a date, but I suddenly wanted to break it. "Yes, yes I am." I told him.

"Fine. I'll pick you up at eight."

The bell rang, and I excused myself, saying that I had to get back to work. As Helen and I left, Jim called out, "Hey—you forgot to give me your address." My face turned red as I walked back to the table and wrote it down for him, and on the way up to our floor in the elevator, I told Helen that I had made a fool of myself.

"No, Rita," she said, winking. "You played it perfectly. Just wait and see."

It seemed that she was right. Jim and I went out that night, and we were together almost every evening both the weeks that followed. Since we were both new in Hartford, we spent our weekends going around to all of the landmarks that the local people never bother visiting, and we found that we enjoyed each other's company more than anything else in the world.

Then, one night about two months after we first met, Jim handed me something when he came to pick me up for one of our dates. It was an envelope, and I could see by the look on his face that something was wrong.

"What is it?" I asked him.

"Read it, Rita," he said. "You'll see."

The letter was from the draft board that Jim was registered with back in Chicago, and it said that he was being called for active duty in thirty days.

"Thirty days—there must be some mistake. Why, you've just moved. They can't do this to you."

"They can, honey," he said, taking me in his arms, "and it looks as if they are. There's nothing that I can do about it." My eyes filled with tears, and I couldn't keep from crying. "Come on, Rita," Jim said, kissing the tears away. "Don't cry. I'll be back."

"I'm sorry. I—I don't want to make it worse for you. But it isn't fair, Jim. It just isn't fair."

I clung to him, and he moved his hand along my hair and back. "I feel the same way," he said. "You know, if this hadn't happened—but what's the use? It did happen, and just when I found a girl I wanted to marry."

"What did you say?" I asked, pulling away from him.

"I said that I want to marry you, Rita. It's too bad that this came up, but when I get back—"

Suddenly I had an idea. "Let's not wait, Jim," I said. "Let's get married now—tomorrow."

"But I will be going away in a month. I can't ask you to sit around and wait. After all, Rita, you're a beautiful girl, and there's no reason why you should miss out on getting some fun out of life just because I got drafted."

"You're not asking me—I'm asking you. Please, darling—we have a whole month. I could take a leave of absence, and we could be together every day. I don't care about getting the fun out of life, Jim. I just care about you."

"Are you sure you want to do this, Rita?" he asked me.

"Surer than I've ever been of anything else." He took me in his arms and kissed me, and I felt happier than I had ever felt before. Four days later we were married by a justice of the peace, with my roommate, Claire, and a friend of Jim's as witnesses. My parents were shocked when I told them the news—I'd written them about Jim, but they hadn't expected marriage. They invited us up for the weekend, and wished us both luck.

We spent our honeymoon in Jim's apartment, trying to cram in as much of being together as we could before he left. We had talked a lot about ourselves ever since that first date, but we suddenly found that there were lots of things that we still wanted to learn.

There didn't seem to be time enough for all that we wanted to do. We spent a weekend with my folks in Augusta, then a few days with Jim's parents in Chicago. When we got back to Hartford, we were busy making plans about the apartment. Our company had gotten Jim a really great place with a living room, a bedroom, and a den when he got his transfer, and since he had signed a lease on it, Claire suggested that I move my stuff over and stay in Jim's place while he was in the army. A girl at her office was looking for a new apartment, so she wouldn't have any trouble finding a roommate.

Jim helped me pack up my clothes, and we spent a whole week buying furniture and arranging it. Then, almost before we knew it, it was time for him to leave. The night before he had to go I lay in his arms, unable to control my tears.

"Don't cry, darling," he said. "It's only two years. We have the rest of our lives to be together."

Only two years. As I pulled into the parking lot of our apartment,

I remembered how short two years had seemed at the time. Jim was right—we were both young. He would be 25 when he got back, and I would be 23. We had a lot of time ahead of us.

But after he left, every day seemed to be a month. Suddenly I was different from the girls at work, unable to share their excitement about dates. When I went back to the apartment at night, I was lonelier than I had ever been in my life, and instead of feeling better as time passed, I only felt worse.

When his basic training was over, Jim came home for a week. I was thrilled to see him, but those few days we had together only made me realize even more how much I was missing. After that we had a few weekends together, and then Jim was transferred to the Presidio in San Francisco. He had been there for six months when he finally got a week off, and he had come home to tell me something that made the waiting worse—he was being sent to Vietnam as a member of the Signal Corps.

I got out of the car and walked toward the apartment, and I could see that there was something in the mailbox. My spirits rose as I fumbled in my purse for the key, but when I opened it the familiar feelings of loneliness and disappointment returned. There was a magazine, some bills, and a letter from my mother, but no letter from Jim.

I turned to walk into my apartment, but just as I was opening the door, somebody called me. It was Margie Gates, my neighbor down the hall.

"How are you?" she asked, smiling. "Late getting out of work?"

"Oh, I just rode around for a while. I had some thinking to do."

"Everything's all right, isn't it?" she asked. "I mean, Jim's okay?"

"I suppose he is. I haven't heard anything in a couple of weeks. They must be in the field."

Margie nodded sympathetically. "I'm sure he's just busy, Rita.

Look—are you doing anything special tonight?"

"No, why?"

"Well, Bob and I are having some people over for dinner. We'd love to have you join us."

"Thanks," I said. "I'd like that."

"Great. See you around seven-thirty."

I went inside, and once again the terrible feeling of loneliness hit me. But instead of sitting down and feeling sorry for myself, I went into the bathroom and took a shower. At least tonight will be different, I told myself. At least I won't have to be alone.

When I rang the doorbell Bob Gates said, "Come on in." There were two other couples in the living room, and he introduced me.

"Are you single?" somebody asked, and I found myself explaining about Jim's being in Vietnam—the very thing I had wanted to forget.

Bob made me a drink, and as I sat down, the conversation got back to what the couples had been talking about before I came in. I sat listening to them, and suddenly a strange thought struck me. I didn't belong with them. I was as much out of place here as I was with the girls from the office. Just as I couldn't talk about dates, I couldn't join in the discussion about married life. I was an outsider.

Margie must have sensed how I felt, because at dinner she sat me next to her and tried to keep me busy talking. But I couldn't help looking around the table and noticing that everyone was nicely paired off, husband and wife, man and woman, Mr. and Mrs. I stuck out like a sore thumb.

"That chicken was terrific, Margie," Fay Roberts, one of the guests, said over coffee.

"Oh, it's a cinch to make," Margie answered, smiling with pride. "I can send you the recipe, if you like."

"Thanks. I'll have to tell the mailman to make room for it in our box."

"What do you mean?" I asked, completely baffled.

"Well, Dave and I seem to be on more mailing lists than you can count. We always get so many brochures that if someone sent us a letter, I don't know where the mailman would put it." She took some letters out of her purse and put them on the table. "Look—here's today's mail. I took it just as we were leaving tonight. Somebody wants us to buy a set of encyclopedias, somebody else wants us to buy land in Florida, and Harrod's wants me to 'spend an exciting weekend meeting swinging singles.'"

"Harrod's?" Marge asked. "Isn't that the new resort in the Berkshires?"

"That's the place," Faye said. "They run all of those singles weekends. You know—you go up and just let yourself go all weekend. And from what I hear, most people go pretty far. Of course no married couples are allowed."

"See that?" Marge said. "They're always spoiling our fun. Maybe we could leave our husbands at home and try it sometime."

"And maybe we could leave our wives," Bob said. Everyone laughed, and then I had an idea.

"I wonder if the girls in my office know about it," I said. "They're always looking for new ways to meet men. That place sounds as if it would be just right for them."

"Here," Faye said, handing me the brochure. "Why don't you take it for them? I'm certainly not going to use it."

I thanked her and slipped it into my purse, and for some reason I found that the thought of the resort excited me. When I left Margie's apartment an hour later, I was still thinking about it.

"Meet guys and girls from all over New England. Join others like yourself in a fantastic get-away-from-it-all weekend of fun that you'll never forget." As I lay in bed, I read the brochure over twice. It showed young couples sitting by the indoor pool, eating in the dining room and dancing. Everyone seemed to be enjoying himself, and I envied the people in the pictures.

"Well, Helen should be wild about that place," I said aloud, but even as I said the words another idea came into my head. What if *I* were to go up for the singles weekend. I could forget about my loneliness and the way I missed Jim, and I wouldn't really *do* anything.

It's ridiculous, a voice inside me said. You're *married.*

I turned out the light and looked at the empty place beside me on the bed. I was another year older, and I was lonely. I dreaded the thought of coming home each night to an empty house, and it would be a year before I saw my husband again.

Was that what being married was supposed to mean?

The next day, Saturday, Claire called up and asked me to go shopping. Afterward we went back to her apartment, and we talked the way we used to when I was living with her.

For those few hours I was able to forget my problems, and we discussed clothes, our jobs, and people back in Augusta. Even when Claire started talking about the guys she was seeing, I didn't feel left out. She talked about bars and parties, and we discussed the best ways of meeting single men.

"By the way," I asked her, "did you ever hear of a place called Harrod's?"

"Sure," she said. "Judy, my new roommate, goes up there a lot."

"What's it like? I heard some of the girls in the office talking about it, and I was wondering." It was a small lie, and it would be a lot easier than explaining about Faye and her mailbox.

"It's supposed to be nice, if you like that sort of thing."

"What sort of thing?"

"Well, you know," she said. "Everyone goes up there with more or less the same thing in mind—sex. The guys you meet expect you to be interested in it, or you wouldn't be there."

"But it says in the brochure that you can 'make meaningful relationships'—I mean, that's what the girls say it says."

I had slipped, but luckily Claire hadn't caught it. "Sure, you can make them, but they don't mean much more than sleeping together for one weekend. You just go up and have a good time with no questions asked, and then you come back and forget about it. Either that, or you plan to go again the next weekend."

Claire changed the subject, and I didn't want to seem overly interested, so I didn't press it. We talked awhile longer, then I went home.

That night as I sat watching television, I found that my thoughts were straying to the idea of going to Harrod's. I shut off the TV and went into the bedroom, and I picked up the brochure from the night table.

It was a crazy idea, I told myself, and maybe I should be ashamed for thinking about it. But was it really so bad? What harm would it do if I just went up for one weekend and flirted a little? After all, I could certainly take care of myself, and if anybody tried to get too friendly, I could always say no.

Maybe Jim had been right. Maybe we should have waited until he got back from

Vietnam before we got married. That way I would have been able to go out, to have a little fun while he was gone. It wouldn't have meant that I loved him any less than I did now. He was my husband, and I wanted him.

But I had to face the fact that Jim wouldn't be around for a long time. The loneliness I felt would grow and worsen. I had been lonely too long already, and one weekend of fun wouldn't hurt anybody—Jim would never know.

I called Harrod's the next day and made a reservation for the following weekend. "Will you be coming alone?" the man on the other end of the line asked me.

"Yes, yes I will."

"What name, miss?" For a moment I was panicky, and I wanted to hang up. What name would I use? I couldn't use my own or

Jim's—it just wouldn't be right. Then I thought of Helen.

"Mathews," I answered at last, "Miss Rita Mathews."

During the week that followed, there were many times when I wanted to forget all about going to Harrod's. I'd tell myself that it was a stupid idea, and that if I could even think about it, I didn't deserve a man like Jim. Then I'd hear the girls at work talking about the dates they had had and about going out every night, and I'd think of the way I spent my evenings alone. It just wasn't fair.

On Thursday there was a letter from Jim waiting for me, and seeing my name written in his handwriting almost made me cry. How could I think of doing such a terrible thing, of betraying his trust in me?

Dear Rita,

This will have to be short, because we're finally getting a chance to go into Saigon. We've been stationed on the outskirts for some time, and at last we'll get to see the city. It'll be great to see people again—people out of uniforms, that is. I have to go now, the guys are waiting for me. I'll write later and tell you all about it.

Love, Jim

Somehow it just didn't sound like a letter from a husband. It was more like Jim was writing to a sister or to a friend. The more I thought about it, the more that Jim seemed to be a stranger to me, and I began to think that maybe that was part of the trouble.

If we had had more time together before he went away, we might have drawn closer. As it was, we seemed to be drifting farther and farther apart. All he had to say to me was that he was glad that he was getting a chance to see people, to get away from the monotony of his daily life for a little while. Was it so different from what I wanted?

I packed and made my plans to leave from work the next evening.

As I signed the name *Rita Mathews* in the guest register, the man behind the desk said, "Dinner is in an hour, afterward there's a dance."

A bellboy came over and took my suitcase, and I followed him to the elevator. "Your first time here?" he asked as we rode to the third floor. I nodded. "I knew it. If you had been here before, I wouldn't have forgotten it." It was probably just a silly line he used on all the girls, probably so that he would get bigger tips, but somehow it made me feel good. My room was small, but it was clean and comfortable, and the first thing I did was to take a shower.

I had had my hair done at lunch, and when I got out of the bathroom I felt great. I put on one of the new dresses I had bought especially for the weekend. When I had put the final touches on my makeup, I looked at my reflection in the full length mirror.

"Not bad," I said aloud, smiling with pride. I had a good figure, and my face looked as attractive as it ever had. I left my room, determined to make the most of the next two days.

There were about ten people waiting for the elevator that would take us to the dining room, and when it came down from the fourth floor, it was pretty crowded. "Sorry," a handsome blond guy said, stepping out onto our floor, "there's only room for one more."

Before I knew what was happening, he grabbed me and pulled me inside. Everyone smiled as the doors shut, and my face turned red with embarrassment.

"Don't you think that such gallantry deserves a reward?" the man who had 'rescued' me asked.

He sounded like a real wise guy, but I decided to relax and play by the rules. "That depends. What did you have in mind?"

"Well, your name, for starters."

"Rita, Rita Mathews."

"I'm Jerry Eagan," he said as the doors opened and we got off at the main floor. "The dining room is this way." He put his arm around me and led me down the hall.

"You seem to know a lot about this place. Do you come here

often?"

"Oh, I've been here a few times. This is your first time, isn't it?"

"Yes," I answered. "How can you tell?"

"By the look on your face. Most of the regular girls have a sort of desperate expression. It really turns me off."

"And what do the regular guys have?"

Jerry smiled. "Stick around and see."

We walked into the dining room and sat down. There were large tables that seated eight people in the center of the room, but there were tables for two on the side. "Do you mind?" Jerry asked. "I hate crowds."

Over dinner Jerry told me a lot about himself. He was 24, and worked as an engineer's assistant in Springfield, Mass, He explained that he liked coming to Harrod's because "people drop their pretenses when they are away from home."

"What are those pretenses?" I asked him.

"You know—just look around you." He motioned to the crowded dining room, and my eyes glanced around at the various tables. "If these guys and girls were home," he said, "they wouldn't act the same. They'd have to be introduced, or meet through their jobs. If I walked up to you on the street and said, 'Hi. You're a nice looking girl, and I'd like to go out with you,' you'd either walk away or hit me with your bag or something. But here I just met you, and we're having dinner together."

He had a point. Back in Hartford or in Augusta, I would have thought that he was just the kind of guy who thinks he's irresistible, and I wouldn't have given him a second thought. He was much different from Jim, and different from any of the guys I had gone out with before him. But the very aggressiveness that might have annoyed me in the city seemed natural at Harrod's, and although I recognized it, I didn't mind it a bit.

As we ate I looked around at the other tables, and I noticed that nearly half of them seemed to be made up entirely of girls. "Don't they get many guys here?" I asked Jerry, and he laughed.

"There isn't a one-to-one ratio, but it's not as bad as it looks. Lots of guys don't eat in the dining room on Friday night—they're afraid of getting stuck with one girl too early. They come down later, when the field is wide open. You'll see them later."

Later turned out to be right after dinner. Everyone went into a large hall that had chairs and small tables arranged around the sides of the room. At the far end, a band was playing. Jerry asked me to dance, and for a moment I hesitated. The last time I had been dancing was when Jim and I had dated, and I was afraid that I had forgotten how.

Finally I gave in, and once we got on the floor it was easy to follow Jerry's steps. He was a good dancer, and from the envious looks we got from a lot of the girls, it was obvious that we made a nice couple. I watched the girls sitting at the tables, and I laughed to myself.

"What's so funny?" Jerry asked me.

"Oh, I was just thinking—it's a lot like high school, isn't it?"

"What do you mean?"

"You know, the girls sitting on the sidelines, everyone dancing in the gym—it seems pretty similar to me."

"Maybe it is," he said. "But some people have a more adult attitude. The evening doesn't end with Daddy picking you up in his car." He stopped dancing for a moment and looked at me. "Are you one of those people?" he asked.

I knew what he meant, and I thought that it was really a vulgar remark. But for some reason it excited me. "Maybe," I told him, matching his stare. "Why don't you wait around and find out?"

As it grew later, the dance floor became more crowded. Several guys besides Jerry asked me to dance, but after the dances were over, he was waiting for me. The music gradually changed from fast numbers to slow songs. Jerry held me tight in his arms, pressing his body against mine.

"I've got a bright idea," he said, "slip up to your room and get into a swim suit. The pool should be deserted at this time of night.

He was right. It was. He pulled me down onto a chaise lounge next to the pool and began to nuzzle at my neck. I have no idea how long we stayed there, bodies pressed close together, limbs entwined. . . But later, much later, he said.

"When you've had enough of this, let me know," he whispered, kissing my neck as he spoke. "We can leave whenever you're ready."

I had an urge to run away, to leave Jerry, Harrod's and forget the whole idea. For a moment I felt cheap and dirty, but then the feeling passed. Instead I found myself saying, "I'll go now," and Jerry led me from the pool.

Even then, I felt as if we should go up the back stairs or something, but Jerry took me to the main elevator. Other couples were waiting for it, too, and it was obvious that they had the same idea we did.

It's not wrong, I said to myself. *It's not wrong at all.*

"Relax, honey," Jerry said, taking off his shirt. We were in my room, and he was sitting on the bed. I knew that I should go over and sit beside him, but I kept pacing the floor, unable to stop.

He stood up and came over to me, and when he put his arms around me, I couldn't stop shaking. He kissed me, tenderly at first, and then more passionately. As he kissed me, his hands moved to the zipper of the dress I had put on over my swimsuit, and in a moment I was standing in only my suit.

Jerry flipped off the light switch and led me to the bed, and as I ran my hands over his broad, muscular back, I could feel desire mounting in me. I forgot all about Jim and about everything. There was no question of right or wrong—it didn't even matter who Jerry was.

He was just a man, and I had been without a man for too long. He kissed me again, and I knew that even if I suddenly had wanted to stop, I couldn't have controlled the needs of my body.

The sound of a radio playing woke me up, and I turned and saw Jerry, naked except for a sheet that he had thrown over himself, sitting up in bed. "Hi, baby," he said, bending down and kissing me.

I remembered about the night before, and I pulled away. "What's the matter, honey?" he asked. "Do you melt in the daylight—or should I say freeze up?" He bent over me again.

"Leave me alone," I said. "I'm not even awake."

"I'll wake you up," he said, smiling, and his hands moved over my body.

Just then the music on the radio stopped.

"Here's a special bulletin from our newsroom," the announcer said. "We have further reports on that terrorist bombing that claimed the lives of ten United States army men, on leave in Saigon. In addition to the ten killed, thirty were wounded when enemy terrorists threw a homemade bomb into a Saigon movie theater."

Jerry reached over to turn the radio off, but for some reason I found that I had to listen. I pushed his hand away.

"Several of those wounded were from the New England area," the announcer continued. He read off a list of names and towns, none of them more than a few hours away from Hartford. ". . . Private Louis Valdez, New Haven; Private Phillip Johnson, Meriden; and Lt. James Mitchell, Hartford. Stay tuned for further bulletins."

Lt. James Mitchell. My heart began pounding, and I felt sick to my stomach. It was Jim! He had been expecting a promotion, and he must have gotten it. He had written about going into Saigon for a few days on leave, and now he was lying wounded somewhere, maybe even dead, while I was in bed with another man.

I had to get out. I had to go home and try to find a way to get more information. But Jerry wouldn't let me go.

"Hey—you look sick," he said, switching off the radio and pushing me back on the bed. "Don't let those news reports get you down. After all, we're not over there." He lowered himself onto me, and I tried to pull away.

"What's the matter with you?" he asked, sounding angry. "Last night everything was fine. Now, just because some guys were hurt in Vietnam, you don't want me to touch you." He held me tighter, and I knew that it was useless to struggle.

"Please," I begged him, "you don't understand."

"What don't I understand?"

"One of those men," I said, sobbing, "is my husband."

He gave me a look of surprise, then disgust. Without saying a word, he put on his pants and shirt, then left the room, slamming the door behind him.

I couldn't move. I sat on the bed, crying, and then I looked in the mirror. My makeup was smeared from the night before, and as I held the sheet to my body I remembered all of the movies I had seen about tramps. That was the way I looked, and even more, it was the way I felt.

In my mind I could see an article in the newspapers. *Mrs. Mitchell could not be reached with the news of her husband's injury. She was in bed with another man.* Then I had another thought. Instead of feeling sorry for Jim, I realized, I was feeling sorry for myself.

I picked up the telephone and called the desk. "This is Rita Mathews," I said, almost unable to say the false name. "I'll be leaving in a few minutes. Please have my car ready."

I got dressed and got my suitcase, then I went downstairs to pay my bill.

The trip back to Hartford seemed to take forever. On the way, I thought of the sudden realization that had come to me in the hotel room after Jerry had left. I hadn't only felt sorry for myself when I heard about Jim—I had felt sorry for myself as soon as he had been drafted.

I never once thought that maybe he felt as bad as I did about going—probably worse. Instead of giving him faith and encouragement while he was off fighting for his country, I had written him letters about my loneliness. I had tried to find love and comfort in the arms of another man, instead of thinking of the love of my husband.

But it was no use thinking about it now, I told myself as I drove into Hartford. It was too late. Jim had already been hurt, and I had been punished. The memory of hearing the news as I lay in bed with Jerry, a stranger, would haunt me for the rest of my life.

I had to stop for a light at a busy corner where a newsboy was selling papers. "Two local soldiers hurt in Vietnam," he called out to the passing crowds. "Read all about it." The light changed, but I didn't move. Instead I jumped out of the car and ran to buy a paper. Other drivers were honking their horns at me as I got back into my car, but I didn't pay attention. I had to look at the paper.

My fingers were trembling as I held it in front of me, and then I saw something I couldn't believe. There were pictures of two men I had never seen before. Under one photograph were the words *Phillip Johnson of Meriden*. Under the second it said *James Mitchell, Hartford*.

But that James Mitchell wasn't my husband.

The James Mitchell who had been wounded in Vietnam was another man who lived in a different part of the city, but I felt for his wife and family. Only a few days before I would have been glad that it wasn't my husband, and my feelings would have stopped there.

But those terrible minutes before I learned the truth made me realize that I had been thinking about myself for too long—it was time I thought of other people as well.

Nothing can ever make up for the terrible thing I did by going to Harrod's and sleeping with Jerry. I know that now, and I am ashamed. At first I thought that I would tell Jim about it and let him decide what to do. I don't deserve him, I told myself, and he has every right to leave me.

But I've decided that instead of hurting him, I'll put what I've learned to use. Feeling that I lost Jim made me realize how much I loved him, and how little I had shown that love.

Now I know what it means to care about somebody else, someone you love, more than yourself, and to care about your marriage. When Jim gets back, I'll put that knowledge to use, I've already made a beginning deciding to stop feeling sorry for myself, and by realizing how lucky I am to have Jim.

I haven't been a good wife while Jim's been gone, but I will be when he gets back. I think that I've learned how.   THE END

*You may condemn this woman—but if you have a heart,
if you have ever loved a man—you'll understand...*

AM I A WIFE – OR A WIDOW?

Linda married Mike when she was just nineteen, and got pregnant just before he was sent to Vietnam. Right after she delivers twins, she's dealt a double blow: First, an army officer arrives to inform her that Mike has died in combat. Then, just as she's made up her mind to become "the very best mother and the very bravest widow I could," she receives a telegram stating that Mike's actually missing in action, possibly a prisoner of war.

Four years later, what's Linda to do when she's fallen in love with another man, one who loves her and wants to marry her?

When this story was first published, Linda's final decision must have struck many readers as heartless, and many others as the most realistic option given her circumstances. Even today, it's not easy to accept her choice without a twinge of misgiving, or to condemn that choice without a trace of sympathy.

It's five-thirty, time to call the boys in and get them cleaned up for dinner, but I can't seem to make myself take that first step toward the door. The pot roast will be done exactly at six; Frank will be here before I even have a chance to run a comb through my hair if I don't get a move on.

You're happy, I try to convince the tear-stained face reflected in the just washed kitchen window. Happy, do you hear me? With a quick angry twist of the gold band on my too slender finger, I paste a smile on my face and open the back door.

"Jerry, Michael—it's time to come in."

"Aw, Mom—"

"He'll be here any minute." As if by magic, my sons scramble in the door and obediently run to wash up and change out of their grubby playclothes.

Frank *is* magic to them and to me. He's tall and strong, understanding but firm when their little boy mischief needs disciplining, fun to be with when it's time for a picnic in the country. He's the kind of father any sons would love and respect, the kind of husband any wife would thank heaven to be married to. But Frank is not my sons' father and he's not my husband!

The gold band belongs to another man, not so very tall or handsome. Michael Vincent Harris, the quiet man who made me a nineteen-year-old bride, a twenty-year-old mother of twins and a twenty-four-year-old resident of a horrible limbo world where I don't know if I'm a wife or a widow.

I knew it was wrong to lie, but lie I did from the first moment the twins and I boarded the bus and came to this town. "Mrs. Vince Harrison—I'm a widow," I told the nice man who rented us this little house. Mrs. Harrison, a brave widow with twin sons who was determined to build a new life in this town. A new life because Linda Harris, who had never before told a lie, was too young and too lonely to go on hoping that somebody would suddenly pop out of the blue and return her to the old life.

One more telegram, one more "maybe" or "I'm sorry" or "you'll have to be patient" and I would have lost my mind. Mike had no business going off to war in the first place, but as soon as he was called he went without a thought of trying to get out of it. I guess he was almost afraid to stay with me. We were both so young that the thought of a family was almost as frightening as that war. Mike had worked hard at whatever jobs he could get from the first day we were married, but even with the small check from my folks and the rigid budget we figured out, our money was always gone before the month was over. And then with a baby on the way—

Mom came and sat with me the day Mike was shipped out. She said I was lucky, that Mike would have a lot of time to grow up over there and when he got back things would be different. I tried so very hard to believe her, so very hard not to cry like the little girl that I was and beg her to stay with me.

I couldn't tell from Mike's letters how much growing up he was doing, but I was sure doing my share. Dad was killed in a loading dock accident and Mom, my strong comforting Mom, went to pieces. There was a funeral to be arranged and so many details that had to be attended to. To this day, I don't know how I managed. Mom and I moved into a small house with a den that could be converted into a nursery for the baby. The way it had happened was awful, but I had Mom with me now and I was glad.

The doctor kept saying that it would take time for Mom to get over her grief, a little time and she'd be just fine. He was wrong though. Eight months pregnant, I couldn't even bend down to put flowers on her grave. The woman at Red Cross was very kind; she said she'd do everything she could to get Mike emergency leave so that he could be with me when the baby was born. She also warned me not to get my hopes up; sometimes there was just too much red tape and too little time. She was right.

I was never more alone than that morning when Jerry and Michael were born. I'd expected to at least hear from Mike, but there was no word the five lonely days I spent in the hospital.

At home barely a full day, I pounced at the phone when it rang, thinking it might be Mike. It was just a neighbor and while I was trying to politely get rid of her so that the line would be open, the doorbell rang.

I saw the blur of a uniform through my happy tears. "Oh Mike!"

"Mrs. Harris?" It wasn't Mike at all; just some polite cold stranger telling me that my husband was dead. He didn't know what to say to comfort me so he just sat there stiffly and silently, as some imaginary clock ticked off the required amount of time. Then he left and I was alone again—this time for good.

I cried till I thought the little house would just float away and then I cried some more. I don't know if it was my carrying on or hunger that woke the babies, but that decided it for me. I had to go on living. Pats on the back were in order but there was nobody left to care enough to congratulate me. I got myself up and set about being the very best mother and the very bravest widow that I could.

That's when the telegram came. "Missing in action; possibly a prisoner of war." I picked out the words that were most important. At first I was happy! There was a chance that Mike might still be alive, might come back to me and our babies. So long as there was a chance, however slim, I could hold on; I could wait.

Weeks became months and being alone with two constantly crying babies and impossible stacks of dirty diapers seemed to be too much for one person to handle. But what else could I do? Wear black on alternating Thursdays and cultivate the friendships of the eligible young men in town? Trying to be brave and cheerful and spending my nights alone in a cold double bed was becoming an insane routine. That's when I packed up and came here. Then I met Frank. I never meant to mislead him, to let him fall in love with me thinking that I was free. I never meant to, but I did.

"Mommy!" From the whine in Jerry's voice, I can tell it's not the first time he's called.

"What, Jerry?"

"I can't reach the towel and Mikey says Frank won't give me a hug if I don't hurry."

I reached the towel, delivered a small lecture on brothers being nice and helpful to each other and flipped on the TV so the boys can watch their favorite cartoons. The boys are growing so fast now, Mike especially. As they get older they begin to wonder why they don't have a daddy like everybody else. Yesterday Mike wanted to know why I had to go to work instead of staying home and baking chocolate chip cookies like his friend's mother. Jerry chimed in with his request for a baby brother or sister like "Tommy's mother's gonna get for him."

It would all be so simple if I were really the widow I pretend to be, if I could somehow be sure that it was the man in the uniform who told the truth and not a crumpled sheet of yellow paper.

Frank's car chugs to a familiar coughing stop in the driveway and I run to meet him. He takes me in his arms and kisses me lightly, well aware that we have an audience.

"Frank!" the boys squeal in excited unison. Frank scoops them up in a gigantic bear hug. I'm so very lucky to have found someone to ease the loneliness for me and for them. Frank is the only father they've ever known and though I sometimes can't admit it to myself, more of a husband than Mike ever was.

Three years of pretending and still there's no end in sight. If I'm going to retain my sanity, I've got to start believing my own lies. You're happy! I tell myself as our "family" sits down to dinner.

Frank fusses over the pot roast just as though it was something fancy, plays with the boys while I clear the table and even dries the dishes while we talk. After we put the twins to bed, I pour two steaming mugs of coffee and settle down on the couch with my man. Guilt or no guilt, lie or no lie, I am certain of one thing. This is the man I love, the *only* man I love.

With the twins sound asleep and the coffee long gone, Frank turns all his loving attention to me. I couldn't feel lonely or afraid now if I tried. If only Frank didn't have to pick up his shoes and tiptoe out. If only he could stay all night tonight and every night.

"Babe, are you asleep?"

"No."

"Linda, I've been thinking. It's taken time, but business has finally picked up. The store's made a decent profit three months in a row. We wouldn't live like kings, but I can afford to make an honest woman out of you and you know how I feel about the boys."

"Oh Frank!" He mistakes my sobs for tears of joy, my silence for a yes to his proposal. "I'm already married," I try to say, but the words won't come.

He was alone trying to start a new business; I was alone trying to start a new life. From the first moment, it seemed comfortable and right. Suddenly it all seems so wrong.

"Frank, I need some time to think."

"I'm not getting any younger, Linda. If you want us to have any kids of our own—"

"I know, Frank; I promise it won't be long." Frank's older than I am by twelve long years, but as far as I can tell that only makes him centuries more loving and more understanding than any younger man I've ever known and that includes my husband, especially my husband.

It's one thing to pretend I'm a widow when I have no way of knowing for sure—and another thing to marry again. That would mean breaking the law, dragging Frank and the twins into the kind of trouble love shouldn't lead to. What am I going to do? I can't marry Frank, but now that he's proposed I don't think he'll settle for our arrangement much longer. He's ready to settle down and raise a family on a full-time basis.

My eyes are red from crying and framed with ugly dark circles of sleeplessness when I drop the twins at nursery school. Mrs. Reynolds takes one look at me and offers to keep the twins late "so that you can get a little rest, honey." My boss overlooks the seemingly endless errors in my typing and even tries to give me the afternoon off.

"I'll be fine," I lie. "I think I'm coming down with something."

"That settles it; get lost. We can get a fresh start tomorrow morning."

"Thanks." The house is terribly empty and quiet without the twins and if I break down and call Frank this early, he'll know something's wrong. Without realizing quite what I'm about to do, I change into a simple navy dress and rummage in my drawer for a decent pair of white gloves.

The woman at Red Cross, like another woman so very long ago, listens patiently to my tale of woe. I can tell she doesn't know what to do with me. Doesn't she believe me?

"Mrs. Harris—Linda, it's going to take time to check on your husband's status. Give me your address and phone number and I'll be in touch." Just one more speech about being patient and not losing hope. My patience was used up a long time ago and what in the name of heaven should I hope for? Could I live with myself if my selfish wishes meant that Michael would have to be dead? Should I pray that he has an almond-eyed girl waiting to ease the pain of his lonely need?

What I should do is go pick up my boys and start being a mother to them. They're the ones who suffer when I start wallowing in memories of the past.

"Can we go to the park?" The boys out number me and for once I give in. Fresh air and sunshine, swings and slides, keep us all so occupied that it's five when I finally glance at my watch. Dinner was supposed to be chicken, which I was supposed to thaw but didn't. No supposing about it, Frank will be on my doorstep promptly at six and he'll be starved.

Lamb chops save the day as far as putting a meal on the table is concerned, but my poor deflated wallet warns that this is going to be another month when nothing can possible help me stretch my paycheck far enough.

Jerry and Mike are anything but sleepy when the clock insists it's bedtime. Frank obliges with a bedtime story and leans down for a goodnight kiss.

"Night," Mike whispers.

"I love you, Daddy," says Jerry sleepily. It seems that my kids have a few pretend games too.

"I'm sorry, Frank; he was just half-asleep and didn't know what he was saying."

"Linda, don't you know that I want them to be *our* sons? I think it's great that Jerry already thinks of me as his dad."

Sure it's great, really great. Piece by piece, my whole world of lies is beginning to fall in on me. Frank suggests a Sunday picnic and hints at some sort of a surprise.

Jerry and Mike would never forgive me if we couldn't go with Frank. Mothers aren't ever supposed to be sick or tired; just ask a four-year-old. It must be the awful waiting for the phone to ring or for a letter to come that makes my stomach so jumpy.

Sunday is a beautiful day; the sun is bright but a breeze keeps it cool. The park will be so full. I wonder if the boys would settle for a backyard picnic. Frank says not to worry about crowds; he has a surprise. That's the second time he's hinted at something special.

We pile into Frank's station wagon and ride for what seems like an hour. Finally we stop in a large grassy field with huge shade trees.

"Honey, don't you think we'd better find another place to eat? I'm sure the owner would be furious if he caught us here." Maybe Frank didn't see the "No Trespassing" signs.

"I don't think the owner would mind a bit. As a matter of fact, I happen to know that he's going to build a house right over there for his lovely bride and her handsome twin sons and—"

"Frank!" So that's the surprise. I don't deserve his love and I'm going to have to find the strength to tell him that before he starts building a house we can never live in. Frank's thirty-six; if I keep putting him off, it's going to be too late for the babies he wants so much—babies I want so much too.

Another woman, a woman without a maybe of a husband, could give Frank the babies and the happiness I can't. There's only one right thing to do, but instead of drawing away from Frank I find myself holding him tighter and kissing him harder as the weeks go by. I hope against hope that when the woman from Red Cross finally contacts me, she'll tell me Michael is alive, but he wants a divorce. Such a perfect dream to solve all my problems and ease my guilt!

I pray for my perfect dream to become reality, but it's a nightmare that the woman from Red Cross offers when she calls. "One of the local peace groups has some film I think you should see. It's possible that your husband could be one of the prisoners." She tells me the address and wishes me luck though she can't possibly realize how foolish that is.

A young man with long brown hair answers my knock. He hands me a booklet explaining his group's activities and guides me to an old and not very sturdy wooden chair.

The film is of poor quality, the men all so pale and thin that I'm not sure I'd recognize Michael even if he were there. Eyes, sad brooding eyes, Michael's eyes! Of that I am certain. So much for my new life and happy dreams. I'm still a wife, Michael's wife. I try to look happy and mumble the appropriate thank yous. The young man asks for my signature on some sort of petition and mentions a peace rally that he urges me to attend.

"Perhaps you'd like to speak, tell what it's like to live alone and wait for your man to come back—" He's still talking as I shut the door and hurry to my car.

My "friend" from the Red Cross is waiting when I get home. Everyone wants the impossible from me—Frank wants me to marry him; the young man for peace wants me to tell the world what a devoted wife I've been and this woman—what does she want?

"I thought I'd better check back with you. Did you recognize your husband?"

"Yes."

"I don't know of any easy way to tell you that film of this sort is not always an accurate means of identification. Very often, the same man is identified by a number of different women who all swear that the prisoner couldn't possibly be anyone other than their husband. I'm afraid we don't get the sort of cooperation from the peace group that we'd like. They need the relatives of prisoners to help get their message across so they're reluctant to discourage any identification. Some of the men have died since the film was made."

"Then why in the name of heaven did you ask me to go in the first place?"

"Once we could determine if there was a definite possibility of your husband being in that group of prisoners, we could check it out through official sources. I'm sure you realize that would narrow our investigation."

"I'm not sure what I realize at this point. You really haven't told me anything new. My husband is alive or maybe he's dead. I've heard that before. Tell me something new. Give me some definite fact to live with. Make me a widow or make me a wife waiting for her man to come home—but don't leave me trapped in this horrible limbo of not knowing!"

"I'm sorry, really sorry, but we're doing our best."

That isn't enough, not nearly enough. I can't even manage a forced "thank you for your efforts." Oh God, I think I'm losing my mind!

I live in a nightmare world of trying to smile at the right times, do my job and be some sort of mother to my sons. Frank questions my dark mood with concerned eyes, but he never presses me for an explanation. He just tries a little harder—taking the boys to "help out" at the store on Saturdays so that I can have some time to myself, surprising me with a bag of groceries when he senses the days of the month stretch farther than the pennies of my paycheck. It seems the nicer he is, the harder it becomes to try to tell him the truth.

I dream of Frank's loving tenderness until a nightmare image of Michael's face wakes me with a scream. "Mommy just had a very bad dream," I explain as I put the twins back to bed and try to keep from crying. If only Frank could have stayed, just this one night. I need his strong arms to comfort me.

The cup of instant cocoa I make myself just won't stay down. I've been fighting this virus for weeks, the nausea and the dizziness. Maybe I should give in and see a doctor. No, that's out of the question. The boys need new shoes and that's more important.

I sit in the kitchen waiting for morning to come, then shower and get dressed. Despite the meals I couldn't force myself to eat and the battles I lost to nausea, the skirt that used to be too big will hardly button. An impossible thought flashed through my mind; I can't possibly be pregnant! Precautions. I was always so careful—even when I was tired and upset and needed Frank so desperately? There's only one way to be sure.

Dr. Owens smiles so reassuringly that I'm confident there's nothing to worry about. "Congratulations, Mrs. Harrison, you're about seven weeks along. You're a little run down, but we can fix that with some vitamins and an injection the nurse will give you."

No! I scream to myself. "Thank you, doctor," I say aloud. Abortion. That's what you do when the baby is an accident and won't have a name. Abortion or adoption, but of course I can't seriously consider either. This baby is Frank's—Frank's and mine; I won't give it up!

There's no reason to trap Frank in my nightmare of hopelessness. It would only mean pain for him to find out that I was going to have his baby, a baby who couldn't be born with his name. It's time to move on again, but this time I'm going to leave the lies behind. I used to think that nothing could possibly be worse than the loneliness, but now I know I was wrong. It's worse to pretend and to involve a perfectly wonderful man in your private little games. It's worse, much worse, to know how very close you've come to ruining his chance at happiness.

Jerry and Michael are furious when I tell them we're going to move to a nice town where they'll be able to make all sorts of new friends. They seem to know without my telling them that Frank won't be coming with us and that's what turns my sweet well-behaved boys into monsters. "You're the meanest Mommy in the whole world!" is the answer to even my most convincing explanation of our new life in another place. My children are too young to realize that this is all for the best; they're going to fight me every step of the way.

If only I could just leave and let a letter to Frank do my explaining, but with the kids upset like this—well, I guess I'll have to do my last bit of lying in person.

The store is empty; it's that quiet time before the after-work crowd. Frank's taking inventory; he doesn't even look up when the bell tinkles.

"With you in a minute," he hollers over his shoulder. "Honey, why didn't you say something? If I'd known it was you—"

"I wasn't in any hurry." Those are the first and last words of solid truth to escape from my lips. All my carefully practiced lies about thinking he's a very nice man and will make some other woman a wonderful husband are forced out into the open. Never mentioning the precious secret of my pregnancy, I tell Frank that we're leaving town. It wouldn't be fair to stay when I don't love him, I explain. We're going to stay with some relatives of my late husband, I add so that he won't worry too much about us. Then I turn and try to walk slowly, normally; try to keep myself from running as fast and as far as I'd like. Please, God, don't let Frank come after me.

I sell whatever won't fit into my small car; that's practically everything but clothes and the boys' toys. We'll get a small apartment in a nearby town. With a baby on the way just a few working months from now, I can't possibly swing the rent on even the smallest house.

My boss gives me a glowing recommendation; my doctor the name of a doctor he knows. I leave my name and a message for the woman at Red Cross. "Here's to all your lovely hollow promises. Will be in touch when I have a new address. Please—only facts; no more promises you can't keep." The note says what my cowardly self never could in person. If there's any definite news, I want to know, have to know, but I won't let myself in for any more maybes.

Despite the twins doing everything in their power to prevent it, we do leave town. The apartment house my pocketbook chooses is old, but clean. The manager is a sweet old man who loves children and says the boys can even have a dog here if they want. Maybe a puppy would help ease the separation from Frank. For kids, I guess one warm cuddly bundle of love is just as good as another; I wish it could be the same for me.

I give my real name and say nothing about my husband. I still wear my ring and that seems to be enough to prevent questions that I can't answer. "Where's your husband now?" "Will he be joining you later?" are bits of nosiness from which I have so far been spared.

It's beginning to be obvious that soon there will be four of us in the tiny apartment. Jerry and Mike are still not pleased with the move, but the promise of a puppy and my news about a baby brother or sister seem to brighten their moods. Someday I'll have to explain to them that no matter how much I love this baby, it was wrong to become pregnant. I'll have to make them see that I had no right to become involved with Frank in the first place. Someday, but not today.

My new boss is demanding and more than a little unreasonable, but the pay is a little better and he's grudgingly agreed to give me two weeks off to have my baby. This time, in this town, we're going to make it.

There's bright pink-checked fabric on sale at the dime store. I spend Saturday transforming it into a maternity shift while I keep an eye on the boys. I've promised that we can go look at puppies today and that promise has put the twins on their very best behavior.

The doorbell rings and Jerry and Mike have a quiet argument over whose turn it is to answer it. Mike wins, but Jerry tags along right behind him. "Daddy!" Jerry squeals. Jerry never saw his real father so there can be only one man at the door—Frank.

He's thinner than I remember and there are new wrinkles around his eyes, but he's still Frank and I'm not at all sure I can trust myself to be alone with him. There's so very much I want to tell him but can't.

Just standing here, I tell him one thing; I'm pregnant. He can't help but notice that, can't help but realize it's his child.

"I figured it was something like this that made you leave town, but why? We could have gotten married."

"No. No, we couldn't." And now I have to tell him why. Frank listens patiently, says nothing and his face is blank of any clue as to what he's thinking. Suddenly those strong arms reach out.

"Linda, I came to take you and the boys home. I still want to do just that."

Home. That's exactly what this three bedroom house is—or will be when Frank and I get through with it. We're living together now, living as a family, because that's exactly what we are. Whether or not Michael is dead, Frank and I and the boys are a family.

Frank has hired a lawyer to find out if we can be legally married, but that's not really important right now. What's important is being together, being a family. The newest member of our family, Francesca Robin, is a beautiful baby girl who may grow up without ever knowing how hard it was for her parents to get together.

I still don't know for sure if I'm legally a wife or a widow, but with Frank's love and three wonderful children to raise there's very little opportunity to dwell on the dark possibilities. If Michael is dead, I'm sorry just as I would be sorry to hear of the death of anyone I knew a very long time ago. If he's alive, I'm glad for his sake. But he'll have to understand that there's no longer a place for him in our lives. He'll have to understand that we're Frank's family now. I have to believe that Michael could understand that, that we could make him understand. I hope with all my heart that we are given a chance to try. THE END

Even from on high, in his final, eternal flight, my daddy in uniform was watching over me

DAUGHTER OF AN AIR FORCE MAN

My exploration of the True Love *and* True Romance *archives is far from complete, but so far this is the only ghost story I've come across—the only story, really, with even the slightest indication of giving credence to the supernatural. Both magazines seem predominantly focused on the "true" aspect to their stories. Sure, you can point to all sorts of stories that seem excessively melodramatic and barely believable. But even those stories tend to be grounded with just enough realism that you can convince yourself that they're still within the realm of the possible. (Okay, I remember what I said about Kathy's story a few chapters back, but you get my point.)*

Even this story, apart from the ghostly presence of Lindsay's father, is loaded with enough emotional detail to make the young girl's pain—and the dilemma she gets caught up in—feel utterly plausible. It's very different from the other soldiers' stories in this collection, but it's also an excellent reminder that a soldier's love extends further than girlfriends and wives.

Visiting the Oak Grove Cemetery on Memorial Day was a family tradition that went back several generations. My grandparents, Howard and Beverly Mitchell, still went there every year, placing flowers at each of the family headstones. Every year for the past ten years they had asked me to go with them. And every year, I turned them down.

"No," I told them angrily. "I can't. I won't."

My eyes were filled with sparks, my voice hot and edgy. All I could think about was how my father and mother had both left me, just when I'd needed them the most. Even my stepmother had left me. So why should I honor their graves?

Each time I said no, Grandma Beverly would lay a gentle hand on my arm and look at me with her sad, blue eyes and turned-down mouth. Her voice was as sorrowful as her eyes. "You can't go through life hating your parents, Lindsay. It just isn't right."

"It wasn't right for them to leave me, either. Especially my dad; I'll never forgive him for it. Never."

"But it wasn't his fault, Lindsay. It's not like he—"

"I don't want to hear it, Grandma."

And yet, I didn't always feel that way. In fact, I used to love my father very much. Even now, ten years later, I can still remember how he looked back then—tall, strong, and so handsome. He was magnificent in his crisp, blue Air Force uniform. I loved the glittering captain's bars, the mirror-like sheen that glistened off the bill of his cap, the silver aviator wings, and the rainbow of ribbons that were pinned above his heart. I loved his deep voice, his gentle hands, and his warm, strong hugs.

"One of these days," he'd often say, his bottomless brown eyes smiling into mine as he swept me up into the air high above his head. "One of these days, Lindsay, you and I are going to fly away, just the two of us. We'll go as high as the moon and as far as the stars. And we'll never, ever come back."

It was a dream, of course. Reality was something else. Because my father did, indeed, fly away. But he flew away alone.

And he never came back.

I never knew my birth mother. She died while giving me life. The doctor's report—which I found many years later in a jumble of old family documents—brushed off her death with cold, meaningless words like *complications*, *circulatory stress*, and *aneurysm*. All I knew growing up was that I didn't have a mother like all the other kids did.

Luckily Marie, the woman my daddy married when I was three, tried very hard to make up for the loss of my birth mother. She was successful, too; to my young mind, she never really was a stepmother. To me, she was just plain "Mama."

Unfortunately, I lost her, too. But that was later on. And that loss was not nearly as bad as the loss of my father was on me. When Daddy went away, my whole world fell apart. Home, friends, school—suddenly, everything just swirled down the drain like greasy dishwater.

And it was all Daddy's fault.

Looking back, it's hard to believe that everything could've changed so quickly. At that time, the three of us—my father, my mother, and I were living in a breezy, comfortable, ranch-style home in sunny California. Despite its western adobe look, our sand-hued home was actually located on an Air Force base, the base where my father was stationed. As far as I was concerned, the house was absolutely perfect.

Our life in California was perfect, too. I had lots of friends at Oceanside Elementary School. And I was on the Sunfish swimming team. Mama would drive me to tennis and ballet lessons twice a week, and my father and I would go horseback riding nearly every Saturday morning. And there was never a doubt in my mind: My perfect life would go on forever.

Then, late one afternoon, my father came home looking very grim. His blue necktie had been jerked crookedly away from his throat. His uniform, usually so crisp and smartly creased, now looked wrinkled and stained with sweat. For a moment, he stood in the middle of our living room, his shoulders slumped. He had a sheaf of official-looking papers in his hand as he looked at Mama with sad, weary eyes.

"I'm being shipped out," he said hesitantly, as though his words were knives that would pierce our hearts. "To Arabia."

Then he looked down at me. Instead of a strong and sturdy god, my father suddenly looked like a weary, old man. Even his voice had aged.

"I'm sorry, princess," he said. "Your daddy has to go away for a while."

I stared at him in disbelief, and then I stared at Mama. Her face had suddenly turned to icy marble. Tears welled up in her large, dark eyes.

"Oh, Rudy," she breathed, shaking her head in disbelief. "Not now. Please, not now." She pressed her knotted fist against her swollen stomach. "The baby," she said. Then her words were lost in sobs.

I was only seven then, and war was something that happened to other people, in other lands, far across the ocean. War was something you saw on television. It was like a movie; it had nothing to do with my daddy. My daddy was in the Air Force, yes. And he flew an airplane. But he flew it here, in this country. My daddy had nothing to do with war.

But back in 1991, the Persian Gulf War was not something that happened to faraway people. It had suddenly become a clawed hand that ripped through my very own life, and it snatched my daddy away.

"Please don't go!" I begged the morning he left. "Please, Daddy, *please!*"

He lifted me up in his arms like he did every morning. That morning, however, his eyes were shiny and wet. His voice was thick with emotion.

"I *have* to go, princess," he said. And then he hugged me tightly against his chest. "But I'll come home again, soon."

I hugged him back as hard as I could. The coarse material of his uniform was scratchy against my cheek. Then I pushed him away.

"Promise, Daddy," I said fiercely, my eyes burning into his. "You have to promise me you'll come home. And then you have to cross your heart and hope to die."

Daddy's eyes were lit by a tiny twinkle. His grim mouth softened slightly as he shifted my weight to his left arm. His right hand crisscrossed his ribbon-covered heart and then went up in a Boy Scout pledge. "I promise, princess," he said, smiling. "I'll be back before you know it."

Two months later there was a firm knock on our front door. My mother and I could see a tall, shadowy shape beyond the translucent glass. I glanced at Mama, looking for confirmation, hoping against hope that Daddy had come home to us, once and for all. But what I saw in her face was neither joy nor hope. What I saw was fear, maybe even panic.

With tight lips and an urgent hand, she pushed me toward the kitchen. "Wait in there, Lindsay," she said stiffly. "I'll only be a minute."

"But why, Mama? Maybe it's Daddy. Maybe he's come home."

Mama shook her head. Her face tightened even further as she pushed me through the kitchen door. "Stay there, sweetie," she said, her voice thin and brittle. Then she firmly shut the door, closing me in the kitchen.

I heard more knocks at the door. They were louder now, more insistent. Then I heard the front door open. There was a deep, resonant voice; it was not my father's voice. The words were hushed and firm, but very soft. I couldn't make them out.

Then I heard Mama. But what I heard was not words. What I heard was a sudden, sharp intake of breath, and then a cry of pain. For a moment, I thought the man had punched her in the stomach.

"Mama?" I cried loudly. My cry bounced off the kitchen walls. "Are you all right, Mama?"

"I--I'll be there in a minute, Lindsay. Mama has to—to talk to the man. Stay in the kitchen, okay, sweetheart?"

The deep voice murmured more words. Then Mama began to weep openly.

And then my world came tumbling down.

Grandpa Howard flew all the way to California from his home in Maine. Then he and Mama and I met another plane; this one landed on the base runway. It carried no passengers, only a small crew and four flag-draped coffins. One of the coffins held my daddy.

We had to leave the base, of course, Mama and I. Our house was needed for another pilot, another wife, another little princess. The Air Force arranged everything. They flew Mama, Grandpa, the coffin, and me back to Maine. They packed up all of Mama and Daddy's furniture and shipped all of it back to Maine, too.

I don't think Mama really wanted to move in with Grandpa and Grandma Mitchell—at least not permanently. But there was nowhere else for us to go. And a baby was on the way. I didn't want to live with my grandparents, either. All they ever seemed to talk about was religion. All they ever wanted to do was go to church and pray about Daddy. And they hardly ever smiled. They looked even glummer when Mama had a miscarriage.

But it wasn't just my grandparents that made me hate Maine. It was the weather, especially the winter weather.

In California, the grass was always green, the flowers were always blooming, and the sun came up every single day, bright and warm. The weather in Maine was like a frigid nightmare that wouldn't end. The days were short and bitterly cold; the sky was always gray. The wind blew, the rain turned to ice, and the snow came down like an endless, smothering shroud.

I hated Maine. I hated God. I hated my grandparents. I even started to hate my daddy.

"It's all his fault!" I exploded whenever something bad happened. "If he hadn't learned to fly those stupid planes, if he hadn't gone off to Arabia, if he hadn't gotten himself killed, we wouldn't be in this terrible place!"

I knew Mama felt as I did about living in Maine. She was born and raised in southern California. But for my sake, I guess, she couldn't express her despair.

"We'll get through this, Lindsay," she'd say, over and over again, trying to sound strong and confident. She'd hug me, her eyes blazing with false hope. "We'll be happy again, sweetheart. I promise."

"Stop it!" I finally screamed once. "Don't you see? Daddy made a promise, too. He promised me he'd come back. But he didn't. He lied to me! Promises always get broken!"

Mama tried to soothe my rage. "Don't say that," she said sadly, her eyes glistening. "I know your daddy made a promise to you; everybody makes promises. But sometimes, things happen even when we promise someone that they won't. But that doesn't mean that your daddy didn't love you, sweetheart. He loved both of us with all his heart and soul. And he always will, Lindsay."

"Well, I don't love *him*. I *hate* him. I hate him!"

A few days after that outburst, I hurled my father's framed photograph across the room. I don't remember what caused the outburst; all I recall is the rage.

What made it even worse—it was the only photo that Mama and I had of Daddy. It'd been taken shortly after he'd joined the Air Force, and he looked very proud and very handsome in it. But in the grip of that powerful rage, I didn't care about anything or anyone. The frame bounced off one of the ponderous, old, steel radiators that labored, unsuccessfully, to keep my grandparents' house warm in the wintertime. The glass shattered, the frame bent, and the photo got torn, nearly in half.

But even that didn't satisfy my rage. In a matter of seconds, I turned Daddy's ripped, but beautiful, face into a pile of colored confetti. Then I flushed the confetti down the toilet. And then I cried and cried.

Later that afternoon when Mama came home from work, I told her what I'd done. And then we both cried. But it was too late. The only photo we'd had of Daddy was gone forever, just like Daddy was gone forever, too.

The horror got even worse. For a while after I tore up his photo, I could still pull up an image of Daddy in my mind. But slowly, inexorably, even that began to slip away from me. The more I tried to concentrate, the more I tried to remember his face, the more the image faded. Until one day, when I woke up to a terrible realization: I could no longer remember what my daddy looked like!

That's when I started having that awful dream about him. I could see him, just as clear as day. I couldn't see his face anymore, but I knew it was him. In my dream, I was running down a long, empty gravel road. It was closed in on both sides by a thick forest of gray and winter-naked trees. The clouds were heavy with snow; daylight was fading.

The strangest thing was that in my dream, I was trying to run *away* from my father. He was far behind me and he seemed to be floating above the road; he was calling my name, over and over again. As I ran, I kept glancing back over my shoulder. But no matter how often he called out to me—or reached out for me—I wouldn't stop.

"Come back, Lindsay," Daddy called. His voice was as hollow, as sad, and as empty as the road. "Come back, come back."

The wind blew his words away as my feet kept pounding the gravel. My breath came out of me in great, frosty gasps. I felt like I was running for my life.

Gradually, the distance between us increased. The faster I ran, the farther back my father drifted. Finally, when my breath was almost gone, he had disappeared completely. But I could still hear his voice; I could still hear him calling out to me, pleading with me to stop. I felt just awful hearing him, but I couldn't stop, wouldn't stop. And yet, I didn't know why.

I continued to have that dream for several years after I tore up Daddy's photograph—oh, not every night, but often enough. For a while, I even dreaded going to sleep, for fear I'd have the dream again.

And while the dream plagued my nights, my life during the day was also plunging downhill like a sled on ice. Even at school, things got worse. In California, my grades had always been A's and B's. I was lucky to get C's in Maine, even in classes that I'd used to love, like history and English.

I blamed my poor grades on my classmates. The kids at Oak Grove Elementary were consistently cold, brittle, and stand-offish. They were glued together in tight little cliques and clannish groups; there was no room for an outsider. They made fun of the way I dressed and walked. They made fun of the way I talked, too, which was crazy—they were the ones who had funny accents, not me, I thought.

As my grades continued to plummet and my behavior became increasingly erratic, Mama was summoned to school several times for parent-teacher conferences. Even my guidance counselor threw up her hands when I failed to keep up my end of an anger management agreement. By the end of that first year in Maine, the principal of Oak Grove Elementary—an austere-looking, thin woman named Leticia Frarningham—had insisted that my mother seek psychiatric advice to correct my belligerent and irresponsible attitude.

Mama wrung her hands and looked very sad when she confronted me with this latest development. "Can't you just *try* to get along with your classmates?"

"Why should I? They don't try to get along with me. They *hate* me."

Mama shook her head and tried to lay a gentle hand on my shoulder. "I'm sure that's not really true, sweetheart. If you'd only—"

"They do hate me! The kids, the teachers—everyone! Even my guidance counselor hates me!" I tightened my lips and squared my shoulders. "Well, I'll show them," I said haughtily. "I'll just quit. I'll never go back to school again!"

Of course, I did go back to school again; I had to. It was either that, or run away from home forever. And I wasn't quite ready for that just then—not in elementary school.

Then a week before my fifteenth birthday, another crisis struck. That's when my second mother left me.

Mama was on her way to work that day. The weather was miserable, as usual—heavy snow, blustery winds, and black, icy roads.

The police were never sure about what actually happened. They found deer tracks in the snow beside the road, near the skid marks. They also found the footprints of a dog and a man. Perhaps, the police surmised, Mama swerved to avoid hitting one of them. But they could never be sure.

Whatever happened, Mama lost control of the car. It slid off the road and slammed into a tree. Mama died instantly.

Now I was completely alone and totally cut off, even from my grandparents. That's when the prospect of running away from home grew clearer in my mind. I knew I couldn't run away in the dead of winter, of course, when the temperature hovered around zero. So when it was that cold outside, I'd just hang out at the mall every afternoon. The mall was only a short walk from school, so I'd go there as soon as my last class ended. I'd stay at the mall till it closed. And that's where I finally made some friends, just by hanging out at the mall.

At first, I'd just wander through the stores, pretending to be a customer. I'd try on shoes and coats and anything else that caught my eye. But when the sales clerks finally realized that I never bought anything, they started watching me very closely. I'm sure that several of them thought I was a shoplifter; I could see it in their eyes. A female detective at one of the stores even followed me into the ladies' room once and threatened to call the police if she ever saw me in her store again.

After that, I started hanging out at the mall's central hub: the food court. There was a big fountain in the center of the hub, with lots of plants and trees and benches scattered around a circular pool. For a while, it was nice just sitting there, surrounded by warmth and light while a frigid and gloomy winter raged outside. The sound of the sparkling, splashing fountain was very soothing; it made me feel peaceful and calm, and it helped my mind to drift, unfocused and free.

Some afternoons I'd spend my hoarded lunch money on a triple-dip ice cream cone, or a couple slices of pizza from Sbarro's. Or else I'd buy one of those huge cinnamon buns they sold in mall food courts. Whatever I bought, I'd eat near the splashing waters. I never thought about school, or about the homework that I seldom did. I didn't think about my father, either, or my mother. I didn't even think about Maine, or about the awful weather. Munching on good food beside a huge fountain in the midst of an artificial garden was like being in another world for me. And in my mind, I could really *be* in another world: I could go anywhere, do anything, and think whatever I wanted to think. I loved it there beside the fountain.

But even peace and idleness get to be boring if they go on too long. At least, they did for me. I guess that's why I almost welcomed the intrusion one afternoon in early February when I was sixteen.

I was deep in thought, and about to take a bite of one of Granny Fanny's huge soft pretzels. That's when a voice cut through my reverie.

"You got any money?"

I looked beyond the half-wrapped pretzel poised before my mouth. "What?"

I supposed it was a girl, but I couldn't be sure, at first. She—or *it*—was wearing a very baggy sweatshirt under a long, and even baggier coat. The coat was open down the front, all the way to the torn-jean knees. She was wearing scuffed and heavy boots, too—the kind you see on combat soldiers. Her hair was green and spiky, and her skin was pale, with dark shadows beneath the eyes. I couldn't tell if the shadows were simply the result of poorly applied makeup or if they were an indication of ill health or lack of sleep. I could also see some kind of mythical horned beast tattooed along the side of her thin, corded neck.

"What are you staring at?" the girl demanded. Her voice had a raw, coppery edge to it. "You think I'm some kind of freak?"

I could feel my face growing hot and red. "No—not at all. I—I just wasn't really sure…" I let my voice fade and quickly reached for my purse. "Um, I think I have a couple of bucks left. You hungry?"

Without waiting for a response, I opened my purse and pulled out my new wallet. It was the one that Grandma Beverly had given me for my birthday; I could still smell the slightly acrid scent of the new leather as I pulled out several bills. There was a five and four ones; I pulled out the ones and thrust them at her. My bright, cheery smile felt phony, even to me.

"Go ahead," I insisted. "Take them. Get whatever you want."

The girl stared at me with dark, suspicious eyes. Then she jerked the bills out of my hand. Her only thanks was a curt, barely perceptible nod. A moment later, she turned away and disappeared into the crowd.

A week passed before I saw her again. This time, I was sitting on a bench in a different part of the mall, away from the senior citizen-jammed fountain area

"You got any money?" she asked me, just like before. She was standing directly in front of me; this time, she gave me a slight, crooked smile, almost like she was joking about the money.

I smiled back and patted the bench beside me. "First you have to tell me your name. Then we'll both get something sweet and sinful. Deal?"

She sat down hesitantly, on the edge of the bench, and glanced around. Her hooded, narrow eyes watched the passersby intently; she appeared to be searching for someone, someone she did not want to see. Then, seemingly satisfied, she finally settled back more comfortably on the bench.

I stuck out my hand. "My name's Lindsay. I go to Oak Grove High, but I don't think I've ever seen you there."

The girl ignored my hand and looked down at her own for a moment. Her knuckles were raw and dirty; her fingernails looked like she'd been gnawing on them for years.

"I don't go to school anymore." She glanced up at me again, searching my eyes for some reaction. "I quit."

"I've been thinking about quitting myself," I said casually. "I hate school."

The girl shrugged slightly and looked at her grubby fingers again. "I didn't actually *quit*. I guess you could say I just stopped going about six months ago. I used to go to Carson. It's on the other side of town."

"What did your parents say? About you quitting, I mean."

She snorted. "Like they care. I haven't seen my dad since last August. He got cut up in a bar fight and spent a couple of days in jail. Then, when Mom bailed him out, he just took off. We haven't seen him since."

I nodded sympathetically. "My dad left me, too. What about your mom? She doesn't care that you quit school?"

"I hardly see her. She's a waitress at the Eight Ball. But she hangs out there all the time, even when she's not waitressing. She's looking for another man. She says she's looking for Mr. Right, but all she ever brings home is Mr. Wrong. Creeps, every one of them."

"I'm sorry," I said quietly, and I really was. The girl's eyes were like large, bottomless wells, filled to capacity with unshed tears. But when I laid a comforting hand gently on her arm, her eyes erupted with sudden, unexpected fire. She jerked her arm away and glared at me.

"What are you, queer?" she asked harshly.

I stared at her, shocked and hurt. "No," I said quickly. "I'm not like that at all. I just was…" I struggled to find the words. "I just was…I felt bad for you. That's all."

She glared at me for a long moment, and then finally began to relax again. "Sorry," she finally muttered. She glanced at me sideways. "I don't mind gays. But I don't want them coming on to me. You know?"

I nodded stiffly. "Anyway," I said lightly, "the deal still stands: Tell me your name and I'll buy both of us one of those giant cinnamon buns." I nodded toward the food court.

She smiled. Despite the garish hairdo and smudgy eyeliner, there was shyness in her eyes suddenly. Her smile was almost sweet. "Mikey. That's what they call me."

I grinned back at her, feeling suddenly grateful. "Well, Mikey, I think it's time for a sugar high."

After that, Mikey and I started meeting at the mall nearly every afternoon. There was never anything official about our meetings; I mean, we never actually said, "See you here tomorrow, okay?" We'd just show up and then hang out together.

I soon learned that Mikey's name wasn't really Mikey; it was Michelle. But she hated that name because it was her mother's name, too, and she hated her mother.

Mikey and I would talk about all sorts of things, but mostly about our families—or, rather—the shortcomings of our families. Mikey was also into astrology and spiritualism and other kinds of weird stuff. She even believed in ghosts.

"Get serious," I said jokingly as we shared a bag of doughnuts one afternoon. "Ghosts?"

She just shrugged. "You'd believe in them, too, if you'd seen the things that I've seen."

"Like what things?"

"Like my dog, Chief." She licked the coating of powdery sweetness from her fingers and then reached into the bag for another doughnut. "He was a big black Lab. I had him since I was two. Then when I was seven, Chief got hit by a car. But I still see him, every year, usually on my birthday."

"That's crazy." I laughed uncertainly. "It's probably just another Lab, one that looks like yours."

Mikey shook her head. "It's Chief, all right. He still has this strange patch of gray fur on his left leg, too, just like he had when he was alive." She paused for a moment. Her eyes looked distant and strange suddenly. "I've seen my Uncle Frank, too. He was a logger when I was just a little kid. A tree fell on him. Squashed him flat."

I was starting to feel uneasy. "When do you see him?"

"Mostly at night. Sometimes he's standing at the foot of my bed, just looking down at me. A couple of times I've seen him at my bedroom window, looking in."

An awful chill went down my spine. I laughed awkwardly. "Let's talk about something else, okay?"

Mikey shrugged. "Whatever. But they're real, all right."

A couple of weeks later, Mikey introduced me to some of her friends. They all looked kind of freaky, too, with their strange hair, raggedy clothes, and dangling chains. Most of them also had tattoos. Naturally, they all stared at me when Mikey introduced us.

"Where'd you find the geek?" one of them asked Mikey, looking me up and down. He was a big kid, maybe sixteen, and kind of fat. He had a goofy sort of grin that made you want to grin back at him.

Another one laughed. "You know Mikey—she's always picking up strays. She should be a damn vet or something."

Mikey grinned and gave them all the finger, but it was easy to see that they all really cared about each other. And before long, I began to think that they really cared about me, too, even if I did dress like a dork.

I knew that Grandma would have a fit if she saw me with green hair and shredded, dirty clothes. But at the same time, I wanted to fit in with my new friends. Mikey solved the problem by bringing me a set of her much-too-large clothing one afternoon. Then she showed me a bank of wall lockers near the ladies' rest room in the mall.

"You can keep the rags in one of these lockers," she said casually. "If you don't want to take them home."

"My grandma would have a heart attack if she saw me wearing an outfit like this." I grinned as I held up the huge, paint-smeared sweatshirt. It only had one full-length sleeve; the other sleeve had been cut off above the elbow, the edges raw and straggly. There was a faded and vaguely obscene logo on the back of the shirt. The faded jeans had several slashes on the legs. One of the back pockets had been torn off, leaving a small, but gaping, hole on the right buttock. Mikey winked and wiggled a finger through the hole.

"If you wear a scarlet thong under this, you'll drive the guys berserk!"

I laughed. "I think I'll stick with my plain, old, white panties. I might patch up the hole, too."

Mikey laughed good-naturedly. "Chicken!"

My new friends and I soon established a regular afternoon mall routine. Like me, a couple of the other kids still went to school, so we all started meeting near the mall fountain every day at four.

Mikey was usually the first one there, and I was usually the second. She always immediately followed me into the ladies' room. While I changed into the grungy clothes she had given me, she'd jabber away about her mother's latest creepy boyfriend. Then the two of us would hang out at the fountain and wait for the other kids.

A week or two later, one of Mikey's friends—the fat kid named Neil who always wore bike chains around his waist—came up with a great idea.

"Let's go skating out at Arrow Lake," he suggested. "We'll get some pot and beer, and we'll go during the day while the school dorks are still cracking books. We'll make it a party. And we'll have the whole place to ourselves."

Everyone high-fived each other and agreed that Neil's idea was way cool. I'd never been ice-skating in my life, but I had to admit the idea sounded great to me.

"But I don't have any skates," I blurted out.

The other kids looked at each other like they'd never heard such nonsense. Simply *everyone* in Maine owned ice skates, they assured me. Then Mikey laughed.

"Not a problem. I'll get you some."

She didn't explain just *how* she'd get them, and I didn't ask. I guess I just assumed that she had several pairs at home and would loan me one. Then another thought crossed my mind.

"But how will we get out to Arrow Lake? It's miles from the mall."

Mikey shook her head and glanced around at the others. "This kid worries too much, don't you think?" She laughed and punched my shoulder.

I felt the hot flush of acceptance filling my face when all the kids laughed along with Mikey. Neil finally said with a wink, "I'll get my old man's van. He's in the slammer again, so he won't need it."

I didn't say anything to Grandma about our ice-skating party. *What she doesn't know won't hurt her,* I thought. Besides, she and Grandpa didn't approve of my mall buddies. One of Grandma's church friends had seen me with Mikey one day after school by the mall fountain. There's no telling what kinds of descriptions and comments she passed along to Grandma, but whatever she said, Grandma clearly didn't like what she heard.

"The youth groups at church are just *filled* with wonderful kids," she'd coaxed. "Productive kids, decent kids—nice young people who know where they're going in life."

"Are you saying my friends are irresponsible jerks?" I'd asked her stiffly.

"Of course not, dear," Grandma had replied gently. "I can't

say that because I don't *know* them. I just don't want you getting involved with the wrong kind of people, that's all. And besides, you might enjoy meeting the kids at church. I know they'd enjoy meeting you. And they're always doing things together—bowling, line dancing. You know, having fun."

To get her off my back, I told Grandma that I'd think about it. But I had no intention of giving up my friends for a bunch of teenage Holy Rollers.

The next morning I skipped school altogether and met my friends at the mall entrance. Mikey presented me with a pair of gleaming, white skates that still had a price tag dangling from one of the blades. I accepted the skates reluctantly, staring at Mikey.

"You bought these for me?" I asked her in disbelief.

Mikey laughed. "Are you kidding?"

"But—they're brand new. Where did they—" And then it hit me. "You didn't steal them, did you?"

Mikey laughed. "Let's just say I borrowed them, okay? Anyway, what's the big deal? My mother shoplifts all the time and she never gets caught." She jerked her head toward the parking lot. "Wanna hit the road? Neil's got his old man's van, all gassed up and ready to go."

I hardly said a word during the drive out to Arrow Lake. While the rest of the crew was popping open cans of beer and passing around the bong, I sat staring out the rear window of Neil's dumpy van. I still couldn't believe that Mikey had actually stolen a pair of ice skates. For me! Did that mean that I was partly to blame for the crime?

I glanced around the van and tried not to think about the skates. I glanced at Neil, who was driving with one hand. His other hand was wrapped around an open can of beer. Between gulps, he was talking rapidly. So were most of the other kids, and nobody seemed to be listening. In a matter of minutes, the van was filled with acrid smoke and the pungent smells of beer and pot. I was beginning to wonder what I was doing there. I liked the kids well enough, but I was beginning to question the things they did.

The drive out to Arrow Lake seemed to take forever because the lake itself was way out in the boonies and surrounded by dense woods. It wasn't easy to get there, either. First we had to follow this blacktop, two-lane road for miles. Then we had to turn off onto a long, narrow logging road that a timber company had put in years ago. And as the miles slipped by, the kids got more and more insistent with me.

"What are you, some kind of religious freak?" one of them—a girl named Jessica—asked me. "The least you can do is drink a beer with us." She was clearly annoyed when I shook my head at the proffered can.

"I just don't like the taste of beer," I said, trying to sound casual.

One of the other kids, a skinny boy with several rings in his nose, started to get belligerent then. His beer-fumed breath rolled toward me like a brown, fusty cloud. "Looks to me like we're not good enough for her," he sneered to the others. "Little Miss Prissy-butt."

Suddenly, all of the kids were glaring at me, their bloodshot eyes vaguely blurred by the alcohol and pot. I looked to Mikey for support, but I didn't get it. Her eyes, too, were strangely distant despite her vacant smile.

"Wouldn't hurt you to have just one," she slurred drowsily.

She reached down between her legs and pulled another can of beer out of the cooler. When she popped the top, a cascade of foam poured out of the can and down over her hand. She shoved the dripping can at me.

"Whaddaya say, Lindsay Old Girl?" Her laughter was not entirely pleasant. "Gonna be a buddy? Or a stiff-necked prude? It's your choice, babe."

Reluctantly, I reached out and accepted the cold, slippery can. That prompted a wild cheer from everybody, even the skinny kid with the nose rings.

"Next thing you know, she'll be wanting a toke," he said with a crooked grin. He was looking at me as he exhaled a cloud of acrid smoke and held up the small, hand-rolled joint. "Well, you ain't gettin' any of this," he added. He looked over at Mikey, who was also smoking from an elaborate, psychedelic-looking, glass bong.

Before I could protest, Mikey had thrust the bong at me. "Go ahead," she insisted. "You might like it." She laughed. "It'll also make the trip go faster."

She was certainly right about that. Time did start to speed up after I'd had a few sips of beer and a few puffs of pot. I still didn't like the taste of the beer or the pot, but at least the beer was wet; the pot made my throat burn and my eyes water. The beer, at least, cooled the burn. I rolled down the window a crack and the frigid air soothed my watering eyes. My head was starting to feel light and fuzzy, but it wasn't really a bad feeling at all. In fact, it was kind of nice, actually.

Before I knew it, the van had lurched off the main highway and onto the narrow, gravel logging road. I could hear the frozen stones as they splattered up against the bottom of the van, clunking and thunking. For some odd reason, the noise suddenly seemed hilarious to me, and I began to giggle.

"They're playing our shong," I slurred. "Anyone wanna dance?"

Then suddenly, everyone was laughing, and I began to feel very warm as I washed down the final, acrid puffs of smoke with several more big gulps of beer. I dropped the short, brown stub of a joint into the beer can and heard it hiss. Then I crushed the thin aluminum in my hand, cranked down the window, and tossed the can out. I giggled as the image of Grandma Beverly's face appeared before my eyes. She was looking very displeased and shaking her index finger at me.

"Aloom-alum is not bio—dede—degradable," I said clumsily. "Thass what my grandma always says. And she should know, too." I was having a hard time making my mouth work, but it didn't seem to matter because I was also starting to feel very pleased with myself. I tilted my head back against the worn, vinyl headrest and let my eyes drift out of focus.

The barren landscape seemed to drift by beyond the cold window like a surreal drawing, all grays and blacks and washed-out blues. Even the snow looked lifeless and gray, detached somehow, like the way I was starting to feel. I tried to focus my mind, but it wasn't easy. With a great deal of effort, I concentrated on the gravel road, and then the lake. I remembered Mikey telling me earlier that the old road completely encircled Arrow Lake. To get to the picnic area, she'd said, we would have to drive nearly all the way around the lake. Sometimes the bumpy, rutted road rambled so far away from the lake that the glittering, frozen surface disappeared completely behind the trees. At other places, the road veered very close to the rocky shoreline. If I'd had another empty beer can, I probably could've tossed it right out onto the ice.

After awhile, my eyes got heavy and I let them slide shut. I also let my mind drift aimlessly. I felt isolated; but at the same time, I also felt surrounded by a flood of chatter and laughter. Words were flying all around me like wisps of colorful smoke—laughter, crude jokes—one girl was even talking on her cellphone. But it all seemed so far away from me suddenly. A moment later, I could feel myself falling asleep as my head bumped lightly against the frigid glass of the van window.

I don't know how long I dozed, but I was suddenly jerked awake by the sound of a car horn blasting. My eyes snapped open and I lurched forward; my hands flew up automatically and found the back of the driver's seat.

Neil was pounding the horn with his fist as obscenities spewed out of his mouth like lava from a volcano. He jerked the wheel hard to the right, and I immediately saw why: There was a man in the middle of the gravel road. He was directly in front of the van, not ten feet from our front bumper.

My fuzzy brain cleared instantly as a charge of adrenaline surged through my entire body. "Neil!" I shouted. "Look out!"

Neil cursed again and jerked the steering wheel even harder. The tail end of the van seemed to slide sideways; I felt my shoulder crunching into the handle of the van's sliding door. Stones and ice exploded into the air; they clattered against the van, bouncing off the metal and glass.

"What the hell's going on?" someone shouted.

Mikey and one of the other girls were screaming something, but I couldn't make out the words. All I could think about was the man in the road. He was looking directly at me, his eyes locked onto mine. He was wearing an old uniform of some sort; it looked like a mailman's uniform, and I wondered, briefly, *What's a mailman doing way out here?* There wasn't a house around for miles.

Out of the corner of my eye, I could see Neil still struggling with the steering wheel. He was still pounding the horn, too. Miraculously, the van slid by the man in the road with only inches to spare. The mailman's face shot directly past my window; it was a tired, weary face, and the eyes were still locked onto mine. His hand was raised and his lips were moving. He seemed to be saying my name.

The fat kid behind me was shouting angrily, "What the hell's wrong with you, Neil? If you can't stay awake, let me drive!"

"Didn't you see him?" Neil shouted back. "That old dude just popped up out of nowhere! I thought I was gonna run him over!"

"What old dude?" the fat kid asked, looking around. He snorted unpleasantly. "You're crazy, Neil, you know that? I've been watching you for the past ten minutes, dude, and you've been driving like a psycho!"

"But you must have seen him," Neil insisted, pointing at the road. "He was right there. In the middle."

"I didn't see nobody," the fat kid growled, settling back into his seat again. "And neither did you. Or anybody else. Freakin' loony, that's what you are."

I twisted around in my seat and looked out through the van's rear window. I couldn't believe that the fat kid hadn't seen anything. The mailman was still there, still standing right in the middle of the road. His hand was still raised, his mouth was still moving. His eyes were just as sad as before, and still locked onto mine.

And he was still saying my name. I know it sounds crazy because I couldn't hear him with my ears exactly, and yet, I *could still hear him*. It was like his words were somehow going through me, like a shaft of light. They were touching something deep inside of me.

"Come back, Lindsay," he was saying. "Come back before it's too late." And then, in an instant, the mailman was gone, dissolved like a puff of smoke.

The fat kid jerked around in his seat and looked out the back window. "See?" he shouted. "The road's freakin' empty, Neil! And you're a freakin' wacko!"

I could feel eyes boring into me as I faced forward in my seat again. I glanced up at the rearview mirror and saw Neil's eyes, watching me intently. "You saw him," Neil said directly to me. He was angry, aggressive. "Well, didn't you?" he pushed.

Suddenly, I was confused, hesitant, and befuddled. "I—I don't know. I—I thought I-"

Mikey screamed, "A deer!"

The huge, gray animal leaped out of nowhere. The front of the van caught it in midair; the heavy body crashed instantly through the windshield,. The glass caved in slightly and spoke-like cracks radiated in all directions.

Neil jerked the wheel again and this time, the van plunged off the road and down a steep embankment. Everyone was yelling and screaming as the van leaped and bounced and teetered sideways.

The windshield was completely blocked by the deer's body. The antlers had somehow poked through the breaking glass, and the rest of the windshield was completely obscured by the gray-brown fur of the deer's enormous frame. Neil yanked at the wheel and desperately fought in vain to regain control of the vehicle, but he couldn't even see where he was going.

I frantically looked out the side window and shouted, "Oh, my God—the lake!"

The van was swerving sideways. I could see trees and rocks sliding past the window as the engine roared and we veered even further out of control. And then I saw the shoreline—

It was behind us.

The van was out on the ice!

An instant later, there was a groaning sound, and then a loud *snap*. Then the front of the van quickly tilted downward at a steep and crazy angle. The windshield gave way completely then; somehow, the deer's body had been flung aside by all of the bouncing, but now a torrent of freezing water came gushing in through the shattered windshield.

Suddenly, everyone was screaming and pounding against the side windows. "Open the doors!" someone shouted. "Open the damn doors!"

I reached for the door handle on my side of the van, but the shock of the icy water pouring over my legs and stomach took my breath away. Suddenly, I couldn't move; I couldn't breathe. I couldn't do anything. And in an instant—

I knew I was going to die.

My hand was still clutching the door handle, but I couldn't pull it back. It was badly jammed, and I suddenly knew that it was hopeless. We were all going to die and there was nothing that I or anyone else could do about it. I was vaguely aware of the thrashing and screaming and pounding that was going on all around me. I could hear huge bubbles erupting somewhere. I could hear more glass shattering and collapsing; I could hear metal groaning and bumping. And yet it all seemed so distant from me, so meaningless, so totally…pointless.

I felt my hand slip away from the door handle as the frigid water reached my throat, my eyes, and then quickly covered my scalp. As I slipped under the numbing, green flood, I suddenly felt peaceful. I felt like I was sliding downward. I felt like I was slipping into an endless, warm, and welcoming deep sleep…

I'm sorry, were the only words that came to my mind. *I'm so very, very sorry…*

I closed my eyes and embraced death.

But death didn't come.

Instead, I felt the inside walls of the van giving way. Somehow, the sliding door had been wrenched open; it was slipping silently backward, and then a powerful hand was clutching my arm.

An instant later, I felt myself being pulled sideways and upward, out through the open door and up through the icy, green water. Before I could fully comprehend what was going on, my head had broken the surface. Then I was choking and coughing and gulping air, all at the same time. Someone was in the water beside me, yanking me forward, pulling me jerkily, stroke by steady stroke to the shore. Chunks of broken ice floated all around us.

"You're all right," a voice was saying, over and over. "I've got you, Lindsay. You're all right now. You're safe."

Then other hands were grabbing me, pulling me. I could feel my knees and elbows banging and scraping painfully against hard things beneath the water—frozen, razor-edged rocks. My fingers reached out like claws, clutching at anything, anyone. Then several people were pulling at me all at once, dragging me up out of the water and onto the narrow, rocky beach.

"Thank you," I gasped, blinking my eyes, trying to clear them of water. The last thing I saw was the mailman. His hair was dripping water that was fast turning to ice. His skin was pale, almost blue. His uniform was sodden and dark. He looked exhausted. But his smile was the warmest thing I had ever seen; I could literally feel its warmth pouring into me.

He was the one who'd saved my life!

And then everything started to fade to gray, and then to black.

When I woke up in the hospital, Grandma Beverly and Grandpa Howard were both there, standing beside my bed. Their faces were drawn, their eyes weary, but they were both smiling at me.

Grandma reached out and grasped my hand in both of hers. "Oh, Lindsay!" she cried. "I thought we'd lost you for sure!" Tears were streaming down her lined cheeks, but her smile was full of hope and joy.

"The mailman. Is—is he all right? He saved my life."

Grandma and Grandpa glanced at each other, their brows furrowed. "Mailman?" Grandpa said. He shrugged his bony shoulders. "Nobody said anything about a mailman, honey."

I felt confused for a moment, and then decided that I'd ask the doctors later. "What about my friends? The kids in the van? Are they all right?"

Grandma and Grandpa exchanged glances again. "They're fine, dear," Grandma said grimly. "Most of them just ... got banged up a bit." I pushed myself upright against the pillows. "What do you mean *most* of them?"

Grandma looked at Grandpa. He frowned and took a deep breath. He let it out slowly. "One of the boys didn't make it, honey," he said sadly. "One of them drowned."

I stared at him, not believing the words. "Who?" I managed, my voice shaking.

Grandpa's frown deepened. "I think the police said his name was Neil, honey."

"Neil drowned?" I said in disbelief.

Grandpa nodded sadly. "I'm so sorry, honey."

I was released from the hospital the next day with only a few scrapes and bruises. The other kids were mostly okay, too, just like Grandma had said. The fat kid had a concussion. Mikey had a broken arm. And two of the other kids had bruised ribs. But we were all just devastated about Neil.

Grandma and Grandpa took me to Neil's funeral several days later, but none of the other kids showed up. I called Mikey on the phone later, and she sounded very distant, almost like a stranger. She told me that she had wanted to go to Neil's funeral, but her morn's car had died, and she'd had no way of getting to the funeral home.

"You should've called me," I told her. "Grandma and Grandpa and I would've taken you."

"Forget it. Doesn't matter. Look, I gotta go, okay?"

"But when can I see you? I mean, we can still hang out at the mall…can't we? Like before?"

"I don't know. I'm kind of busy. Mom strained her back, and I've got this broken arm…things are kind of screwed up around here." She paused, but only for a second. "Look, I'll see you around, okay?"

"Mikey, wait!" I said frantically. But she had already hung up. And when I tried to call her right back, nobody answered the phone.

For the next two weeks I went to the mall after school, anyway, but Mikey never showed. None of the other kids showed up, either. I saw the fat kid once, and I know he saw me. But he ignored me completely, and disappeared into a knot of bustling shoppers.

"I don't understand," I said to Grandma Beverly. "It's like they don't even want to see me anymore."

"Maybe they just don't want to see *each other*," Grandma explained gently. "Maybe they just don't want to be reminded of the accident, or the death of your friend."

"But that's crazy. It wasn't anybody's fault; it was an accident."

Grandma nodded sadly. "Sometimes kids have a hard time accepting death. They're convinced they'll live forever, and when someone dies—someone they know very well—they just don't want to face it."

"But why?"

Grandma smiled her sad smile. "Because it hurts too much, I guess. Because it's too frightening. And because it makes them realize that death can happen to anyone, not just to old people." She looked at me steadily. "Sometimes it even happens to people you love."

I met her eyes for a long moment and then changed the subject. I didn't want to think about that just then. "I still want to find the mailman," I told her determinedly. "He saved my life. The least I can do is thank him."

My search, however, led me from one dead end to another. I checked all the newspaper articles about our accident, looking for his name, or even for some brief mention of how he'd saved my life. But there wasn't a single word written about the mailman in any of the articles.

Then I looked up nearly everyone who'd had anything to do with the accident. First I found the deer hunter who'd been out hunting nearby when our car went into the lake. It turned out that he was the one who called 911 on his cell phone.

"The only uniforms I saw," he told me on the phone when I called him, "were the ones the cops and paramedics were wearing when they got to the lake."

The paramedics couldn't remember having seen a mailman on that fateful day, either. Nor could the doctors at Lutheran Memorial.

"We treated a lot of kids for exposure that day," the tall, good-looking intern I spoke with told me. "Plus a deer hunter and two cops. But no mailman."

"But that's crazy. He's the one who saved my life; he's the one who pulled me out of the water."

The intern shrugged. "Sorry."

I even went down to the post office and talked to the personnel manager. "He's one of your people," I insisted. "There's got to be some kind of record."

The personnel manager frowned at me and turned back to her computer. She scrolled quickly through a long list of names and mail routes and incident reports. "Nothing," she said after a few minutes, shaking her head. "As a matter of fact, we don't even *have* a mail route out at Arrow Lake. Nobody lives out that way—not permanently, at least."

"But he *must* have been from this post office," I said impatiently.

She shrugged. "Maybe you should talk to the cops."

But there was no record at the police station, either, no report of a mailman being questioned about the accident.

"But my friend, Neil, saw him, too," I told the beefy, red-faced officer. "Neil's the one who was driving the van."

"Then maybe you better check with Neil."

"I can't. Neil's dead; he was killed in the crash."

For weeks after the accident, finding the mailman became an obsession with me. I thought about him at school. I thought about him at home. I thought about him before I went to sleep at night; I thought about him the minute I woke up in the morning.

Surely somebody knew who he was, and where he was. *A person can't just disappear from the face of the earth*, I thought. I just had to find him.

And when I finally did, I could hardly believe my eyes.

It happened the day Grandma decided to do her spring housecleaning—during the last week of April. By then, the winter chill had finally given way to milder temperatures. Most of the snow was gone; the mud was drying up. The combination of my erratic behavior, however, plus the harsh winter and then the accident, had all been so hard on both Grandma and Grandpa. They were starting to look haggard and worn, so I quickly volunteered to help.

"The first thing we have to do," Grandma said with a firm lift of her chin, "is air out the house. The whole place is starting to smell like a musty cellar."

"I'll get the bedroom windows, Grandma," I said quickly.

"Thank you, dear," Grandma said as I started up the stairs. "One window in each room should do fine. And only for an hour."

When I reached the upstairs landing, I ran into my bedroom and tried to open my only window. It was stuck, of course; it hadn't been opened in months. But I finally managed to jiggle it up about halfway. Then I went into Grandma and Grandpa's room.

As I opened the door to their room, a thought suddenly struck me: In the ten years I'd been living with Grandma and Grandpa Mitchell, I'd never really been in their bedroom before. Suddenly, I felt like I should knock on the door, even though I knew they were both downstairs. Their bedroom just seemed so private to me, so personal. I felt like an intruder, standing before the entrance to a sacred place.

Awkwardly, I pushed the door open and stood in the doorway for a moment, transfixed. The whole room looked like something out of a very old catalog. The curtains were made of faded and shabby lace; the walls were covered with ancient wallpaper. There was a long, worn doily on top of their scarred, mahogany dresser.

There was also a silver picture frame propped up near the mirror. But it was the picture itself that nearly yanked my eyes out of their sockets. As if in a trance, I stepped into the room, and my mouth dropped open. I gasped.

The guy in the photograph—was the mailman!

I stood before that dresser for the longest time, just staring at that old photo. I was barely able to breathe because there was simply no doubt about it: It really was the mailman.

I recognized him instantly. And yet, there was something different about the photograph, something that didn't quite fit. The deep, sad eyes were the same eyes that had probed mine that horrible day on the gravel road. The warm, sad smile was the same, too. And the hand, raised in a gentle wave. And the hair, so wavy and dark. And the postal uniform, so crisp and—

"The uniform," I said aloud.

I stared at the picture a moment longer. Then I raced to the scarred dresser, snatched up the photograph, and rushed back out into the hallway again.

"It's him!" I shouted, running down the hall. "It's the mailman!'

I could barely breathe as I clumped down the stairs, taking them two at a time. "Grandma, Grandpa!" I yelled when I'd reached the bottom of the stairs. "It's him! It's him!"

My grandparents hurried into the living room, their ancient faces lined with worry. "Lindsay?" Grandma said. "What's wrong? What are you shouting about, dear?"

"It's him!" I thrust the photograph at them. "This is the man who saved my life!"

Tentatively, Grandma reached out and took the framed photograph into her hands. She looked at Grandpa, her mouth a tight line. Grandpa's face, too, was rigid and grim.

"Well?" I said impatiently, mystified by their lack of response. "Surely you know him. I mean, his picture was on your dresser."

Grandma gazed down at the photograph for a long time. Then she smiled sadly. "Of course we know him," she said softly. "He's our son. He's your father, Lindsay."

"What?" I snatched the photo out of her hand. I stared down at it, suddenly feeling as though I'd been kicked in the stomach. In the same instant, an icy chill shot up my back. "But—I don't understand. The mailman's uniform . . ."

Grandma smiled and shook her head slowly. "No, Lindsay—it's not a mailman's uniform. That's an Air Force uniform, dear. Your father was a pilot. You remember that."

"But he died—ten years ago. How could he be…?"

Grandma shook her head slowly. "I don't know, Lindsay," she said softly. "I really don't know."

The question has tumbled through my mind countless times since I found that photograph. I've looked at it countless times, too, and I know, in the end, that Grandma and Grandpa were right; after all, that photo was an exact copy of the photo I'd torn to shreds in a fit of rage so many years before.

And the man in the photograph really was my father—the same man I'd seen, night after night, in my dreams so many years ago. The man in the photograph was also the man I'd seen on the gravel road out at Arrow Lake.

He's the man who plunged into the icy water.

He's the man who saved my life.

Thinking about it still sends shivers up and down my spine. None of it makes any sense to me, because I still don't believe in ghosts. And yet, I *know* that I saw him with my own eyes that day on the road out to Arrow Lake. Neil saw him, too. But Neil died in the crash.

Sometimes I think, *Well, maybe that's why Neil and I are the only ones who saw him—because death came so close to both of us.*

Certainly, death took Neil, and certainly, it almost took me, too. I realize now that the only reason I didn't die is because Daddy saved me.

But why did Daddy come back? Why did he save my life? The answers to those questions are still swirling around in my brain. But I'm beginning to think I understand.

I'm beginning to think that Daddy came back and saved my life because he wanted to give us both one more chance at forgiveness. I had to forgive him for leaving me, and he had to forgive me for leaving him.

Because I did leave him. I thrust him out of my life. I tore up his picture; I blamed him whenever anything went wrong. I decided that my whole, miserable life in Maine was all his fault. And then, as if all of that's not bad enough, I even forgot what my daddy looked like.

Surely, all of those things caused him pain, too. And it may sound strange, but I really do believe now that pain is not something that only the living can feel. I do believe that the dead feel it, too. And by that, I mean that the spirits of those who have died can still feel pain. Especially when those who are left behind continue to harbor all kinds of negative feelings toward that deceased person—feelings like anger and blame and guilt. Once those feelings are released, however, the pain that afflicts that restless and unhappy spirit is also released. And then the spirit is finally able to rest and heal in the hereafter.

My primary goal now is to make sure that Daddy's spirit is finally able to rest and heal. To do that, I realize that I am the one who has to forgive. And that's precisely what I'm learning to do.

I forgive my daddy for being a pilot. I forgive him for leaving my mother and me alone. Most of all, I forgive him for dying.

This year, things are going to be different. This year, I will be going to the Oak Grove Cemetery with Grandpa and Grandma. And I'll put lots of flowers on Daddy's grave. I'll talk to him. I'll pray for him. And I'll forgive him. Because I know now that he really does love me.

I also know that I love him, too, and that I always will. THE END

Don't judge a book by its cover!
MY SON WENT FROM MARINE—TO BEAUTY QUEEN!

Although True Love *and* True Romance *both tended to be culturally conservative when it came to sex and relationships, they could be relatively progressive on some topics. In the early 1970s, for example, gay men didn't come in for condemnation, even though in many cases their stories involved deceiving their wives about their true inclinations. Granted, pitying them for their lonely, loveless lives wasn't a huge improvement, but it was as compassionate a portrayal as they'd be likely to get from a mainstream magazine.*

By 1998, the situation had improved so significantly that True Love *could run a story about a mother coming to terms with her son's cross-dressing without going into a massive gay panic. Of course, Dean's mother has her suspicions, and she and her husband do go through some anxiety when they discover his life revolves around fancy dresses, but it's presented in the context of honest emotional confusion about why their happily engaged son makes his living as a female impersonator. ("We couldn't even begin to comprehend how Paige could continue to love him," Dean's mother laments, "when frankly he wore a dress better than she did.") Soon enough, they're cheering him on at drag pageants, and all his gay best friends become their best friends, too.*

Dean's stint in the Marine Corps actually plays just a background part in this story, and even his little sister wonders if he signed up "so he could prove he's a man." But his military service and his drag life would naturally have to be kept separate—in the early days of "Don't Ask, Don't Tell," when this story was set, getting caught in women's clothes would surely have led to a swift discharge.

"**H**as anyone seen my black skirt?" my daughter Jeanie called from the top of the stairs.

"Did you check the laundry room?" I called.

"It's not there," she yelled back. "I already checked."

I put an apple beside each sandwich I'd made and went to help Jeanie look for her skirt.

"I thought I hung it in my closet," she said as I looked under her bed. She was going through her dresser drawers. "I hung it next to my blue sweater."

"Well, it's not my size," I said. "I'm sure you just misplaced it."

"Sure," she said, "like I misplaced my beaded *vest* last week and my red sweater the week before."

There did seem to be a problem with clothing disappearing in our house lately. I'd recently lost a pair of pearl earrings, and I couldn't swear to it, but it seemed as if someone had been rifling through my lingerie drawer recently.

"Do you have something else you could wear?" I asked.

"Jeans," Jeanie said. "The same old jeans."

"I'll look for your skirt," I promised. "It's probably in the wash, or maybe it fell behind the dryer."

Dean was already in the kitchen when Jeanie and I went downstairs. "Hey Jeanie," he said, "you want a ride this morning?"

I began putting the lunches into paper bags and handing them to my children. Jeanie was a sophomore in high school. Her brother Dean was a senior. He was very proud of his first car. I was proud of him, too. He'd begun saving money for that car when he was barely into his teens. And Dean was a good student, too.

By contrast, his sister's grades were okay, but I'd known even before she went into the first grade that Jeanie was more interested in socializing than academics. We'd struggled through some difficult years; years in which Jeanie wanted to play, and my husband Race and I wanted her to study. During her first year of high school, two girls in Jeanie's class had dropped out to have babies. One of them was Jeanie's best friend.

"Oh, Mom," Jeanie had cried after she'd been to see her friend, Julie, and her new baby, "you should see how she lives! She's in this dinky apartment all day long. She and Mark can't even afford cable TV, so she's just stuck there all day with nothing to do but watch that baby!"

"She'll go back to school soon," I'd said softly. "It's going to be rough, but I'm sure she'll do fine."

"She's not even any fun anymore!" Jeanie had declared. "She didn't want to talk about school or boys or music or anything!"

"Her life has changed," I'd replied.

"*I'll* say," Jeanie huffed, "and not for the better! I'm going to make sure I have a good job and a good life before I have a baby!"

From that time on, we didn't have to beg Jeanie to study. She seemed to understand that school was about her future. It wasn't just something her old fogy parents wanted her to do for the fun of it.

I waved to my children as they drove off. Race and I were so lucky. We had two bright, motivated children, good jobs, and wonderful friends. What more could a couple ask of life?

The morning went by quickly as I cleaned up the kitchen, did some laundry, and vacuumed. I hadn't located Jeanie's skirt, but I wasn't worried. I was pretty sure I'd find it soon enough. It was probably on the floor in her bathroom, or at the bottom of the laundry hamper.

I was hanging some shirts in Dean's room when something at the back of his closet caught my eye. There was Jeanie's skirt—and her red sweater. What were they doing in Dean's room?

I stood there for a full minute before I shook my head and

realized I must have put them in the wrong closet the last time I did laundry. What would Dean, our football-playing son, want with his sister's clothes?

I put the incident out of my mind until a few weeks later, when a bottle of foundation and a tube of my lipstick disappeared from my vanity table. I looked high and low for them—even accused Jeanie of taking them.

"I swear I didn't touch your makeup, Mom," she said. "We don't have the same coloring anyway, so why would I want your foundation?"

She had a point. I had sallow skin, and I had to balance it with a foundation that had a pink base. Jeanie had more peach tones in her skin, and my foundation would have made her look feverish. But since it wasn't the sort of thing I carried around with me, I knew I hadn't left it in a purse somewhere.

The next morning I was halfway through getting ready for work when I realized the bottle of foundation was back where it belonged. So was the lipstick. I stood in the bathroom holding both of them and wondering about their sudden reappearance. I hadn't just overlooked them: I *knew* they hadn't been where they were supposed to be when I'd been looking for them before.

Then I remembered finding Jeanie's skirt in Dean's closet, but I dismissed my fears as nonsense. Dean had never shown any indication that he was interested *in* women's clothing. If anything, he made it a point to avoid the subject of fashion altogether.

When asked what his date had worn to the junior prom, he'd said, "Some blue thing—lacy, I guess."

When I'd seen the pictures taken that night, I'd been surprised by how pretty Dean's date had looked. Her blue dress was simple in design, but Mindy was a knockout in it. I'd chuckled a little at Dean's inability to remember how pretty she'd looked.

Then about a week before Dean's graduation, I came home from my part-time job early one afternoon. I'd gone to work with a pounding headache that morning, and it hadn't gotten any better even after I'd taken several pain pills. Mr. Foster, my boss, had suggested I go home.

"You can come in tomorrow if you feel better," he'd said. "I get migraines once in a while myself. The only thing that helps is to lie down in a darkened room."

I decided he was right. I grabbed my pocketbook and headed for home.

Dean's car was parked in the driveway. *That's odd,* I thought. *He's usually not home at this time of the day.* Then I remembered: It was final exam week, and the kids didn't have a full schedule. I hurried into the house. I planned to make myself a nice cup of tea, and then I'd relax for the rest of the day.

What I saw when I pushed open my bedroom door nearly stopped my heart.

My son—my big, strong baby boy—was wearing panty hose, a pair of high-heeled pumps, a black satin teddy, and a full face of makeup.

"Oh, I—oh!" I couldn't even form a complete sentence, the shock was so great.

"Mom," Dean said softly, looking at me, "I'm so sorry."

He ran from my room into his own, slamming the door behind him.

I fell across my bed sobbing. How could I possibly live with what I'd just seen? My husband and I had had such hopes for our son.

Okay. I thought after I'd cried myself out, *I've read enough advice columns in the newspaper to know that he wants and needs acceptance.*

This might be hard to accept, but I was going to try.

"Dean?" I knocked lightly on his door.

"Come in," he said. He was sitting on his bed. His face was scrubbed clean of makeup, and he was wearing his own jeans and a white T-shirt. He had his knees drawn up to his chest as he leaned against the headboard. I could see he'd been crying.

"Honey, is there something you want to tell me?" I asked carefully, kind of lingering in the doorway before I moved hesitantly to take a seat near him on the bed.

"No." he said quietly, looking down at his shaking hands.

"Okay," I said. "I just want you to know that I'm available if you want or need to talk about anything at all. I won't judge you, Dean. I love you."

"Mom," he said slowly, after a long moment, "I should have—asked permission to get into your things. I'm really sorry. I'll wash them and get them right back to you."

"That will be fine," I said. I hoped I was doing things the way the advice columnists always recommended. I didn't want to jeopardize my relationship with my son. Dean cleared his throat and said hesitantly, "We're doing a skit—on class night, the night before graduation. I've—got one of the lead parts. I sort of—well, if it's not too much trouble--I need to borrow your things."

"That's what this is about?" I asked. The relief I felt was indescribable. "You're in a play of some kind?"

"Well, yeah," he said, looking up at me as if I should have known. "It's a sort of Monty Python thing. You know, those British guys who were always playing female roles?"

I laughed. "I do know. Your father loved Monty Python. He thinks that parrot sketch they did is the funniest thing he's ever seen."

Dean brightened, but only slightly. "I got you two tickets," he said. "And one for Jeanie, too."

I didn't say a word about Dean's play to Race or Jeanie. I knew it would be even funnier for them to see Dean in drag if they weren't expecting it. Our local high school always devoted the night before graduation to a showcase of talent within the out-going class. It's also when many seniors received awards and scholarships. I hoped Dean would be among those so honored.

"So, what's Dean doing in this thing?" Race asked the night

of the show when we'd found our seats in the packed high school auditorium.

"Oh, some little skit," I said in a bored voice.

"He's never been in anything before," Jeanie remarked. "Is he going to become an actor now?"

"I've been meaning to talk to him about his plans," Race said. "He hasn't seemed thrilled with the college acceptances he's received so far, and a couple of them are from really great schools. Do you think he's depressed?"

"No," I said softly. "I don't think he's depressed. Maybe he's just burned out from so much studying."

"That's probably it," Race agreed.

The emcee strode on stage just then, and for the next forty minutes, we were regaled with song, dance, and the presentation of numerous awards. Then the lights went down, and we were taken on a hilarious romp through the eyes of our children as they made caricatures of their high school teachers. Dean played Miss Kratzenberg, a teacher known for her many male admirers. Dressed in my teddy, the pumps, and an elaborate Dolly Parton-style wig, he sashayed across the stage like a professional.

"You boys better behave!" he warned. Then, in a fabulous imitation of Mae West, he purred, "Even if I do think a bad boy is more interesting!"

Dean brought down the house that night. We laughed until we cried, and the whole family was just so proud and impressed with this new talent of Dean's that we'd never seen before. We were even prouder when he received a full scholarship to a very notable college in our area. I was thrilled beyond words.

"You were fantastic!" Jeanie said as she hugged her brother when we all trouped backstage to congratulate him. "I didn't know you had it in you!"

"It was fun." Dean grinned bashfully.

We all praised his tremendous performance. Then we watched

as he went off to be with his friends. He was moving away from us in so many ways, and I found myself trying to memorize every aspect of the moment, not wanting to ever forget how it had felt seeing my son enjoying a few moments of real acclaim.

The next few weeks flew by. We went to the lake for part of the summer. Dean and Jeanie immediately renewed their friendships with the other teens at the lake; kids who'd been coming there with their families for almost as many years as we had. We spent our mornings boating and fishing, and our afternoons sprawled across the comfortable furniture on the screened-in porch, reading and talking and just enjoying each other.

Through it all, I sensed there was something troubling Dean. The last night of our stay, he finally told us what it was.

"You might not approve of this," he said slowly and carefully, "but I guess I'm man enough to have made my own decision, so now I have to stick to it."

"What is it?" I asked. My voice trembled.

"I've enlisted in the Marine Corps," he said. "I go to boot camp in August."

"No!" I cried. "You can't be serious, Dean! Wh-what about college? What about your scholarship?"

"College is important to me," he said calmly, "but there are some other things I feel I need to do as well. While I'm in the Marines, I'll be saving up money for college. I scored very high on my tests, so I'll get some really good training—"

"Garbage!" Race roared. "Of course you scored high on your tests! Any baboon could pass a test! A Marine is nothing more than a target! Is that what you want to be, Dean? You want to go to war and get shot at?"

"No, sir," Dean said softly. "It's just something I need to do."

Race got up and walked into the house, slamming the door behind him.

"I'm not sure I understand," I whispered to my son across the suddenly vast and terrifying expanse of the screened-in porch. "Are you sure about this, Dean?"

"Yes, Morn," he told me plainly, his strong, confident gaze meeting mine without so much as a blink. "I've never been more sure of anything in all my life."

Dean went to boot camp. It was tough letting him go. I felt completely unprepared for the quiet house, the change of routine. I moped around for a few weeks. Jeanie did her best to try and cheer me up, and I quickly realized it wasn't fair of me to ignore her just because I was concerned for my son.

"Why don't we take an entire day and just go shopping, and go get our nails done, and just do girl stuff?" I finally suggested to her one morning over breakfast.

"That would be great!" Her eyes shimmered with anticipation. "When?"

"Today seems like a good day," I said. "You have the day off, and so do I."

We were having our nails done in a salon at the mall when Jeanie completely caught me off guard with a question.

"Mom, do you think Dean joined the Marines so he could prove he's a man?"

I stared at her as the woman applied the finishing touches to my French manicure. "I don't know what you mean," I said. I couldn't believe she was asking me a question about such a personal family matter in front of the nail technicians.

"Well, he said a few things to me once about how he wished he'd been born a girl."

I colored slightly as my nail technician looked up at me, then made herself look very busy with a bottle of clear acrylic topcoat.

"Perhaps he meant that he thinks men have a tough time deciding what they want to do with their lives, Jeanie. You know, society is often kinder to a woman who takes her time making that decision. Some women choose to get married young and have their families before deciding on a career. Other women choose the career first. Men don't really have the luxury of those choices."

"Dean said he wished you and he had days like this." Jeanie said. "The last time we did this, he told me he was jealous."

My stomach tightened with fear and questions I wouldn't allow myself to ask. "Now we're talking about sibling rivalry!" I forced an uncomfortable laugh that didn't sound convincing even to me. "He just wanted my full attention, Jeanie."

"And your teddy," she said softly.

I suppressed the urge to snap at her and tell her that she was wrong. Dead wrong.

That night, Dean called us. We took turns talking to him, and he told us he was doing well, even though he said the drill sergeants were working him to death.

"Wait till you see me!" he said. "I've got a shaved head and washboard abs! I bet you don't even recognize me!"

We laughed, and I could tell that in spite of his initial resistance, my husband was very proud of our son. He immediately told Dean we'd all be attending his graduation from boot camp.

"That would mean so much to me, Dad," Dean said earnestly. "I'm kind of excited, actually. I've done well enough to qualify for advanced electronics training. If I do well in that, I'll be able to do my time in the Marines, and then I can get out and get a really good job, or I can go to college like I planned."

"You've given this a lot of thought," Race said.

"I suppose I have," Dean replied. "I've always admired the way you got your training, and then went right to work. I guess I'm impatient, and couldn't see spending four years in college trying to decide what I want to do."

Race's voice was choked with emotion as he told Dean how proud he was of him. We all sat staring at the speaker phone after Dean had hung up. For a few wonderful moments, Dean had been with us. That phone call had meant more to us than all the college scholarships in the world. And his lighthearted comments about his muscles and his shaved head had alleviated a lot of my fears. Dean still was, and had always been, a confident, terrific young man.

Dean's graduation from boot camp was a highpoint for all of us. Race clapped him on the back at least a dozen times and told him how proud he was. Even Jeanie kissed her big brother's cheek and told him she thought he'd made the right decision.

I cried. Dean laughed at me, but I couldn't help myself. My baby, all suited up in his dress uniform, was now a strong, powerful man. Boot camp had made him grow up. I'm sure he would have been embarrassed at such a display of affection, but there were plenty of other mothers crying that day because they felt the same way about their sons.

Dean's training had him moving around every few months. We wrote letters and sent him care packages. He called often. When he finished his training, he was sent overseas.

Jeanie, now in her junior year of high school, was utterly preoccupied with her part-time job and her friends. Although I had my work and my church activities, I felt at loose ends. My children no longer needed me the way they had when they were younger. In an attempt to stave off depression, and the empty nest syndrome, I signed up for some classes at the local community college.

The first night of class, I met a lovely young woman. I told her all about my dashing young son the Marine, and I could tell she was interested. At the next class, I showed her Dean's picture and encouraged her to write to him. She did, and I was tickled that they seemed to hit it off right away. Amanda and I were nearly delirious with excitement when Dean said he was going to be coming home on leave. She already felt as if she knew him, and wanted more of a relationship with him than their correspondence had allowed. I was ecstatic; my son was coming home!

For two wonderful weeks, I cooked Dean's favorite foods, asked him questions about his job and his travels, and watched him like I'd never seen my son before in all his life. There was no sign that anything was amiss. I decided Jeanie had just been rattling off empty words at the salon that time. Dean didn't seem jealous of the time Jeanie and I had together. In fact, he seemed more at ease with himself. I was a little disappointed that after just a couple of dates, he and Amanda weren't seeing each other anymore. She'd seemed so perfect for him.

We all hugged each other at the airport, and then I watched my son get on the plane and head back to his post. He'd brought us lovely gifts from Germany, and he'd raved about the fabulous food, and all his friends over there. I wondered, if he'd become involved with a girl stationed there. Perhaps he'd even fallen in love with a German girl.

I hadn't been courageous enough to ask. Dean, who'd always been rather open about his feelings, hadn't confided in me during his visit. About the only thing he'd said about his plans was that he thought he'd extend his tour in Germany, because he wasn't in a big hurry to come back to the States.

I wondered if he'd confided in Amanda. I knew I shouldn't pry, but I couldn't help myself. After class one night, I asked her what had happened between the two of them.

"Oh, you know how it is," she sighed. "You write to someone and you think you know them, but then you actually meet them, and they aren't exactly what you were looking for." Her voice was heavy with disappointment.

"What was wrong with my son?" I forced myself to ask.

"Oh, no, Irene—nothing like that, honestly," Amanda had rushed to protest. "Dean is a perfect gentleman—a wonderful, terrific guy. But look, Irene—I don't want you to be upset, but there's a lot you don't know about Dean. He's established a wonderful life for himself in Germany, and I just couldn't see myself moving over there, and I couldn't see myself loving a man who—well, let's just say I couldn't see myself with Dean in the long run. He's just not my type, Irene—and to be perfectly honest---I don't think I'm his type, *either*."

I wondered what she meant, but I eventually told myself Amanda and Dean just weren't truly right for each other. Two long years passed before Dean returned home. He was nearing the end of his enlistment by then, and we were all anxious to hear about his plans for the future.

"I'll be living in Nevada," he said. "I've got a job in Las Vegas."

"Las Vegas! What will you he doing there—gambling for a living?" Race joked.

"I've got a job working for one of the biggest and best hotels and casinos." Dean explained. "I'll be working as a computer programmer, and I love that area—I love the mountains and the desert, and a couple of my friends are already working there. You can come visit—"

"Of course we will," I said quickly. "We're so proud of you, Dean! I guess we just expected you to come home and live and work here for a while before you figured out what you really wanted to do."

"I love Minnesota," he said, "but there's really nothing for me there. Anyway, only be a hop, skip, and a jump away— by plane, that is."

Reluctantly, Race gave his blessing. That night as we lay in bed, I reminded him that some of our friends hadn't been fortunate enough to have children who made their own way in the world.

"Just the other day, Renee told me that her daughter is moving home again," I said—. "She jokes about Kirsten's suitcases wearing out before she does, but I think Renee's really tired of it. One minute she's got her house to herself, the next she's got Kirsten back in with her."

"I just worry about the boy," Race said. "What do we know about these friends of his? What do we really know about his life?"

"We know that he's earning his own living, and he's responsible enough that he's already secured a job," I said.

"That's something," Race agreed. "But what if he falls in with the wrong crowd? I mean, it seems to me he could get in with some really rough characters in that part of the country."

"We've got some rough characters right around here," I countered. "Didn't you see the news tonight? Didn't you watch the story about those teenagers who beat and robbed that poor grandmother?"

"I saw it," he replied. He sighed heavily before conceding, "I guess he'll be okay. I mean, the boy is a *Marine*, after all."

I didn't tell Race I was worried, too. Since leaving home, Dean hadn't told us very much about his life, and I couldn't help but wonder about it. He said all of the right things when we were together, but there was a lot he *wasn't* saying. He didn't mention having a girlfriend or even dating, and this concerned me. I was kind of hoping for some grandchildren.

Jeanie went to visit her brother during the summer. When she came home, she excitedly told us all about the clubs Dean had taken her to, and all of his nice friends.

"Is he seeing anyone special?" I asked.

"Yes," she said. "Someone you'll really like." Then she refused to tell me anymore. "You'll have to go see him for yourself," she told me. "He really wants to see you and introduce you to his friends."

That night I suggested to Race that we take sonic vacation time and go visit our son.

"You just can't wait to get to his apartment so you can frill it up," Race teased. "But okay, let's take some time off and go see him. But I'm warning you, Irene: I'll turn right around and bring you back home if you try to smuggle him any frilly bathroom stuff!"

I laughed. Race was always teasing me about my need to decorate every little space. One year I'd even wallpapered a closet, because I'd seen an article about pretty closets in a magazine!

The truth is, I would have embarrassed myself if I'd come prepared to decorate my son's apartment. As it turned out, Dean had developed exquisite tastes during his time away from us.

"This is beautiful!" Race *exclaimed* as Dean took us on a tour of his spacious condominium.

"I kind of play around with color." Dean grinned. "It helps me impress the girls."

His reference to girls had me immediately asking if there was someone special in his life.

"There is," he said proudly, "and I can't wait to introduce you guys to her."

That night at dinner, he did just that. We instantly fell in love with Paige. It was clear she adored Dean, and the two of them made the announcement I'd been waiting and praying for. They were going to be married at Christmas time.

Dean was working nights. Every evening at six o'clock he headed for his job. He was always dressed in casual khaki pants and a polo shirt. He'd come back to the condo somewhere around four in the morning, sleep for a while, and then he'd get up and go to the gym. He didn't tell us much about his job, but he did tell us not to make any plans for the weekend. He said he had a big surprise for us.

On Saturday night, Dean took us out to a big club at the hotel where he worked. Paige met us there. We had just ordered dinner and drinks when a young man approached the table. Dean introduced him as a coworker. The young man seemed upset. Dean tried to brush him off, saying we'd made plans, but the young man insisted there was a problem that needed to be attended to.

"You go ahead," Race encouraged.

"We'll be fine here with Paige."

"I hope you enjoy the show," Dean said.

He kissed Paige. Then I heard him whisper to her, "This isn't the way I'd planned it."

Paige smiled and told him that everything would be fine. I wondered what she meant. What was the big deal? One of the computers must have broken down, I figured, and Dean was being called to fix it.

When the stage show began, the Superstar Diva Revue, I nearly choked on my sirloin steak. An entertainer who looked like Cher, sounded like Cher—but had an Adam's apple that Cher *doesn't* have—came on stage and sang. Then a man who looked just like Joan Rivers came out and told some really bawdy jokes.

At first, Race seemed a little uncomfortable; but as he laughed at the jokes, I could see him relaxing. Men dressed as female celebrities from Liza Minnelli to Barbara Streisand entertained us for a good two hours. We applauded wildly. It was a fantastic show.

Then suddenly the lights dimmed so that we could barely see the curvaceous silhouette of a singer in a long, shimmering gown sitting on a stool on stage. In a soft throaty voice, she began to sing. As the lights came up, my heart stopped and started again. I gripped Race's hand so tightly, I worried later that I'd broken some bones.

There on stage in sequins and a feather boa, for all the world to see, was our son.

Dean wore a blond wig; huge, thick, glittering false eyelashes; and stiletto ruby rhinestone heels that sparkled in the spotlight.

He sang, he danced, he smiled seductively at the audience. I had to turn my head away when he approached our table. Race sat staring with his mouth hanging open.

We left the club immediately after the show.

Neither of us knew what to say, not even when Paige remarked, "Isn't he fabulous? He's one of the best entertainers on the Strip."

I cried. Race wondered where we'd gone wrong. We spent the entire night trying to figure out how our macho Marine Corps son could pull on panty hose every night and transform himself into a woman. We couldn't even begin to comprehend how Paige could continue to love him when frankly, he wore a dress better than she did.

"At least now we know why Amanda broke up with him." I was laying in bed in the guest room, crying in Race's arms as he just held me and sighed heavily every now and then. Dean wasn't home yet, and Race and I had bid a strained good night to Paige and left her sitting downstairs in the living room. "He's not right—Oh, Race, we'll never have grandchildren!"

"Jeanie will give us grandchildren," Race said quietly.

"I guess you two have a lot of things you'd like to say to me," Dean said from the doorway. Neither of us had seen him standing there, and I wondered anxiously about how much he'd heard. "I'm really sorry about tonight, Mom and Dad. I thought I'd done pretty well to arrange a Saturday night off. My plan was to take you to the show, see how you liked it, and then decide if I'd tell you about my job. I never intended to hurt or embarrass you. Believe me, that's the last thing I would ever want to do—especially where this is concerned."

"What I want to know," Race said in a quiet, controlled voice that sounded like thunder rumbling on the horizon, "is how the hell you expect us to feel, Dean? What you're doing is—is—hell, I don't even know what to make of it!"

"I'm sorry you feel that way, Dad," Dean told him "I work very hard. I enjoy my work."

"How long have you been dressing like—like a woman?"

"Most of my life," Dean said. "In secret."

"Well—it's not—not right!" Race sputtered. He moved away from me and rose from the bed. "Get your things, Irene; we're going home. I've said what I had to say."

I got to my feet. For a few moments, I stood between my husband and my son and wondered what to do. As a good wife, I thought I should go with Race and figure out how to talk to Dean later on. As a good mother, I wanted my son to know that I had been shocked, but I was also a little—well, more than a little—proud of him. According to Paige, he was a gifted entertainer, and I'd certainly seen that for myself in the Superstar Diva Revue.

"I can't go with you," I said to Race all of a sudden—before I'd even thought about saying it. "I love you dearly, Race, and I'm sorry you're so upset, but right now, I need to talk to Dean. Running away isn't going to change the fact that he's a female impersonator."

"He's a—he's acting like a crazy man!" Race stormed. "I just want to go home and think of him as a Marine!" he blurted out, and then, all at once, the fight and the fire seemed to drain out of him, and my husband sank down on the bed in lost defeat.

"He's our son, Race," I said plainly, tears shimmering in my eyes. "Or have you forgotten that because you can't deal with the fact that he's chosen to make his living in a way you never imagined?"

Race slumped down even further, as if that were possible. "I don't know," he muttered finally. "How am I ever going to tell my friends what my boy is doing?"

"You can tell them I'm a computer programmer," Dean said. "In my spare time, that's what I do. I do freelance work, and as a matter of fact, I just started designing home pages for the Internet out of my home office. Why would your friends need to know any more than that?"

"Is this what you've always wanted to do, honey?" I asked in a timid, hesitant voice that didn't sound at all like mine.

"I didn't know what I wanted to do for the longest time," Dean admitted. "You see, for as long as I can remember, I've enjoyed putting on women's clothes. That's the honest truth—and it's just as simple as that. But nobody I knew ever did this—or at least, nobody ever talked about it. So I just kept it a secret.

"Then when I went to Germany, I met two guys who dressed like women on the weekends. We had to keep our activities secret because we were enlisted men, but I went to some clubs in Germany where men dressed like women, and that's where I found the—courage, I guess you'd call it—to try my wings as an entertainer. I loved it all right from the start—the sound of the applause, the spotlight, the rehearsals—everything. The audiences were very appreciative and very kind to a newcomer like me. So, I perfected my act, and when I came back here, I got a job in one of the smaller clubs here in Vegas."

"Are you gay?" Race asked.

"Many of my fellow entertainers are," Dean said. "But I'm not. I wish I could explain it, but when I'm offstage, I don't want to dress like a woman. What I mean is, I don't want to dress like that all of the time. I think of it as a uniform—something I put on because of my job—because it's what I'm good at."

"I have to think about this," Race said after a long, silent moment.

"Well, there's something else I need to tell you," Dean told us. "This coming weekend, there's a beauty contest—"

"Sheesh!" Race blew out a whoosh of air. "Don't tell us you're going to be in it!"

"It's a benefit," Dean said. "For AIDS research. How could I refuse?"

"A beauty contest?" Race's silvery eyebrows shot up. "You mean like in a bathing suit, and an evening gown?" My heart went out to my husband then, who was fumbling with words and trying so desperately to understand our son.

"Something like that." Dean smiled. "I'd love it if you'd both come."

"We'll be there," I said. "Won't we, darling?"

Race nodded his agreement. I knew this was difficult for him, because it was hard for me. But I felt that our son needed our support. What kind of parents would we be if we turned away from him now?

"Is there anything I can help you with?" I asked Dean later that day. "I mean, for the pageant?"

Dean chuckled. "I'm getting my legs waxed Friday afternoon, my nails done at the same time—" He stopped abruptly and began to laugh. "Mom!" he teased. "This is our big chance! You and I can spend a day at the salon together! I'll pay for everything—we'll even get massages and facials!"

"They won't mind my being there?" I asked. I assumed it was a special salon frequented only by female impersonators.

"It's just a regular salon, Mom," Dean said. "And Dad, while we're getting beautiful, how would you like to spend the day playing golf with a former pro?"

"You mean it?" Race's eyes were shining with excitement.

"He's a friend of mine," Dean explained. "I'll arrange it."

One of the things I admire most about my son is that he doesn't do anything halfway. Not only had he arranged for Race to play in a foursome with a former pro he'd met at the hotel, but he'd already arranged to pick up the tab at the clubhouse for Race after the game.

The spa he took me to was so beautiful, I had a few moments of anxiety when we first went in.

"I can't believe a small-town woman like me is in such a beautiful place!" I whispered to Dean.

"This is something I've always wanted to do for you, Mom," he told me, taking my arm in his. "You deserve to be pampered."

The attendants soaked me in mud that smelled like gardenias; massaged me until my muscles felt like melted butter; steamed my skin till it was pink and glowing; advised me on what vitamins to take and what kinds of food to eat; did my hair, my nails, and my makeup. I felt like a movie star when Dean and I left five hours later.

"That's just the appetizer," he teased in the car as we drove along the desert highway. "Now we've got to get you a suitable dress."

"I've got a little black dress I can wear," I said. "With my pearls."

"And you look great in it," he said. "But let me buy you something new—something outrageous."

"I don't know if I can *do* outrageous," I said. "I'm not young, and I'm not exactly small."

Dean drove us to a small boutique. Big Mary, the seamstress, greeted us at the door. Mary, Dean explained, had taken the name as her given name after her sex change.

"I'm delighted to meet you, Mrs. Dawson!" she gushed, ushering us in.

When Dean told her what we were looking for, she grinned. "You're about a size twenty, Mrs. Dawson—is that right?"

"How did you know?" I asked.

"I've been sewing since I was old enough to hold a needle," she said. "This year alone, I've done eight of the ten costumes for our little beauty contest."

"Mary was last year's contest winner," Dean explained. "It was ironic, since she designed many of the gowns the other contestants wore."

"Did you do my son's gown?" I asked.

"I did," she said. "Dean's a delight to work with. And I just *love* Paige. I'm hoping she'll ask me to design her wedding dress."

I felt a tingle of excitement about the wedding: Then I joked, "Well, maybe you should design one for Dean, too!"

We were all laughing when Mary said, "Well, here's what I have in mind for you, Mrs. Dawson." She held out a navy blue dress that was so lovely, I gasped.

"I could never wear such a gorgeous gown."

"Please," Dean whispered. "You'll be so pretty Mom. We'll have pictures made."

How could I refuse my son?

Race let out a low whistle that night when I twirled around in front of him in the navy dress with the silver stars handpainted on it.

"You look like a princess, or a goddess!" he said, taking me in his arms for a wonderful kiss.

"Dean picked it out," I said. "The designer says she's hoping to design Paige's wedding dress."

"What's Dean wearing tonight?" Race asked.

I laughed as I admitted I didn't know. "I'm sure it will be lovely, though," I told him. "Since when did you become interested in fashion, anyway?" I teased.

"Since my son became a knockout," he said gruffly. "I'm still not sure about all of this, but I'm going along with it tonight because I think the contest is for a good cause. I don't know how I'm going to feel after I get home and I've had some time to think about it though."

Paige picked us up and drove us to the club. She told us that she'd helped organize the event.

"I'm so glad you've agreed to stay," she said. "I love your son very, very much Mr. and Mrs. Dawson. He's a kind, generous, wonderful man, and I can hardly wait to spend the rest of my life with him. He talks about you all so much, I guess I'd be devastated if we couldn't work this out."

"He's always going to be my son," Race said gruffly. "I just never expected this in all my years. You've got to give an old man like me some time to deal with it."

"You take all the time you need, Mr. Dawson." Paige smiled warmly, and I squeezed Race's hand.

A young woman took the stage before the pageant began. Ironically, she was dressed in jeans and a tank top. She explained that she had HIV, and told us she'd contracted it as a result of a heterosexual relationship. She reminded the guests how important it is to practice safe sex, and she emphasized that many innocent children are being born with the disease. We applauded her for her courage and her message.

Pageant officials then explained how the money collected that night would be spent to further the search for a cure for this dread disease.

The pageant began with all of the contestants parading on stage in their formal gowns. I was so proud of my son. Dean wore a deep blue satin gown that brought out the color of his eyes. His hair, a custom-made wig, fell in soft black waves around his shoulders.

Two contestants lost their rubber breasts during the bathing suit contest. Race and I laughed along with the crowd as they quickly scooped them up and stuffed them back in good-naturedly. Dean looked stunning in a bright red, one-piece bathing suit.

"He's got good legs," Race observed. "Never thought I'd say that about my own son, but if I were a judge. I'd give him some high marks for that."

"I hope he wins," I said, crossing my fingers underneath the table. I was tingling all over with excitement. I was no longer thinking of Dean as a Marine, or as my son; I was thinking of him as a beauty contestant and I desperately wanted him to walk off with the crown.

The talent portion of the pageant was next. Contestants weren't allowed to lip sync, which is common practice in many of the clubs, so they had to demonstrate their own real talent. One contestant twirled flaming batons; another danced. Dean sang a song he dedicated to Race and me. I immediately recognized the melody. It was an old Burt Bacharach song that I'd always loved. His voice was strong and clear, and my heart nearly burst with pride as the audience gave him a standing ovation.

The emcee told some jokes after that, and there was a short slide show highlighting moments from the previous year's pageant. At the end of the short program, there were photographs of those contestants who volunteered their time to help those who have AIDS. Race squeezed my hand as a picture of Dean flashed on the screen. It turned out that Dean had donated more than one hundred hours of his personal time to the local AIDS hospice.

I thought I would faint as I waited for the judges to announce their decision. Dean, dressed in a simple white gown with a gold bugle-bead trim, was, in my opinion, the most beautiful and talented contestant. I desperately wanted the judges to agree with me.

The third runner-up was a young man from Ohio, who cried when he was given his small crown and his bouquet of roses. The second runner-up was dressed in a silver gown so tight, it didn't leave anything to the imagination. The first runner-up was one of Dean's friends, Nathan, who wiped tears from his eyes as Big Mary placed the small crown on his head.

Then, amidst a drum roll, the winner was announced. There was a moment of complete silence. Then the crowd and Race and I went crazy. We screamed, and cheered, and jumped out of our chairs and raced on stage to hug our son. We carried on for a good five minutes. Then, we went back to our chairs while Dean took a long walk down the runway and waved to the crowd, the tiara sparkling atop his gorgeous hair.

"He won!" Race exclaimed. "Our son won!" He excitedly pointed to Dean as he announced to anyone within range, "That's my boy! That's my boy up there!"

We returned home with a suitcase full of souvenirs from our trip. Most prized was the portrait we had taken of Race, Dean, Paige, and me. Dean and I were in our formal gowns.

"Let's hang it in the entryway," Race suggested when I showed him the large framed picture.

"Aren't you afraid of what people will say?" I asked.

"Not in the least," he snorted. "Because if they say one word against my boy, I'll tell them all about how he donates his time to the hospice, and I'll tell them about his fiancée, and if that doesn't shut them up, I'll tell them how much money he makes!"

It hasn't always been easy. Some of our friends were blatantly unsupportive, and a few even distanced themselves from us when we told them about Dean's career. Those reactions stung, but Race and I quickly realized that people who are so quick to condemn, probably aren't people we want to be friends with in the first place. How can they understand that the values we wanted our son to have—honesty, ambition, kindness—are all there; Dean just likes to package them in a dress from time to time.

In a few weeks, Race and I will return to our son's home. It has become a yearly tradition for Race and me to attend the annual beauty pageant that benefits AIDS research, and fills so many lives with a renewed sense of faith in the human race. Many of the young men we've met have been disowned by their families because of who, and what, they are. I feel sorry for them, but most of all, 1 feel sorry for their families, who will never know how truly wonderful these men are. Race and I cheer for them as if they were our own children. A lot of them have taken to calling us Mom and Dad, and that's an honor we truly treasure.

Jeanie presented us with a granddaughter the same week Paige gave us our second grandson. I was so touched when I read the note Dean had sent to his sister to congratulate her on the birth of her first child:

You'd think after two years of experience, I'd be an old hand at parenting. The truth is, Jeanie, I'm not. In fact, I stumble around like a complete idiot in front of little Race. But I think I've figured out that if we can accept our children for who they are, and not for what we want them to be, the way Mom and Dad have always accepted us, then we're going to be the kind of parents our children can be truly proud of. I love you, Sis, and I'm thrilled for you.

I wiped tears from my eyes when I read that letter.

My son, the beauty queen, is everything I could ever have hoped for. THE END

DEAREST SOLDIER: THE STORY OF A GALLANT WIFE

As American soldiers went off to fight in Europe and the Pacific during the Second World War, their wives were expected to make their departures as stress-free as possible. But even when "Dearest Soldier" was first published, some readers must have thought that Marcy was taking things too far by not even telling her husband Jack that she was pregnant with their first child before he ships overseas. Today, it's hard to imagine that any woman would think that's a good idea, no matter how much Marcy convinces herself that "having the baby, planning for the baby, changing my life as it was necessary, that was all mine to do alone."

Overseas duty was a much different experience in World War II than it is today, though. The only line of communication most soldiers and their wives could count on was mailing letters back and forth through the post office—no email, no Skype sessions, not even phone calls. When an American soldier was fighting halfway around the world, he was really gone. And in this case, where Marcy has been living an almost ridiculously sheltered life, being left to her own devices becomes a huge responsibility.

When Jack came home on his last leave, I tried to forget he'd be going overseas soon now—and just remember how thankful I was to have him with me. And that was easy at first, when we were so happy to be together that nothing else mattered, nothing mattered but that we could hold each other close.

After all, we'd only been married a little over a year, and Jack had been away at camp most of that time. The first day he was home, I hated to have him go out of sight. He was just the same. When he went to the post office I went along with him, and when I went grocery shopping he was right alongside me. And all the time we kept reaching out to touch each other—just a light touch on my shoulder, just Jack's hand on my arm—that was enough to send the bright sparks rushing through me, and catch my breath with happiness.

When we got back to the house, the minute the door closed Jack put the grocery bags right down on the hall floor and caught me in his arms. For the moment my world was perfect.

"I haven't kissed you for forty-three minutes," he told me.

"I know it." I said, my hands tight in his crisp hair.

"Your mouth is like honey and fire," he whispered. "How I love you, my darling, my darling."

He lifted me so strongly that I swayed against him, and then he had me clear off the floor, laughing, holding me a long instant before he set me down again. "You're so tiny, to be the most important person in the world," he said. "My little love, my little, little love—"

I stretched up tall till my head almost reached his shoulder. "I'm not so tiny," I said indignantly.

Whereupon he swung me up again. "Stop bragging, Marcy half-pint. Do you love me, Marcy?"

"Put me down," I said. "I won't be blackmailed into answering such a question."

I stood quite close to him, looking up into his face, where the afternoon sun slanted against his tanned cheekbones. Sunlight touched his lashes, lay deep in his brown eyes. The dearest face—

"Loving you, that's my whole world," I tried to tell him slowly. "That's everything that matters—loving you, belonging to you."

"We're lucky," he said softly. "We're so darned lucky, Marcy darling."

And so the first day slipped away through our happy hands, and we were glad together. And that night, close in his arms, I had no other thought but for his tenderness, I only knew he was my own, and he was home again.

When I awakened in the morning, I looked straight into his face. He was leaning on one elbow, staring down at me. The look on his face stilled my heart with happiness.

"Hello, Marcy," he said softly. "Hello, my dearest."

I smiled sleepily back at him. "I knew you were here, Jack. All night I knew it."

"People look so defenseless when they're sleeping," he said. "You're so little, Marcy. And you're only twenty."

"When my great-grandmother was twenty," I told him, "she was dashing all over in a covered wagon, pouring water on Indians."

He grinned, but his face went swiftly back to seriousness. "I can't help worrying about you, Marcy."

"But Jack, why, dear?" I was always telling him not to fret about me, but he couldn't seem to stop.

"After I've gone overseas, I mean," he said then. "I worry about you, all alone here. And it'll be worse then."

"I'll be fine, Jack," I told him earnestly.

But he shook his head. "You'll be alone here by yourself," he said again.

I almost told him, then, that I wouldn't be alone after a few months, that I'd have our baby to keep me company till he came home. I wanted to tell him, wanted to so badly—but Jack had always cared for me, protected me, guarded me; he was ten years older than I, and I guess I seemed sort of young and fragile to him, and not very responsible. Anyway, when we were engaged, he started taking care of me. I was so crazy about the way he did it, maybe I didn't act very grown-up and independent. And when we were married, he planned things so carefully, so I'd be all right while he was at camp. He even made me a budget. Did you ever hear of a man making out a budget, and even writing down the day I should pay the taxes?

He worried about me that way, and was concerned about me. I knew it would make it harder for him to go away if he knew about the baby. That was my job, I'd told myself, to send him off to war without that added burden of concern. I mustn't tell him, but I wanted him to know.

"Jack,'" I said softly, and perhaps I would have told him then, because I always told him everything and we'd talked so often of the children we wanted, and because—oh, because I wanted to share the happiness with him.

But he suddenly caught me tight against him, and held me almost fiercely. "I wanted to give you everything." he exclaimed. "You've had such a rotten time for so many years. Knocking around in schools, and little dabs of vacations with your father, and then another school. And all on your own since your father died. I wanted to take care of you, Marcy. Oh Marcy, I was going to take care of you forever. And now what can I do?"

"Now you're taking care of me, a different way, going off to fight for me," I told him steadily. "And I learned to look out for myself those lonesome years, Jack."

Maybe it had been a mistake—to let go so thankfully when we fell in love, and relax and let Jack do all the planning. Maybe I had been wrong to let him get so used to babying me. But it had been heaven to have his thoughtfulness so warm around me, to know I could drift along and his love would guard me.

And what I could do now, must do, was to reassure him. To send him away with none of his courage drained by worry about me. I could do it, I had to do it. It would be a selfish pleasure, to tell him about the baby when he had to leave me.

"Jack," I said, "look at me, darling."

His brown eyes met mine levelly, and I smiled at him and closed my hands around his face.

"Please, my darling, try not to worry about me anymore," I told him. "Trust me, I'm a woman, not a little girl. Trust me to be your wife, Jack."

"All right, my sweet, I'll try," he said. And he grinned suddenly. "If your great-grandmother really did throw boiling water on Indians—"

"She did," I assured him, laughing back at him. "And I'll do the same for any wolves on the doorstep."

"Only maybe we could sort of plan things for after I'm gone," he said.

"If it will make you feel better," I agreed. "Would you like to start making lists right now?"

"Before breakfast? I would not," he retorted. "Where's my coffee? Where are my four eggs?"

"Beast," I said. "Keep me here talking. And then howl at me for your breakfast."

"Who's keeping you here?" he demanded, reaching for me again.

But I reached the middle of the floor safely, and was on my way. "You'll get coffee in fifteen minutes," I told him.

"You'll get kissed in ten," said Jack.

So another day began, another day with Jack, and still I tried not to look ahead. He was here, here to watch and touch, right in the room with me, turning every so often to me with that slow loving glance.

We saw a lot of people that day: friends of ours, older people who used to know Jack's parents, George Kelly, who owned the radio shop where Jack used to work. They all wanted to talk to Jack. They made a big fuss over him, but somehow they all seemed dim and far away to me. The only person who was vividly real to me was Jack. It was Jack's voice I listened to, and what the others said didn't matter, though I made them welcome.

By the time the last caller had gone it was afternoon, and Jack gave a huge sigh of relief. "Shall we lock the doors?" he asked me.

"People will camp on the front steps," I answered, "Of course they want to see you, Jack. Only—"

"Only we've seen enough people today," he said firmly. "Would you mind very much spending the evening alone with me?"

"I could bear it, darling."

And a few minutes later we were leaving by the back door, very quietly, with sandwiches in our pockets, and taking the back lane out of town. We didn't meet anyone but a couple of boys, by luck, and we took the old towpath along the canal. When the willows closed in behind us, we looked at each other and grinned.

"The boat?" I asked.

"Of course. Where else?" said Jack. Captain Tom's boat was where we always went when we wanted to be alone.

Tom didn't live there, but he used the boat some weekends for fishing. The rest of the time it was moored by the shore where the river widened around a bend, and it was tucked away so well under the curve of the weeping willows that it was out of sight from the towpath.

We got there in about fifteen minutes, and Jack took my hand as we went down the bank. He lifted me across to the deck. We lay there on the warm boards, with spots of sunlight drifting down on us through the trees.

"It's so quiet," Jack said under his breath. "Whenever you get a minute to take it easy, at camp, there's always fifteen fellows around talking at once."

"I come here by myself sometimes," I told him.

So many times I'd stretched out there, watching the slow water of the river, dreaming ahead to when Jack came home, dreaming of when he first saw his son. I never had the slightest doubt we'd have a boy. A boy with Jack's brown eyes, his wide sweet mouth, his determined chin, though he'd have to grow up a lot for that.

"What are you smiling about?" Jack asked me suddenly, breaking the silence.

"What does it look like to you, Jack?"

"Something nice."

"I was thinking about your chin, darling."

"Good heavens," said Jack, running a hand over his chin.

We lay there for a while, Jack smoking contentedly, and watched the leaves and bits of twig that floated past, and made bets on which ones would reach the boat first. Jack's arm was across my shoulders, and I could see the reflection of his face when we leaned way over the side.

"You'll have enough money," Jack remarked suddenly.

"What?"

"You'll have enough money, while I'm away."

"Oh," I said, with a small secret sigh that we had to make plans right then. But if it made Jack feel better to talk things over, that was the thing to do.

"With the allowance from the government, and the extra I send you from my pay, and your library money, you'll be all right. I've figured it all out, for extras, too."

But not extras like having a baby, I remembered swiftly. That was something I'd been figuring on my own.

"It's lucky you like that library work, honey," he went on.

I had a job in our town library, and I could keep it for a few months more, but sooner or later I'd be giving up that work. I felt mean not to tell Jack that I couldn't follow the plans he'd made so lovingly. But how could I tell him that there'd be big expenses, that I'd have to stop my job, while he was across the ocean, and couldn't help me?

"I love the work," I said.

"And we're lucky I inherited the house," Jack said. "No rent to pay. I'll be thinking of you going in our front door, sitting in Mom's big chair by the front window."

That hurt—hurt with unexpected brutal swiftness. Because I wouldn't be there in the house, where he had pictured me, where he would think of me when he was away. That was part of my private planning. I was going to rent the house, and take a room over the candy shop. I could make some of the money I needed that way, money for doctors and nurses when the time came. For the rest, I'd have to hang on to every penny I could, and Jack's budget would be far too generous. I was glad I'd found a way to manage the expenses, but if only I could stay on in the house those months of waiting. If I could be there, where Jack had grown up, where he and I had been so happy. Because I knew how lonesome I was going to be, even if I tried not to look ahead.

I watched a leaf twirl in the water, and didn't look at Jack. "You'll be coming back to our house when the war is over, and I'll be waiting there," I said. Waiting with his son in my arms. Again I wanted to tell him.

"It's important, leaving a real home," Jack said slowly. "Some of the fellows have rattled around since they were kids. They haven't got a home waiting for them. They haven't got a wife like you, Marcy."

I moved my head till my cheek was against his solid, khaki-clad shoulder.

"Something safe and sure to come back to," he said. "Someone dear and wonderful to come back to. Marcy, do you still chew the corner of your mouth when you write letters?"

"I don't know. I never watched myself write a letter."

"You'll be writing me, sitting there at Dad's desk under the green lamp," he said.

And again the hurt flashed through me, because I wouldn't be writing him from our own house, where he could remember me, picture me. I'd be off in a strange little room, where he'd never seen me. And there'd be people in our house, living there, instead of me.

How could I bear to give up our place?

We'd gone, straight there after we were married, and all my dear first memories were warm in those rooms. But I had to have money, and renting the house would make the money possible.

"Talk about after the war," I said suddenly. "Talk about after the war, my darling."

And so we looked ahead, far beyond the war, and planned a life of fun and work and laughter, with long days in the sun and long evenings under the stars.

He would always come home to lunch from work, because then we'd only be apart a few hours. And the weekends would last forever, and all the hours would shine.

"We'll have a garden, where your mother planted the roses," I said.

"I'll have a work shop, in the tool shed," said Jack.

"Every morning I'll wake up, and know, you're home to stay."

"Every morning I'll be amazed because I'll love you more, my Marcy."

"How can we love each other more than we do now?"

"Dearest," he said. Just "dearest."

And then he said the thing that startled me, that gave me a swift uncertainty.

"We'll have a family," he said. "We'll have our own kids, then. Won't that be swell, Marcy?" And there was a wonder and wistfulness in his voice.

"Yes," I whispered.

But my uncertainty deepened every instant. Jack was thinking ahead toward our children, wanting them. Was it fair not to tell him that we'd have our first child soon; before the war was over? Was it fair that he should go away, and not know?

I hadn't realized that he cared so much, but the wistfulness was still there in his face. Did it help a man, going away to war, to know that with all the uncertainties of the future one thing stood steadfast, he had founded a family, he would have a child?

And I wished desperately that I knew what to do. It might be right to tell him, it might be wrong, what should I do? Better wait, I told myself; wait for a while, not tell him yet. Perhaps something would happen before he left, or he'd say something that would help me know what to do.

Jack reached over and tipped my face toward him. "I'm here. Forget about your husband? Don't daydream too long."

"No," I said. "Oh, no, my darling."

And we were silent as the sun sank lower, silent but very close; and I watched the water with Jack's hand in mine, and wondered at how peaceful and safe it was there under the trees, when it could seem so bleak when I was there alone.

After a while we ate our sandwiches, and Jack climbed up the bank and came back with his hands full of tart red apples. "You learn to live off the land in the Army," he said solemnly.

"I can just see you boys, picking peanut butter sandwiches off the bushes," I agreed.

And a long time after that we went home, with a yellow moon at our backs, arm in arm and singing. We turned in at our house and I could smell the roses. We went inside and lighted the rooms. If we could always be home together—

Two more days of Jack's leave went by, two more days and nights, and now I couldn't fight off the knowledge he'd be going soon. And there were sudden silences between us, when he'd say "after I'm gone—" or I'd say "when you're away—" and we wouldn't talk, because we didn't want to say unhappy things.

The couple in the next house came over once or twice. They were nice people about Jack's age, but they seemed so set apart from us because the husband was 4-F. There they were, the two of them. Their life was different, set on a different track from ours —they were together, Jack was going away.

I was taking my vacation from the library, so I could be with Jack all the time he was home. We didn't do anything very important, we refused invitations and we didn't want to take a trip—we just wanted to be together.

We were in love that way, making our own world, finding our own happiness. We cared about everything we did together passionately, even the silly little things, because so soon we wouldn't be together.

The only time Jack went anywhere without me was when he and George Kelly, his old boss, drove over to Clayton one evening. Clayton was the next town, much bigger than ours, and George wanted to show Jack some new radio gadgets a man had over there. They asked me to go along, but I figured that maybe it would be nice for Jack to have some time with George, just men together.

After they were gone I roamed around the house, regretting I hadn't gone, blaming myself for wasting what little time I had, when I could be with Jack. And later in the evening I blamed myself with agonized terror.

I was on the porch, waiting for the men to get back. I saw George's old car come around the corner, under the swinging street light. And I ran back into the house, to the switch that turned our porch light on.

I heard the sound of another car, and a sharp report and a crash. And then there was silence.

An accident — another car had crashed George's car. Fear seized me that Jack was hurt. Do you know how it is, sitting alone so many evenings, wondering if the person you love is all right? Do you know how much fear can pile up, hidden, for all the dangers ahead? So when I heard the crash, all that hidden fear broke free and struck at me. I was sure Jack was hurt, and wild that I had not been with him.

I ran out, forgetting the porch light, forgetting everything but getting to Jack. And then I saw George's car, in front of the house. But it was empty.

I had reached the sidewalk when I saw them coming toward me, walking away from another car. They saw me several feet away. "Hello, honey," said Jack. Nothing had happened to him. He was there.

"Hello, Marcy," said George.

"Hello," I said. And then, "What happened? The crash?"

"Car had a blowout," Jack said.

"Tires probably worn out," George said. "He swerved and hit the fence, but no real harm done."

It was such an anti-climax after my panic that I started laughing in nervous relief. I managed to say good-night to George, but when I turned back to the house with Jack, I couldn't stop laughing for a minute, and I was still shaking with nerves. But I didn't want him to know that I was such a silly, to get scared.

"Did you have fun?" I managed to say.

"You haven't kissed me yet," said Jack. He reached for me quickly. "Why Marcy, you're shaking—what's the matter, dear?"

"Nothing," I said, my voice steady.

"Come clean. What's the matter, Marcy? What's upset you?"

"I was just a crazy silly," I said. "I heard the crash, and I was afraid there was an accident and you were hurt."

"Foolish sweetheart," he said.

And he held me tight till my heart stopped bumping, and I drew a deep breath. "All right, now," I told him.

But he wasn't satisfied, and he took me into the living room and settled me down on the lounge with him. "You mustn't get so scared of things," he said tenderly.

And I realized that once again he was seeing me wrong, seeing me all afraid and nervous and uncertain, and I wasn't that sort of person, really. But I couldn't blame him, this time, because he couldn't know what it was like to be home alone, wondering. "I'm not timid," I told him. "I'm not afraid of anything, except something happening to you."

That was true—my only fears were for him. And suddenly, I sensed something I'd not understood before: Jack was concerned for me, that same way. Not just as if I were a foolish child, but because I was the one who mattered most to him. I was his to look after. And he worried about my being safe and secure while he was away, just the way I worried about him. I guess when you love a person so much you can't help some of that worrying.

But you can try your best to keep the other person from worrying, I told myself. And that was the time I decided, at last and finally, that all the problems of my life after Jack was gone were my responsibility.

I mustn't let him worry about my health. I mustn't let him worry about finances. I mustn't let him worry about my being alone. After the baby had come I could tell him. Then he would have no distress and fear, wondering about me, so far away.

A little peacefulness came to me, now I knew what I must do. Having the baby, planning for the baby, changing my life as it was necessary, that was all mine to do alone. It was my job.

I was sure I was right, but I didn't bargain for what happened when Aunt Chrissy's letter came a couple of days later. Aunt Chrissy was Jack's nearest relative. We had visited her though she lived way off in Maine.

She wrote us a sweet letter, full of good wishes for Jack, and wishing she would see him before he left. Then she said, "And you must come and stay with me as long as you can, Marcy dear."

"She's a fine old gal," Jack said, folding the letter. "Look, honey, I've a swell idea. You've got to spend Christmas with her."

"Christmas is a long way off," I said.

When Christmas came I'd be in the hospital, with old Doctor Bennett looking after me. But I couldn't tell Jack that.

"But it'll be perfect," he exclaimed. "You'd be lonesome, and so would she. I'll be so glad, knowing you're not alone Christmas."

I wouldn't be alone for Christmas. I'd be over in Clayton in the hospital; I'd have Jack's baby, and I'd be writing to tell him. Only what could I say, now?

"Let me plan about Christmas, later," I said and I groped for reasons. "There might be a blizzard," I said.

"You crazy—" Jack was laughing. "Say, you could have her here for Christmas."

Aunt Chrissy was a darling, but she fussed so, and talked all the time in that sweet high voice. Maybe I could have her for a visit, after Christmas, after I got back in my own house again. How soon would that be? But I couldn't invite her to share my small room over the candy shop, and what would I do with her while I was in the hospital?

I found firmness in desperation. "Listen to me, boss. You let me write her."

"All right," Jack agreed, so nicely that I felt remorseful all over again. It felt so wrong, not to tell him, when something so important was going to happen to us.

But watching him find so much contentment in the plans he made for me, I still knew I had decided right. Jack spent that evening making lists of people to get hold of, if something went wrong. I knew how to get the plumber if the pipes froze, and which carpenter would fix the screens. I was to phone George, if I needed any business advice. Yes, but George, with his business hard hit, would have no help for me when I had to pay the hospital. It would be the tenants in our house who would pay those bills.

I had lists telling me what to do, when so many things went wrong. But what would I do when Jack was gone and loneliness struck me? There was nothing on any list to help that. And then I remembered—I would have weapons to fight the loneliness; I would be doing my job.

And I would send him away with no tears, so he would be reassured about me. I must remember—don't let him see you unhappy. So when the last day came, with one more day and one more night, and then he would be gone in the early morning, I didn't say, "We have twenty-four hours left." I didn't say, "Tomorrow you'll be going."

We had a lot of things to do that day —people Jack wanted to say good-by to, errands to get things he wanted, and all that helped. We kept up a surface that it was just any other day. And then, walking along the street, we met Dr. Bennett.

It was crazy, but it never occurred to me that he might meet Jack. His house was out in the country, and there was no reason for Jack to see him. And now all my careful plans could be ruined.

Dr. Bennett was already greeting Jack. "Well, you're off tomorrow, aren't you, Jack." He spoke to me, but he turned to Jack again. "Feeling pretty proud, aren't you?"

I broke in quickly. "I'm awfully proud of him, going off to fight," I said. "Oh, Jack, would you mind awfully going back and getting a loaf of bread?" I had turned Jack around, pulling at his arm as I spoke. And he looked surprised at my impatience.

Dr. Bennett was watching me.

"I haven't told him," I explained breathlessly. "Jack would worry, and I thought I just wouldn't tell him till it was all over. Then I can write and say, 'We've got a baby, Jack'."

He nodded slowly. "Got it all worked out, have you?"

"I'm going to rent the house, and take a room," I said, looking over my shoulder to be sure Jack wasn't coming yet. "I'll make enough money that way."

"I guess we can fix things all right," he assured me. "We'll manage fine."

I asked him suddenly, "Dr. Bennett, you think I'm right, don't you? Not to tell Jack?"

And for an instant his hand patted my shoulder. "You're a good girl, Marcy. You're pulling your share in the team. Time enough to tell Jack, later."

He was gone when Jack came back with the bread, and I

meekly took Jack's teasing for getting in such a dither over a loaf of bread.

"You'll be hungry by dinner time," I said.

But neither of us was hungry at dinner that night, and the darkness closed down too swiftly, and the clock moved too fast. We packed Jack's things, and that was bad.

When at last I lay beside him in the dark, I clung to him desperately, and he held me as tightly. He was here now, but there would be so many other nights—

"You're a good wife," Jack said suddenly in the darkness. "You don't tell me how lonely you'll be. You don't tell me that you can't let me go."

"You know how I'll miss you," I said.

"Some of the wives that live near camp, I've seen them make awful scenes when they said good-by," Jack said. "I've seen what it did to the boys."

"Don't worry, I won't, Jack."

"I know it," he told me. "You've been perfect, all this time. You've made my last leave the way I wanted it."

"I'm glad. Do you know how I love you, Jack?"

"I know how I love you. Oh Marcy, take care of yourself when I'm gone."

"Yes, my darling."

"I'll be coming back fast, and here we'll be again, the two of us, Marcy."

Once more I wanted to say it, I wanted to say, "The three of us." I wanted the sharing, the married sharing of Jack and me.

And I buried my face in his shoulder and didn't speak. I remembered Dr. Bennett saying, "You're a good girl, Marcy." I had to be good a little longer, till Jack's train pulled out. After he was gone, I could cry.

When the morning came, it was all one endless chain of little goodbyes. Because everything was for the last time—the last breakfast, the last look around the house, the last collecting of bags and cap and coat. It was a sort of good-by walking down the path together, though we didn't say a word.

I wondered if I could stand it, not crying, till the train went. I wondered if I could stand it, not telling Jack about the baby.

And then on the platform Jack said the one thing I hadn't expected. The train whistled down the track, and he caught my arm.

"Marcy, I'm not worrying about you, any more."

"Why?"

"You've been different this leave. I don't know, but suddenly I've quit worrying about you. I'm leaving you in charge, Marcy."

So he had somehow caught it—my firm decision to look after myself, some flavor of my quiet planning, some signal that he could trust me.

The train was coming, and people crowded against us, but my dazed misery was gone. There was the sharpness of parting, but there was the peacefulness of his trust. This was the marriage I wanted, this trusting.

"I'll take care of everything," I told him.

"That's my girl," he said.

The train rushed in and ground to a stop. I swallowed desperately. Jack's smile was frozen on his face.

"You're the right kind of a girl, when a guy has to go away," he said, and I knew what he was trying to tell me. He understood why I didn't cry. He knew I was trying to send him away without worries about me, even if he didn't know it all. That was why he was trusting me, because I stood on my own two feet and didn't cry.

"Don't miss your train, soldier," I said.

He kissed me swiftly and turned and was up the steps. He waved once, and the train started and he was gone.

I was still standing there when the train was out of sight. And

I wondered why I wasn't crying. I wondered when I would begin to cry.

I turned and started back up the street toward home. He had gone away reassured, that was what I wanted. And when I wrote and told him we had a baby, then he would know he was right to trust me to take care of everything while he was gone, and he would know why I waited to tell him. He would know I'd done my share of loving and caring, to keep the worries from him.

I walked faster and faster, planning ahead, facing my life alone for a while. Why wasn't I crying now that Jack had gone? And suddenly I knew I wasn't going to cry at all. I was going on straight ahead, the way Jack wanted me to. And I didn't feel alone, because all Jack's love was with me. I could hear his voice saying confidently, "I'm leaving you in charge, Marcy." THE END

SERGEANT'S BRIDE

Here's another take on the American soldier's wife getting ready to send her husband off to fight in the Second World War. This time, though, it's narrated by the soldier himself, and Con is pleasantly surprised by the initiative that Barbie's shown in finding a house in the city near their base camp so they can be together—so pleasantly surprised, in fact, that he can't bear to tell her that he's already got his orders and will be leaving soon.

When she finally finds out, Barbie takes the news in stride, expressing gratitude for the "perfect week" they've been able to spend together, and Con's glad she's taking it so well, when "so many wives make it hard for their men." It's enough to make you think the editors of True Romance *got notes from the Pentagon about how to keep up morale on the home front.*

The crisp tempo of the camp was clicking around me as usual, as I walked through Company I Area that afternoon, headed for the Service Club. I did wonder who the visitor was, waiting there for me, but otherwise my mind was full of strictly G.I. concerns. So it snapped me straight into another world—a hot, exciting, rocketing world—when I swung into the service Club and found Barbie waiting there for me.

"Barbie—" I shouted incredulously. "Barbie darling—"

I grabbed her and kissed her till I lost count, regardless of the pleased grins on the faces of a couple of my pals. She was real—she was extremely real; I couldn't be dreaming the way she hung on to me. Barbie, from half across the country—here with me, instead of staying tucked away with her parents till the war was over.

"You look so wonderful, Con," she was saying. "Are you surprised?"

"What do you think?" I demanded. "Surprised? Lord yes. So you came way out here, to see if you still had a husband."

Barbie laughed and shook her head. "Nope. I know I've got you, no matter where you are. I came—to be with you—Oh Con, I've missed you so—"

I saw one of the boys moving up to get introduced, and I snaked Barbie out of there. Standing outside the door, I looked her over; slim and tall and lovely, in a dark blue outfit that didn't do her figure any harm; with her black hair curling recklessly and her blue eyes bright with happiness. Boy, was I proud of her!

"You look just the same, only better," I told her. "Where's your bag, honey? We're going to have a sweet time, getting you a room at the hotel. But you're here—you're here, my gal, and in two hours and forty-five minutes I'll give you a real welcome—"

"Why do I have to wait that long?" Barbie demanded, laughing. "That sergeant I asked said you'd be back from the rifle range, and all through after Retreat, at five-forty-five. You certainly live by the clock, here."

"I'm on special duty till eight tonight," I told her ruefully.

To my amazement she looked delighted. "That's perfect, Con," she cried. "I came right out to camp, because I couldn't wait to see you. But I'm so glad, that you're busy now—"

"What's up?" I wanted to know.

"You'll find out when you give me that welcome you talked about," she said, and locked up her pretty red mouth and refused to explain.

"Well—I'll meet you in town, about nine," I told her. "Worst luck, I've got to go now. Let's see—I'll meet you—"

"You'll meet me at 23 Polk Street," she told me, grinning at my perplexity. "Remember Kitty? Well, her husband's been here at the same camp, and she's been living at 23 Polk Street, here in town."

"That's fine, you've got a place to sleep," I said, much relieved. "Say—how long can you stay out here, Barbie?"

"I'll tell you tonight," Barbie said. "You can stay at Kitty's house tonight, can't you?"

"Can't I?" I said. "Try to stop me, darling."

So I put her on the bus for town, and kissed her again to last till I got there, and went over to the Orderly Room, and I was in a state to be marked "Highly Explosive." Overnight pass, about three hours to get through—and then Barbie.

And was I lucky, that I could go to town that night, after all the orders and changed orders that had been hitting us lately. After my last furlough, the last time I'd seen Barbie, my unit had been alerted to go overseas. Then that had been changed, and the unit had been put off the alert, and I'd been assigned to a training cadre.

"I guess I'm here for the duration," I'd written Barbie.

Then this last week, to our surprise, we'd been alerted again. I guess more infantry were needed for the big doings in France. I had written Barbie that it was sure we'd be shipped off sometime soon, but my letter must have crossed with her as she came out here.

From now on nothing would be certain—the old stuff—we'd go off and on the alert, till finally it would be the real thing. Right now, for the mysterious reasons of the powers above, I wasn't alerted, and could leave the camp with a pass.

It was good that Barbie was here—I wouldn't have asked her to make the trip, not knowing if I'd have two hours or two days with her, when she arrived. But she'd come anyhow, and we'd have a little time together, before I sailed.

Was I impatient! Everything moved slow time, while I knew Barbie was waiting for me in town. But at last I was on the bus, rolling up the dust and headed for town and Barbie.

I located 23 Polk, and found it was a neat little house, with flowers in front and a lot of cheery light coming out the front window. I hoped that Barbie's friends had been tactful, and taken themselves off to a movie, so I could have Barbie all to myself—so I could hold her tight and forget the war and everything else for a little while, forget everything but how terribly much I loved her. The front door flew open as I went up the steps—and there was Barbie herself —but a different girl suddenly. The blue suit was gone, and she had on sort of a flowery thing, the sort of bright dress she used to wear when I got home to our two-room apartment for dinner. She had a frilly apron over that, and she was the prettiest thing I'd seen since my last furlough, since I said good-by to her.

"Welcome home," said Barbie, reaching for me.

She felt like satin and she smelled like flowers and her mouth burned against mine. I held her tight but I couldn't get her close enough; I kissed her and I never wanted to stop. She was everything I wanted, and at last I had her in my arms again.

"It's been awful without you—" I muttered.

"Darling," said Barbie. "My darling dear—"

I guess it was quite a while before I let go of Barbie with one hand so I could get the front door closed. We were standing in the living room of the little house.

"Welcome home," Barbie said again softly.

I looked around, bewildered, the further I looked. I'd never been in the place before, yet it seemed strangely familiar. There was a framed picture of me on the piano, and what would a friend of Barbie's be doing with my picture? There was a green shade just like ours on the lamp. And there was my pipe rack by the door.

"What cooks?" I said. "What cooks, baby?"

There couldn't be two sewing boxes like Barbie's, with pins stuck like a star on the lid. And the woods picture we'd bought on our honeymoon—I stared around dazedly—and saw a lot more of our own personal things.

"Look here—" I told her. "What's the score?"

She grabbed my hand and pulled me into the next room, and

it was a bedroom, and there were suitcases all over the floor, and dresses of Barbie's spread on the bed, and I saw my red leather house slippers. Barbie was watching my face joyously, her lips parted breathlessly.

"Here I am, bag and baggage—" she said amazingly.

"But darling—" I began, trying to make sense of it all. "You can't spread your stuff all over your friend's house this way. Why, you must have brought half our stuff—"

"The trunks are coming tomorrow," she announced gleefully. "When Lieut. Hadden—"

"Who?" I interrupted her.

"Kitty's husband—Lieut. Hadden—"

"But he's gone," I exclaimed. "He's been shipped out."

"Darling dope," she said, "that's just it. Kitty wired me, and said he'd got his orders. She went to his parents when he left. She asked me if I'd like to have the house for the rest of the lease. And you'd told me there wasn't a room to be had for miles, Con. So of course, I wired back and said 'yes' I wanted the house. Isn't it marvelous? Aren't you surprised, darling?"

"The house—" I repeated like a dope, like the very dope she called me.

"A house of our own," Barbie said softly, with a light on her face. "For the first time—we'll have a house of our own—"

And the whole thing hit me right over the heart. Barbie hadn't got my letter yet, of course. She thought I was stuck there at the camp for the duration, the way I'd told her. And she'd taken that house—and shipped our stuff out—and she was waiting now, with that joyous light on her face, for me to tell her how glad I was. How could I blurt out—that minute—that I'd been alerted to go overseas any day now?

"I never was so surprised in my life," I told her truthfully.

"I didn't want you to know ahead," she said, "I wanted to be here when I told you—" She straightened my big shaving mirror and gave it a little pat. "Oh Con—I can't believe I'm here—I've wanted to be here so dreadfully—"

"I've wanted you," I said slowly, and took her in my arms.

"And every night you'll be coming home to me—" she said.

I held her head down close so she couldn't see my face. How many nights would I be coming home to her?

I knew so well why she cared about the house, besides all our gladness at being together. We'd got married just before I went into the Army, and all the time we'd had together had been a couple of days' honeymoon, a couple of weeks in that two-room apartment I'd sublet from a guy I knew on vacation, and the three times I'd gotten leave. And we'd dreamed —lord how we'd dreamed of having our own place, and it always was a house, not an apartment. Of course—when Kitty offered her house, right here near my camp—of course Barbie caught at the chance.

To be together again—half our letters were about the time when we'd be together. My arms tightened on Barbie. That much was all right; out of all this mess; we were together, as long as it lasted.

"You're here," I said. "You're here, sweetheart—"

"Hold me tighter—" said Barbie.

So I held her tighter, and for a blessed space of time I forgot about the house, and the shortness of time before I'd leave for overseas. There was Barbie—Barbie with her eager hands and glad mouth, Barbie who was my own.

And when at last I remembered that sometime I'd have to tell her that I wasn't training troops any more, I was expecting to go overseas any time—well, that was no time to tell her, not that first night. Because she was so very happy, I wanted her to have a little more time for happiness. And she'd counted so on pleasing me about the house, I couldn't take that away from her the first night. I couldn't let her down.

She rubbed her head against my shoulder like a little girl. "I brought the curtains, the ones we got to keep in my after-the-war hope chest," she told me.

"Did you, darling?" I added hastily "That's swell."

We'd made a game of planning our future after the war. We'd bought little things the times we were together; and Barbie had put them away carefully, for peace, when we'd have a home.

"And some of the wedding presents, the useful ones," she said. "They're coming in the trunks."

Trunks, trunks—what an awful disappointment when she'd have to ship those trunks back east again.

"We have a kitchen with a little dining alcove, and a shiny blue bathroom, and a screened porch," Barbie announced.

"Imagine our having all that—" I managed to say.

"Isn't it perfect?" Barbie said softly.

"You're perfect," I told her, kissing her soft hair. "Come and show me this mansion, baby."

So we went over the house, hand in hand—and it was a neat little place, it really was. And with Barbie in it—and our things spread around already—well, it was home for me.

For that one night, I told myself, I'd quit thinking about the future. I'd be home—with my wife.

We'd both picked up a bite to eat, but Barbie fixed us a snack anyhow, scrambled eggs and coffee, and we sat there in the dining alcove eating, and it was wonderful just to be there.

"If anybody had told me at breakfast in the mess hall that tonight I'd be eating with you, Barbie—"

"In our own kitchen," she added.

"In our own kitchen," I agreed. Because as long as we were there, it was ours, and I got a little comfort out of that.

"Kitty left a lot of food for me," she said. "But I'm going marketing tomorrow—like a housewife. Isn't that funny, Con?"

"Wrinkle your nose again—" I told her. "You're adorable, Barbie—"

"You're the handsomest thing in a uniform, Con."

"It's just the uniform, funny bunny."

"No it isn't either. It's your shoulders under the uniform. And your eyes. And the dimple in your chin."

"That isn't a dimple in my chin—" I shouted, this being an old point of debate. "Well, whatever it is, it's cute."

"Listen here, I'm supposed to be a hard-boiled sergeant, sister."

"Not in this house," she said provocatively.

"That so?" I straightened up and sunk my voice down a couple of pegs.

"Put those dishes down," I barked at her suddenly with my best tough delivery.

Barbie gasped and then chuckled. "But I've got to wash them—"

"Not tonight," I said.

"No?"

"No. Tonight is ours. And—I don't want to waste any of it—"

She put down the plates and ran to me suddenly. "Con—I love you so—"

"Keep on loving me honey, that's all I ask."

"I'll love you forever, Con."

So we were at home, Sergeant and Mrs. James Conroy, of 23 Polk St.— until I reported back to camp next morning—until the moment when my unit was alerted again. How soon would that be? How long did we have together, Barbie and I? I shoved the questions away, and turned out the kitchen light.

"Morning will come too soon," I said softly to Barbie, "a whole lot too soon."

"If you were always near enough to touch," she answered.

"But we have now," I said.

It didn't seem possible that night, that I'd ever go away—because it was so right to have her close to me, so right to listen to her sleeping breath and know she was my own. And next morning, when Barbie said gladly, "I'll be waiting for you, tonight, Con"—

well, it seemed as if nothing could happen to keep me from coming home to her.

"I'll get here by six, tonight," I told her. "Or a little after."

"I'll have dinner ready," she said, smiling at me from the steps. And I took the picture away in my head, Barbie in a red and white checked dress, standing on the steps of the house—our house.

But on the bus going back to camp I read the war news in the paper, and I knew we had a job to do before I could be really home with Barbie. And when I got to camp, going past the officers' huts, striding along on the hard-tramped ground, listening to the familiar sounds—well, I knew I wanted to be in this war with the rest. I wanted to go overseas and get into it.

Only—maybe I'd put off telling Barbie for a few days, if I had that long. Maybe the decent thing to do would be to let her have some time in that little house, time to remember, when I was away, with no shadow of parting on her gladness. It wouldn't be easy, when I'd want to hang onto her fiercely and say, "Barbie, I've only got a little time with you. Barbie, love me for all the time ahead—" But I could do it for Barbie, I could wait, and not tell her yet.

And the minute I got back into routine that morning, as usual we hit such a pace that I had precious little time, even to think of Barbie. We kept swatting at it all day long, and when Retreat came along—and I was hitching a ride to town—then I knew I couldn't tell her yet. She'd be waiting, so happy—I couldn't tell her yet.

This time when I got to the little house, the front door stood open, and I walked right in. Something smelled eating-good and I could hear Barbie whistling in the kitchen.

"Hi—" I called.

Barbie came running. She had a ruffled apron on and a big spoon in her hand.

"Hello, handsome—"

"Hello, cook. Chow ready?"

I took her clear off the ground, lifting her to kiss her. "You're too beautiful to cook," I told her. "You can't be useful as well as ornamental."

"Wait till you try the meat balls," she retorted.

The meat balls were swell, and so was the rest of the dinner, but the best part was looking across the table at Barbie.

"You're a wonderful cook," I admitted when I'd finished. "But I'd rather make love to you, than eat—"

"I notice you didn't say that till you'd had a second helping of dessert," Barbie came back at me demurely.

But when I reached for her she shook her head. "Go smoke a cigarette on the porch, while I clear up," she said.

"Hey, what goes on? Throwing me out?"

"I'll be along. Go ahead, darling, you look tired."

So I stretched out in a chair on the screened porch, lit up, and marveled at the way I'd been provided with a civilian home for my free time. The house came furnished, which was a good thing—Barbie wouldn't be wanting to go furniture shopping.

I could hear her moving about in the kitchen, and it was a swell feeling to sit there and know she'd be coming out pretty soon. It wasn't so bad—not so bad at all—to be able to snatch at happiness for a while. Maybe I could take things as they came, and not look ahead; maybe for a little while, it could seem to me as if we'd be there, Barbie and I and the house, to really stay.

So that evening I threw myself into Barbie's mood, and joined in her planning, and gosh we had fun. She had big ideas for a victory garden, and we measured off the ground, and argued about all the different vegetables we'd plant.

"It'll be wonderful to have our own vegetables," Barbie said. "It's terrific to shop here, Con. The town's so crowded and the food doesn't get shipped in fast enough. Why—I had to go to five stores, just to get the food for dinner."

"It's not easy, living in a town near a camp," I said.

"But I love it," she assured me hastily. "And I won't mind the crowds and hunting for groceries—I'll be doing it for you, darling. Con—you don't know how much it means to me, just to be able to do something for you."

"You're a real partner, Barbie."

"Look who I'm teamed up with," she answered, slipping her arms through mine.

"It'll be dark pretty soon, Con. Do you want to go for a walk?"

"Swell. We could take in a movie."

So Barbie put a bunch of ribbon on her head and called it a hat, and I picked up my cap, and we were off. And you don't know how different a town can look when you're roaming it for the fiftieth time with a bunch of fellows—and when you're walking down the street for the first time with your wife.

But when we got to the movie house, there was a line queued up waiting for seats that stretched clear around the block. That was the only movie house in town, and it looked as if the walls would burst if they got all those folks in.

"Let's give the movie a miss," I suggested.

"We can get a soda," Barbie said.

"I've got it—we'll do some dancing, Barbie."

So I took her to a decent little joint I knew, where there was a juke box and a floor for dancing, and booths with make-believe vines climbing round 'em. The place was pretty packed, but we got a table.

"All the boys I know will be wanting a dance with you, Barbie."

"Not tonight," she said, smiling at me slowly.

"No?"

"Not tonight. I'm dancing with nobody but you, tonight." She made my heart jump through hoops, the way she said that.

She had on a dress with a lot of soft white lacy stuff at the throat, but her neck was whiter than the frill. When she touched my hand, I closed my eyes for a second. I was floating in space—there wasn't any future—there was only Barbie, touching me.

"Let's dance," I said abruptly.

So we swung out on the floor, and I dug a little hole among the couples, and Barbie's face was against mine. Music could do things to you—music and the right girl—and we danced for seven nickels before we sat down and gave our order.

"That was swell," Barbie said. "If I weren't here, what would you be doing?"

"Probably roaming around town, wishing you were here," I told her. "I've done plenty of that."

We had our beer, that is I did, and Barbie had a soda, and then we danced some more, and finally we walked along home again. Going along the dark, quiet streets with Barbie, going home—I passed a couple of M.P.s, and that reminded me of what was going on outside my charmed circle with Barbie.

"They're shipping the boys out fast these days." I said aloud.

Barbie's hand caught mine tightly. "I'm lucky," she said. "You're doing your part in the war—and I can be with you, too—"

And I couldn't tell her that she wouldn't be with me long; it would be cruel to tell her now. And it gave me a sharp-edged wrench inside, remembering how it would hit her when she knew.

Yet I was happy too; how could I help it, just being with her? I unlocked the front door, and stepped inside, and there we were again in our own house. I couldn't blame her for being so crazy about that house; I got a kick out of it, too. Good lord—I couldn't blame her for loving me, when I was mad about her, could I? So—another night was ours, and if I couldn't count on any sure time ahead with her, well, I had that night anyhow.

For a little while it went on that way, I'd just hang on to the time I was sure of, and throw myself into it. I'd work like a horse all day at camp, and then I'd say—"I've got another night with Barbie—"

Four days and nights went by, and then a week and Barbie felt really settled in. She'd got the garden started, and I worked in it evenings. The trunks had come, and the house was familiar and friendly with our own things.

"Our house," Barbie would say, and "our garden," as if we'd lived there for a year. And I caught myself doing it too, it seemed so right and natural.

We had some of the boys over one evening, and they told me what a lucky guy I was. And looking at Barbie—I knew it. That was how I drifted along, till the evening when something Barbie said brought me up short. We'd decided to stay home that evening, and after dinner we'd settled down in the living room, both of us on the lounge where we were in reaching distance of each other. I was smoking and running over the evening paper, and Barbie was writing things in a little notebook.

"I'm certainly getting dated up," she told me finally.

"That so?" I said. "With me, I trust."

Barbie chuckled. "Hen-party stuff, darling. Kitty told a lot of her friends to look me up, and they've been rallying round. I just haven't asked them over in the evenings —because—because—"

"Because what?"

"Because I wanted to have just you—with nobody around," she said.

"That's my girl," I told her, touching her head gently.

"But daytimes, they're keeping me busy," she went on. "What time I don't need for housekeeping is filled full. A Red Cross meeting tomorrow, and next day the committee that looks after entertaining the boys from camp—"

"Hey—" I interrupted. "You're entertaining one soldier. One. Count him."

"Silly, the committee asked me to make some cookies for the Saturday dance. And I'm going to join a Better Buying Club, and we're going to keep an eye on price ceilings and black market sales, but we're going to look for bargains, too."

"Nice gals?" I asked.

"They've been marvelous to me." she said. "They've helped me, about the stores, and where to go. And—they make me feel really at home in this town, Con."

"Fine," I said, wondering how fine it really was for her to get settled in so fast.

"I feel as if I really belonged here," she said suddenly.

That was when I really got jolted into worry. Maybe I'd made a mistake; maybe I'd doped it out all wrong.

I'd wanted to give Barbie a little happy time with me in a real house, just the way we'd always dreamed of living. I'd wanted to give her that to remember and hold on to when I went away. But now, I wondered, if she felt she belonged here, what would happen when she had to be uprooted? And if the reason she felt she belonged was because I came home to her every night—what would it do to her to turn the key in the front door, and go away alone?

All of a sudden I was in a cold sweat, seeing the mess I'd made for Barbie. She was so happy that when I finally told her it couldn't last, the disappointment would be all the worse.

Maybe I'd better tell her quickly—and yet looking at her, sitting there so contented, I wasn't sure. Maybe the harm was done now, and since I'd started, I might as well go on as long as I could. I wished I knew what to do. I wished I knew what was right, for Barbie.

Then suddenly she threw the book on the table, and leaned over against my shoulder. Her hand touched my face and pulled my head down against hers.

"This is so heavenly peaceful—" she whispered. "So many months, I knew if I could just sit close to you like this—"

"I know—" I said.

And I did know, too—and how could I break that peaceful evening? Barbie was such a little girl—she was way out here away from her family—would she go to pieces, when I finally told her?

Her fingers tightened, pulling me closer, and I quit battling with myself, trying to decide what was right. "One more night—" I told myself. "One more happy night with Barbie—" And I turned her face so I could reach her mouth.

The next evening, I'd begun to brace myself to tell her that our happiness had a time limit, when some of the boys came in unexpectedly. When they left it was so late that I put off telling her for one more night.

Maybe I didn't really expect things to happen so suddenly, but anyhow—next morning at camp—flash out of the sky, our outfit was alerted again. We might be sent overseas this time. And of course we couldn't leave the Company Area while we were on alert.

Well, I figured maybe this was more of the previous stuff, and we wouldn't get sent out this time. We'd got sort of used to being ready to go, and then finding the plans for us were changed. So I didn't tell Barbie—not hard and cold over the phone.

I phoned her, and said I couldn't get in to town that night. She was fine about it, cheerful and all, and said she knew she couldn't expect to have me every night.

For forty-eight hours we didn't know yes or no. We carried out orders, and stuck to the Area, and chewed the fat about what was going to happen. And then—then it began to dawn on me that this time things were different.

We were taken off the alert, and half the outfit was given a pass to town that night, and half the next night. I was in the second bunch. And the second bunch got told that we'd be on the alert again the morning after, at six A.M. We were notified—this was the real thing—they were going to ship us out.

So—now I knew. This was it, we were going out. And the next time I saw Barbie—I'd have to say good-by.

I put in a sweet time there, trying to figure how to tell her the best way, trying to imagine how badly she'd go to pieces. She was all settled with her plans for the future, and I was going to take the ground out from under her feet.

When the time came, and I rode to town, and walked toward the house, I went slowly, looking at it hard, wanting to remember just how it looked. Barbie was watching for me. She came running out, and I'd remember that, too.

Now I was going to tell her, and no more waiting. I was going to tell it to her straight and not try to pussyfoot around.

We went inside with our arms around each other, and I kissed her, and held her face in my hands, taking a last look at her happy eyes. She wouldn't look that shining happy in a minute now—

"It's so wonderful to have you back," she was saying.

"Barbie," I said, "Barbie, I've got to tell you something."

"Yes, Con?"

"Barbie dearest—my outfit has been alerted. We're going overseas."

"When?" she whispered, her mouth stiff and slow.

"Leave ends at six tomorrow morning. I can't come home after that, my darling. We'll leave sometime soon. I won't be allowed to tell you when. I'll get a pal of mine to phone you, when we've gone. Barbie—"

Her eyes had that sudden shadow—but somehow, she was still smiling at me. "Oh my very dearest—" she said. "I'm so thankful we've had this week—"

And I caught her close with a burst of thankfulness. "Thank God you feel that way, Barbie. Because I've known we'd have to go sometime soon. And I didn't know whether to tell you, or not."

"I'm glad I didn't know—" she said. "Glad, darling. It's been—a perfect week—the kind of living in a home, that we'll have some day—"

"Yes," I said, "yes, Barbie."

"Let's not talk about it—that you're going—any more now," she told me. "I'll get my breath, Con."

"You're being perfect," I told her. "So many wives make it hard for their men."

"You said we were partners," she answered. "Con, come and eat your dinner. Con—talk about—after the war."

We talked that evening of what we'd do when the war was over. We talked about the house we'd have, a lot like this one, but with another room or so. We talked about the children we wanted, and the work I'd do. We didn't mention the fact that six A.M. was coming steadily closer, till late that night, when we were lying close together in the darkness.

"Barbie," I said then, "Barbie, I hate to think of you packing by yourself."

And then she startled me. "I'm not going to pack," she said clearly.

"What are you talking about?" I exclaimed.

"I figured it all out this evening," she answered slowly. "I'm going to stay here, Con. I'm going to put a cot in the other room. And I'm going to rent this room—to wives who come here to see their husbands at camp, and haven't anywhere to stay."

"That's a grand idea," I told her. "But won't you be lonely, darling?"

"Lonely?" she said. "In our own house?" I held her tight.

After a moment she said, "Of course I'll be lonely—you know that. But less lonely here, than anywhere else. Why—this is the place where I belong, Con. I'll pick the things you planted in the garden. I'll sit at the table and remember how you looked across from me."

"Like that?" I said.

"Like that," said Barbie. "And when you think of me, you can think of me in our own house where we lived, waiting for you. Would—you like that—Con?"

"Crazy about it," I said against her hair.

She sighed and relaxed against me. "Then that's settled. I'm here where I belong, Con. Con, I'm so glad I came—and in just this little time, we made a home."

"Because I love you so terribly," I said.

"Because we love each other so terribly," said Barbie.

Next morning we were up early, but Barbie had the lights on in the kitchen, making coffee for me. She was dressed in the red and white dress I liked best, and she didn't cry—once.

I gulped the coffee down, and got the little things I was taking, and stood looking at her.

"Barbie—"

"Don't say good-by—" she said suddenly. "I mean, not really good-by. Say it as if you were coming home tonight, Con. I'll remember it, just that way. And I'll be waiting for the night—when you come home."

Her eyes were steady, steady, loving me.

How could a fellow help fighting with all he's got, with a wife like that behind him?

"I love you—" I said under my breath. "I love the ground you walk on." Then I took her lightly by the shoulders, and kissed her deeply.

"So long," I said, and I had a job keeping my voice even. "I'll be seeing you, Barbie."

"So long, Con," she said, and all her love was in her voice. "I'll be waiting for you—"

And when I went away, she was waving to me, with her other hand holding tight to the door of our little house. THE END

DAD, I'M A DRAFT DODGER...
But I know about your sins, too!

True Love *didn't have much use for hippies or the peace movement during the Vietnam War era, and it shows in this portrayal of John—a long-haired, bearded college dropout who's prepared to burn his draft card right in front of his father, a proud World War II veteran. John's mother tries to make peace between the two, but there's a deeper family drama involved here, and it's going to take its time bubbling to the surface.*

This story has its weak points—John's refusal to tell the police who borrowed his car and got involved in a hit-and-run accident is totally unconvincing—but it does a good job of ratcheting up the tension until the truth comes out. The ending offers only the barest glimmer of hope... just enough for this family to cling to as they resolve to "come through this, each one of us, with flying colors."

"**W**hat are you trying to do to your father?" I demanded of our son the morning after the trouble. "Ruin him?"

He answered in an ironically evasive way, "What makes you think it has anything to do with him *personally?*"

John's smart-alecky manner may have been just a cover-up for some deeper feelings, but right then it irritated me. "Oh, there's no use talking to you," I commented angrily. "You've changed so much—in just six months. I can't understand why."

In answer, he just shrugged. I had the impression for just a moment that he wanted to tell me something, to reassure me. But then I got just as distinct an impression that he wouldn't ... because of my husband.

That's an odd way of phrasing it, but that's how John seemed to feel about his father lately: as if he didn't want to think of him as his father, but rather as some stranger.

How John had changed in that half-year! It was right after he took that camping trip with some of his college friends. When he returned he was a different young man.

His attitude and manner had changed completely, and that was reflected in his appearance. He let his hair become long, and he grew a beard. His clothes were sloppy, no matter how hard I tried to keep them presentable. He didn't return to school, and hung out with a new crowd of friends, girls and boys as "hippily" dressed as he was.

And the wall between John and his father had gone up overnight, apparently complete and impenetrable. They had never been as close as I would have liked—my husband Robert being so involved in business and civic matters—but Robert was proud of his boy, who always seemed to want to do the right thing and thus win his father's approval.

When John at first wandered around the house aimless and unshaven, his father was puzzled. Then he became amused by it, but his jokes about John's appearance failed either to make the boy smile or to make him clean up. From there, Robert tried sarcasm, and finally angry shouts: "Go take a bath and shave. Try to look like a human being."

From John's side: Nothing. Silence. The Cold War was raging in our home.

Among his many other outside activities, my husband was active in a veterans organization that he had joined after his Army service in World War II. He was a patriotic man, but he also mentioned that many good business contacts could be made in such groups. This year, he had again been elected the commander of the local chapter.

The night of the trouble, there was a peace demonstration scheduled in one of the parks of our middle-sized midwest community. Several anti-war speakers were to be heard, and some young men announced that they were going to burn their draft-cards.

To protest this protest rally, several groups arranged to have members there, carrying American flags and pro-U. S. placards. My husband's veterans chapter voted to wear their uniforms and be on hand.

These counterbalancing groups had formally resolved to be non-violent. But such resolutions from both sides didn't mean much when the confrontation took place.

The speakers talked about the injustice of *all* wars and of the Vietnam conflict in particular. To some of the veterans among the hostile spectators, it all sounded foreign and Communistic. When the bearded young men and their girls chanted, "Hell no, we won't go," these veterans took it not only as an insult to the nation, but to themselves personally, since they *had* gone.

The highlight of the outdoor assembly was to be the draft-card burning. Three young men stepped forward in the bright lights of stage spotlights set up in front of the speakers' platform in the park. With them was a college teacher—one of the anti-war orators—and he flicked on a cigarette lighter as he made a speech about the symbolism of the card burning.

There were newspaper photographers there and television cameramen using their bright lights. All this publicity is something the rally leaders desired fervently.

Watching from the sidelines with other uniformed veterans, my husband was getting angrier and angrier, but was determined not to let any of the men there start a ruckus. That was something else some of the peace demonstrators wanted—TV exposure of themselves being persecuted by unfriendly older people, and by the police.

But tonight, the police and the older people seemed determined to have no such incidents.

Suddenly, however, the man next to my husband whispered to him, "Hey, Bob, isn't that your boy?"

Robert's eyes peered hard toward the cluster of three draft-card burners. They were all pretty much alike—about twenty-one years old, in the same kind of denim jackets, the same long hair and scraggily beards.

"Good Lord, you're right," Robert gasped as he recognized John.

He was frozen by surprise and by hurt pride, and realizing what the other men must think. "Aren't you going to do anything about that?" one of them now demanded, outraged.

"Yes, yes," Robert said, moved to action by the sharp note of criticism in the voices around him.

He pushed through the crowd, hard. He began shouting, "John, John, don't be a fool."

Some people shoved back at him as he elbowed his way along. Others pushed him forward. Only a few in the crowd knew why he was going toward the stage—that he was going to speak to his son. On both sides, those there to hold the anti-war rally and those who were there to oppose it, there was confusion. Confusion added to antagonism was bound to' blaze up into a fight.

Several policemen tried to get to Robert to stop him, thinking he was going to cause trouble. He moved swiftly on, and then John saw who was coming forward, and he stepped to one side and shouted to the policemen, "Let him come closer. Let him watch me do it."

But nobody heard much of this, nor much else that was spoken or shouted then. Because everybody seemed to be shouting at once now, and moving toward the stage. There weren't enough police to keep the two sets of opponents apart, and in the wild surge of the mobs, people were hit and slashed and stomped on. There were shouts and screams and obscenities flying through the air, and physical blows and beatings.

Squads of police cars began arriving and they broke up the melee. The officers used night sticks on some battlers, and there were a few arrests.

But, I thank God, neither Robert nor John was hurt or jailed.

But for Robert, the evening had been a blow as hard as any police billyclub could ever give. In agony he said to me that night, after telling me about John, "Why, Dorothy... why did he do it? What's happened to him lately? What made him change like this?"

I had no answers. Oh, I knew all the reasons given for the unrest in America today, and the rebellion among young people, and the generation gap, and how none of us are supposed to communicate any more. Yes, I knew all that. But it just didn't seem to apply to us and John. And yet there it was—the whole ugly mess blowing up in our faces.

That night, I forced Robert to go to bed right away, before John got home. I didn't think any more talk tonight would be advisable until they both calmed down.

I had hoped that would happen by the next morning, when I made them both sit down to breakfast. It was probably like expecting a miracle that we could just smoothly discuss anything so vital. And it didn't happen.

"All that long hair and those filthy clothes," Robert curled his lips in disdain. "And that wild crowd you hang around with," he accused John.

John was trying to stay cool, and be ironic with his father. "Does it bug you that I can dress like this, when you have to go conduct business in a suit and a tie? As for my friends . . ."

Robert blazed out, "Yes—those kids who are always drinking and having sex."

John almost lost his cool then, but he managed to maintain his hold on himself. "Some of them drink a little, and some of them make-out with girls they love."

"Love?" Robert shot back sarcastically. "Lust, that's what it is. They get drunk and then they fornicate."

"That's a lie," John said angrily. "In the first place, a lot of these kids don't touch liquor, not a drop, because they've seen so many of their parents dependent on alcohol —the ones who have to have several martinis before they can face anything."

"You've never seen me drunk," Robert stated.

"No. But you were lumping all these young people together. You don't know much about them. Some of them are great idealists. They want a better world."

"A better world—in which to dress like bums and fornicate like animals!"

I thought for a moment that John would get so mad that he'd fight back hard, or else just leave the table in disgust. But after a moment of pondering, he seemed to change the subject, although, later, I was to realize that he was following his own logical train of thought, and he was making his point subtly.

John began, "You know, Dad, it's peculiar, but right now I'm thinking of something I heard in a preacher's sermon once. He was talking about the fact that you notice in other people the things that are most prominent in your own thinking. I'm not putting this too well, Dad, but I'll give you an example. I used to lie a lot when I was a kid in grade school."

"You what?" Robert asked, indignant.

"Please let me finish for once," John requested. "I don't lie any more. It's useless But I did then."

"What did you lie about?"

"Oh, like I'd tell kids we went on picnics or that you took me to ball games on the weekends."

"Didn't I do that? I can't remember," Robert mentioned.

"No, you didn't take me. And I remember distinctly."

"Well, I was busy. You know how it is in business."

"Yeah, I know."

"It's fathers like me working hard that give you and those other bums a soft life—while you despise business and everything else that makes things nice for you."

My son just stared at him for a long moment coldly, then asked in contempt, "Are you through with the speech now?"

Robert started to rise as if to strike his son. "I'll *speech* you, young fella . . ." But he didn't hit him. He sat down again.

John continued, "So I lied like that—making everybody in school envy me because you took me to all those places, and you told me so many things. All untrue. But my point was that, as a liar, I became an expert on lying. I mean, I could tell when others were lying, usually, but worse, I began to think that others were liars, because *I* was. That's what that preacher was talking about—about how you project your own faults and fears onto others."

Robert was exasperated. "I just don't understand what you're getting at. I'm talking about you turning into a no-good beatnik with all those phony friends, and you . . ."

John wasn't about to try to explain anything. "Okay, okay," he said, waving his hands as if dismissing the entire matter.

Robert went to work, mentioning how difficult it would be today, what with everybody knowing and discussing his son, the draft-dodger.

It was then that I asked John if he was trying to ruin his father, and got that ironic answer implying that it had nothing to do with his father personally. His answer made me less and less sure that it didn't have something personally to do with his relationship with Robert. But I got no more out of him that morning.

The Cold War between them continued, with no open conflict. Oh, there were a few snide remarks made, mostly by my husband, but he couldn't lure John into a fight. I suppose Robert thought he could clear the air if they had a few more heated words. But things were at an impasse.

Of course I loved them both, my husband and my son, but admit I was feeling more sorry for Robert right then.

I'm not underestimating what John was going through. It was tough being a nonconformist and an anti-war demonstrator in that city. It would be easy for an outsider to see him only as a long-haired coward who didn't want to fight for his country, to which he owed everything. The long hair didn't bother me. To me, it was a fad and a facade. As for the part about him being a coward, no outsider could know as I did that he was a brave kid. And there hadn't been a more sober, loyal and grateful one in the world . . . until... until, as I said, about six months ago. What had happened to change him? I agonized. Would I ever find out?

But, anyway, as for the conflict between father and son, I leaned toward Robert. I sympathized with John, but I had lived for more than two decades with Robert and knew what all of this meant in suffering for him.

Robert had come from a poor family in a small town in the northern part of the state. I didn't know him then, because I was from a different state, but he told me later that he didn't wait to be drafted in World War II, but enlisted in the Army.

After he was discharged, he took advantage of the G.I. bill of rights to get a good education. It wasn't easy, because he had had very poor high school training in that small town, and hadn't even completed what was available, because of enlisting. But he pushed his way through college, working hard at both his studies and at a full-time job at nights.

He needed the income because he had met and married me, and after a few years we had John.

Working night and day after graduation, he made himself a very successful businessman in the city. We had all the good things of life —a very big, very comfortable house, two cars, a lake cottage, a nice vacation each year.

So Robert was very grateful to the country and to the society that made it possible for a poor boy to achieve so many comforts . . . a gratitude he felt should be shared by the son on whom this was all lavished.

I admit that when John now confessed about lying, I had a momentary pang. Looking back, I saw that occasionally I had done the same social fibbing—telling people that my husband had taken me somewhere or had done something for me that wasn't true. I had done it for the same reason John had, so that people wouldn't think that Robert was neglecting me, so they wouldn't feel sorry for me.

Looking back now, I saw how much he was away from us, how often his business commitments kept him from home. And for a youngster, this must have seemed as if Daddy might not love him, because Daddy was not there to do Father and Son activities, or available for Father and Son conferences at which the boy could ask questions and get guidance and advice.

But that was past. What about now? And what about the future? Could they ever get back together?

John continued to see his hippie friends, and be out with them evenings, sometimes very late. I worried about him, but I adjusted to it, and didn't agonize over his every coming and going.

So I was sleeping that night, not knowing he hadn't yet returned home by the middle of the night, when the telephone jangled, awakening me. Robert was answering it.

"Hello," he said. Whoever was on the other end said something, and then Robert pushed the receiver at me, saying sullenly, "It's John. He wants to talk to you."

"John, what is it?" I asked anxiously.

"Now don't worry, Mother, I'm all right. I've just been..."

"Yes, yes, what is it, John?"

"I've been arrested."

"Oh, no! What for?"

"It's a long story, Mother."

"What for?"

"Hit and run. And drunk driving."

"Oh, my Lord, no!"

My husband asked, "What is it?" but I couldn't pay any attention to him now.

My son said, "It isn't true, Mother. I didn't do it."

"What shall I do?"

"Come down and get me out. They've set a bail, but I'm sure you can arrange it with a bail bondsman here. After all," he added with just a touch of irony, "Father's references are very good."

"I'll be right there," I told him, and hung up.

My husband asked urgently, "What is it? What's the matter?"

"John—he's been arrested." I bit my lip. "For drunken driving . . . and . . . and a hit-run accident."

Robert sat down heavily on the bed. "Oh, Lord! How could a son of mine do anything like that?"

"He said he didn't do it."

"What else would he say, calling from the police station?"

As I hurriedly dressed, just a trace of irritation entered my voice, "Well, that's what he says, and before we make up our minds, we could wait until we hear his side."

Robert looked up at me in surprise and hurt. I was sorry to have been so curt with him, especially after his next words, which revealed what was biting at his insides: "And why did he want to talk to you? Why didn't he tell me?"

I had to tell him the truth: "Because you'd have said just what you said to me now—you didn't believe him. You might even have let him stay there, without bailing him out."

He was really in a sorry state now. "I might have. But do you think I really would have? Does he think that?"

"Possibly," I replied, finishing my dressing. "He doesn't know what I do—that you love him."

"Why doesn't he know that?"

"I don't think you've ever told him, and recently, your actions haven't given him any clue either."

I regretted having to leave him on that downcast note, but I had to hurry down to the station.

When I saw John, I gasped and my hand went to my mouth. His face had a cut and several bruises. "What happened?" I asked.

"I'll tell you later. Let's get out of here."

As we were leaving, a young policeman was coming out of an office in the corridor. His face also was bruised, and he and John stopped still when they saw each other, and daggers of hate flew from their eyes at each other. Then the officer went past us without a word.

I began, "John, did you and he... "

"Yes. He hit me."

"And you?"

"Let's get to that later. I'm getting sick of being in this place. Let's go."

They had impounded the car John was driving for evidence, so we got into mine and I drove off. "Well?" I demanded.

"Well, what, Mother? I told you I didn't do those things."

"And you also told us recently that you were a liar."

"*Was* a liar. And I've never lied to you, Mother, and never will."

I was touched, but didn't show it. "You mean that."

"Of course."

"You don't lie to me, John, but will you tell me the whole truth? There's a difference, you know? You could conceal or evade."

"I know. When you want the truth, Mother, just as I do. About the hit and run."

"Don't tell me now. You'll just have to repeat it all for your father."

John was puzzled. "Then what is it? What do you want to

know?"

"Last June," I began, "when you took that camping trip up north, something happened, didn't it?"

"Happened?" he evaded. "What's all this got to do with . . . ?"

"Don't sidestep. Something happened or you learned something that changed you. Isn't that correct?"

"Yes."

"What was it?"

"I can't tell you," he answered firmly.

"You said you'd tell me the truth about anything."

"Anything about me. What you're talking about . . . well, that isn't my truth to tell."

This completely baffled me, but there was no more time to probe further right then. We were home.

In the living room, my two men confronted each other.

"What happened to your face?" Robert demanded.

"A cop hit me."

My husband was in a black mood, and unfortunately he was tending to lecture. "He's not a cop. He's a police officer."

"Okay," John replied in bad grace, "this *police officer* assaulted me."

"Did you start it?"

John's smile was ironic. "That's what *he* said. Dad, you have a cop mentality. Excuse me, police *officer.*"

"Don't smart off to me like a punk."

"Isn't that what you think I am?"

I stepped in between them. "Please. This is getting us nowhere. Robert, let him tell what happened."

My husband shot back, "Let him tell his *story*, you mean."

John narrated, "My story begins when I lent the car tonight to . . . to a friend."

"Who?" Robert inquired.

"I can't tell you."

"Robert, let him finish."

John continued, "I only know what the police told me later—the car was in a hit-and-run accident. An old man was injured. He may not live."

"Oh, no," I moaned.

"Witnesses say the car was speeding and weaving on the road, as if the driver was drunk."

I asked. "Was he?"

My husband exploded. "Was he? You sound as if you believe what he's saying. That he lent the car to a drunken friend who hit some poor old man and..."

John spoke with deadly calm. "She *does* believe me. Why don't you?"

"Do you swear it's true?"

"You—my own father want me to swear I'm telling the truth!"

I said, "Please. Please. John, go on."

"Well, this guy brought the car back to me, not saying anything about the accident, of course, and I was driving a girl home. Witnesses at the hit-run scene got a good look at the car and at the license number, so all patrol cars had the description, and I was stopped."

"And then?" I asked.

"I knew nothing about the hit-run thing, so when we were forced off the road by this patrol car, I was mad. The only thought I had was that they were picking on me because I had the long hair . . . you know, the hippie scene. These two *officers* ordered us out of the car. I told the girl to sit right where she was, and I demanded to know why we were stopped.

"One word led to another, and these two officers pulled us out of the car. I had locked my door, but she'd forgotten to do the same. So one of them opened it and dragged her out. When I saw that, I yelled at them to stop, and I got out and tried to get him to let her go. We got in a fight."

"And that's all?" Robert asked.

"They found an open bottle of whiskey under the front seat."

"But not yours?" my husband inquired in a sarcastic tone.

"That's right—not mine. They wanted me to take one of those tests to see if I'd been drinking. I refused."

I asked. "Had you been drinking?"

"No."

"Then why . . . ?"

"The way they pushed me around and mauled that girl . . ."

Robert shoved in, "The way you probably had mauled her earlier."

John was fiery. "Don't you talk to me about mauling girls. Don't you accuse me of what..."

He looked at me, and then he stopped. He collected himself, and went on, "Anyway, I wasn't about to cooperate in any way with them."

"If all this is true," Robert said, "tell me the name of that boy who borrowed the car, and we'll have you off the hook."

"No. I'm not going to squeal on him."

Robert was almost uncontrollably angry. "You'd rather protect a hit-run driver than save your family name! It's bad enough to have a son who would have burned his draft-card in a public riot, but now to get his story in the paper—a drunken, hit-run driver."

The two of them had more angry exchanges, but John wouldn't back down or reveal the name of his friend.

After a while, we all went to bed, even if we didn't sleep any.

It all seemed a dreadful nightmare. And—joyously for Robert and me—it cleared up by the next day, we thought.

That was because John's friend went to the police station and admitted that he had borrowed John's car and was at the wheel, after drinking, when the old man was struck. He hadn't heard about John's arrest until the next morning when he awoke after a drunken stupor. When he learned what he had done and that someone else was blamed for it, he went right to the police.

"See," I pointed out to my husband later that day, "that boy had a sense of honor, even if he had done those terrible things while drinking."

"Yeah, yeah," my husband dismissed the incident. "Honor in a drunken bum. Well, at least that horrible mess is entirely over, and best forgotten. Isn't that right, John?"

"It isn't over," returned John.

"Of course it is."

"No. I'm going to get a lawyer to sue that cop for assaulting me."

My husband hit the ceiling. "Are you out of your head? You're darned lucky to get out of this at all, and now you're thinking of stirring up more trouble. I forbid it."

"You may forbid it, but I'm going to do it," John emphasized. "You're always emphasizing law and order. Well, he was the law, but he wasn't being orderly. He had no right . . . "

"Have you been talking to some of those leftist civil liberties lawyers today?"

"I've been talking to some lawyers, yes."

"Well, forget this idea of a lawsuit. The officer was doing his duty. You seemed to be asking for trouble, and he gave it to you."

"He assaulted me because to him I was a long-haired trouble maker—a hippie. He and the other one were rough-handling that girl because they think all young people like her are tramps."

"I can't blame him a bit for thinking so," Robert said.

"I know you can't," John returned wearily. "That's why we can't talk."

My husband waved his hands. "Oh, now we're going to hear about the lack of communication, the generation gap."

"Yup, that's right," John said in a steely tone, and he walked out.

I later learned that he went down to the police garage to

get his car, which was being released after being examined and photographed for the trial of the young man who had given himself up for hit-run driving.

Just going on duty, getting his patrol car at the garage, was the young police officer with whom John had fought the night before.

John was going to go about his business and ignore the officer, but the man stopped John. "Do you have a moment?" he asked.

"Why?" John replied hostilely.

"I want to show you something. Come along."

There was something soft in the officer's words and conciliatory in his manner that made John follow him into an office. Since the officer did not know that John intended to sue him in a civil action for assault, John was puzzled by his actions.

The officer began, "I wanted to say I'm sorry about what happened last night. My partner and I were upset. I know that officers in their performance of duty are not ever supposed to have normal human reactions—that's what some people say—but we did. We had just come from the scene of that hit-run that we thought you were responsible for. We'd seen the old man that had been hit, saw the blood, heard the poor old guy's moans as he lay there in pain. Here," he motioned to the photographs in front of them on the desk, "are some pictures of the victim. They aren't color, so you don't get the true effect, and you can't imagine the cries of pain."

John had winced as he saw them. And he could imagine what the young officer had felt who had to try to help this ancient man while the partner radioed for an ambulance. When John got home, he told Robert and me that he had of course abandoned any notion of suing the officer. He could see that both the officer and he had lost control of themselves and both acted badly.

He was about to leave the room, when I stopped him. "John," I reminded him, "you sort of made me a promise that when I asked you about something, you'd tell me the truth—the whole truth."

"Yes, what about it?"

"I'm asking you now—again—about what happened to you to change you after that camping trip."

John looked pained, then evasive, but finally determined. "All right. But I can go only so far. Then it's not my story any more, and not mine to tell."

"Then whose is it?" Robert demanded.

John looked straight into the eyes of his father. "Yours."

Robert war thunderstruck, but silent.

John began, "I told you I was going up north on a camping trip with my buddies. And that was true—up to a point. My real purpose was to enlist in the Army."

Robert almost laughed sarcastically. "You—you who were going to burn your draft-card for the TV cameras?"

"Yes, me. Don't you remember the old me, Dad, the one who respected you and wanted to win your favor in every way I could think of? No. I don't suppose you remember. You hardly knew I was around."

"John, that's not true," Robert said, hurt painfully by his son's words.

"Well, it seemed that way to me at the time. Maybe I was just too sensitive, like a kid will be. But that's how I felt. Anyway, I didn't want to be drafted. And I don't mean because I didn't want to serve in the Armed Forces. I mean I didn't want to be drafted I wanted to enlist. Like you did, Dad. I often heard you tell how you didn't wait to be drafted, but enlisted. I wanted to do the same, and I even wanted to emulate you by enlisting in the same place you did and maybe get in the same division you did. So while I was on that camping trip I went to your home town."

I saw my husband sort of shrivel up onto the sofa. He turned so ashen that I was alarmed that he had been stricken ill.

John finished, "As I say, the rest is not my story."

"What is it?" I pleaded.

In a hollow voice, Robert intoned, "He's saying it's *mine*. He learned all about it up in my home town." He looked up at John. "Tell her."

John faltered, "I can't—not to my mother."

"Tell it," Robert hissed with unexpected energy. "In a way, I'm glad it's out. I'll never again have to fear that she'll find out. She'll know."

"Please," I begged, "tell me what I ought to know."

John was fervent. "You want to know why I changed . . . why I seemed to want to *ruin* my father? Because he's a phony, a hypocrite," he shot out spitefully. "All these years I looked up to him and loved him and listened to his pious rules. Especially those about no drinking and no sex."

My husband looked beaten down, but in a ghastly voice he said, "John, can you ever believe I warned you about those things—not because I was a hypocrite, but because I wanted to save you from the hell that I went through because of them?"

John hesitated just a moment after that fervent statement, but then his anger seized him again. "You escaped your hell. You ran away."

"You can't escape," Robert said wearily. "It remains in your head and heart—that kind of sin remains."

I pleaded again, "Please tell me what you're talking about?"

Robert prompted gently, "Go on."

John did, but much less forcefully and with no rage now. "You know how he was always warning about drinking and sex? Well, it was like I was telling you about me and lying—I know about it and suspect others of it because I'm a liar. That's the way *he* is about lechery."

"Oh, no, don't say any more," I almost shouted, putting my hands to my ears.

"You listen," my husband said. "You have a right to know—maybe even a duty to know it, since it is breaking up our home."

"I learned all about my father in that home town of his. They remember him, all right! I suppose over the years that everything gets exaggerated, like his drinking. Nobody could drink as much as they say he did while he was in high school. But the girls—is that a myth also, Father?"

Robert didn't answer. He looked down on the floor now, stricken.

"Maybe a little," John continued, "but not the nice girl you ruined. She's very real. The nice girl you got pregnant. And so that you wouldn't have to marry her, you enlisted in the Army. Big patriot! You go off to the wars—not waiting to be drafted—you volunteered so that you escape doing the decent thing by the nice girl you seduced."

After he stopped, the silence hung heavy on the three of us. Finally, John spoke again. "I'm going to leave—I don't mean this room or this house. I mean, I'm going to leave the city and this state. I'll go someplace to college or to get a job. But I've got to get away."

My husband spoke heavily, "John, no matter what else you think of me, please don't ever think I don't love you. I do."

John went up to him. "I'm trying to let that sink in."

"Don't hate me."

"I'll never do that," John said fervently. "I was so disappointed about—about what I learned—just *because* I loved you so much. I practically worshiped you. But as for your loving me."

"I know," Robert said softly, "I never told you, but I hoped you'd know."

"Well," said John noncommittally. "Anyway, I think it best if I get out on my own for a while, to think things through."

I finally spoke at last. "It'll be good for all of us."

"Mother, I'm sorry about all this. I hope that what I've done and what I had to tell hasn't ruined things between you two."

Lifting my chin, I said bravely, "No, we love each other. We all love each other. And because of that, we'll come through this, each one of us, with flying colors."

We'll try. And with God's help, we'll succeed in each doing his duty and no one harrying anyone else. In other words, we'll be decent human beings. THE END

FAR FROM HOME:
A STORY OF LOVE, WAR,
AND RECOVERY

Like "In the Arms of a U.S. Marine," this story takes place during the second Gulf War. It's set five years later, though, and no longer feels the need to "argue" about whether the war is justified. Instead, it's able to concentrate solely on the relationship between Josh and Kate—from Kate's anxiety when her fiancé is deployed to the front lines to the raw frustration Josh feels when he's sent back home just a few months later with serious injuries. He tries to push her away, but she refuses: "We were planning to make vows to each other," she reminds him. "Vows about staying together, for better or worse."

The story benefits from the absence of political point making, with a tighter focus on the emotions many readers with loved ones of their own who came home from Iraq and Afghanistan wounded. Like the generations of soldiers' wives and girlfriends before her, Kate is prepared to stand by her man—but that doesn't mean she's going to go easy on him.

In their own way, everyone in our small, everybody-knows-your-business town seemed to quietly prepare for Josh to leave us behind. He would be the first official soldier from our community to leave for Iraq. And we all knew that Josh's tour of duty would likely stretch into months or years.

One day, Josh's high school football coach, Mr. Williams, actually teared-up when he saw Josh, his star quarterback from a few years ago. Right there in the produce aisle at the local grocery store, the old coach first offered his hand, but then grabbed Josh in a bear hug. And when he let go, there were tears in his eyes.

"You know we love you, Son," Mr. Williams said. "Take good care of yourself over there."

Mrs. Bradford, Josh's neighbor and calculus tutor in high school, gave Josh a tiny crucifix to carry in his pocket while he was a world away from all of us. All the guys at the gym, where Josh trained and lifted weights, bought his dinner at least once every week at their favorite sports bar. Josh's grandmother lit a candle at the church in her only grandson's honor. And Josh's mom cried silent tears whenever anyone mentioned that terrible day of goodbyes... the day that was drawing closer and closer.

There were many times I wanted to talk about my fears. While we watched a movie or talked on the phone or shared a pizza, I'd think about the words. But I didn't ever do anything more than think about them. I never said them. I didn't want to seem like I was overly concerned—and Josh hates drama.

Josh probably wanted to talk to me, too. But his concerns were different; like whether I would be tempted to date behind his back. Maybe I would suddenly take an interest in my obnoxious neighbor, the guy who stood by the swimming pool, flexing his muscles in the sun. Maybe he worried that I'd change my mind about our relationship. My concerns, which I kept carefully hidden behind my heart, were for Josh's safe return.

We struggled with how to say goodbye. We have been friends since we were skinny little kids with buckteeth, running through our grandparents' yards to catch lightening bugs in Mason jars. We declared ourselves in love with each other when we were dancing together at our junior prom. And then, a few months after high school graduation, I entered nursing school and Josh came to me with the most serious expression I've ever seen.

"I want to join the Marines," he said. "My grandpa was a Marine.

My dad was a Marine. I'm the only son. And I think I should serve my country."

We were barely nineteen years old. We have never spent more than a week apart. But obviously, this was something that called on Josh's heart.

"If that's what you want, then I will support your decision," I said, as my throat began to squeeze shut.

"Thanks," he sighed a visible sigh of relief. "Thanks for being so awesome, Kate. It's important to me."

"What about college?" I asked, trying to appear nonchalant.

"I'll enroll in college after I serve," he said with a shrug.

After a few moments, he slowly fell to one knee and presented a beautiful ring from his pocket. "I'll marry you, Kate," Josh said with a crooked grin. "If you'll have me, I mean."

I stared at his face and tears burned my eyes. "Married? You and me?" I whispered.

"Sure," he nodded. "We grew up together. We might as well grow old together, too."

"Makes perfect sense to me," I smiled as I framed his face with my hands. "I can't imagine not being with you."

"Here," he slipped the ring on my trembling finger. "It was my grandmother's ring. Do you like it?"

"It's beautiful, Josh," I smiled again. "I love it."

A few weeks after the proposal, Josh spent several miserable months in basic training. We talked on the phone when he got a spare moment. We sent emails, wrote letters, and we knew that in a few weeks we would be together again.

Who knows how I managed to keep my heart beating, but when Josh broke the news that he was being deployed to Iraq, the bottom fell out of my entire world. It was nothing at all like the feelings I had when he left for basic training. This was big. This was a war. This was a frequent topic on CNN, with death tolls.

"For how long?" I managed to ask.

"Maybe a year," he said softly. "Maybe longer."

"How do you feel about it?" I asked.

"I can't say I'm surprised," Josh said. "Of course, I don't want to leave you, Kate. But it's my job. It's the reason I've done all that training."

Every single day since Josh broke the news that he was being deployed, I have felt like hot coals were rolling around in my stomach. Neither of us knew how to cope with what it would be like to be a world apart for at least a year. We never spoke of the incredible pain we both expected to feel at that moment when Josh turned away from me to board the airplane.

"Maybe we should get married before you go," I said, half jokingly. "Let's just skip all that fuss and expense with big wedding plans."

"Your mom would kill us," Josh said with a laugh as he leaned toward me to kiss my nose.

"That's true," I said with a sigh.

"You can finalize the plans while I'm away," he said. "Sorry I won't be here to help."

"You almost sound sincere about missing the opportunity to taste test wedding cake and choose the best shade of blue for the cummerbunds," I said with a smile.

"I love you, Kate," Josh said as he ran his hand through my hair. "I really love you."

"Me too," I said, suddenly feeling like I couldn't breathe.

A giant knot began to swell from my chest into my throat. I was in so much pain, I could not breathe. Tears stung my eyes and I chewed my lip, willing the tears to go away and hide.

Josh placed his hand on top of mine and touched the diamond engagement ring on my left ring finger. "When I get back," he said. Then he stopped to clear his throat, which was crowded with thick tears. "When I get back, we'll have a perfect wedding and a beautiful honeymoon," Josh's eyes softened. "And then, we'll officially begin our lives together." I placed my hands on his face and fell in love all over again with the tenderness of Josh's heart.

"When you get back from Iraq . . ." I said in a whisper. "We'll be okay."

The night before he left, Josh's family and mine gathered for a cookout in his grandparents' backyard.

"You kissed me in that tree house," I said, as we sat together in the porch swing. "Remember that? We were maybe twelve years old."

"Then a few days later, you kissed Max Johnson," Josh said.

"We were playing *Spin the Bottle* at Molly's birthday party," I said with a giggle. "It was pure peer pressure. He meant nothing to me."

"I didn't want anyone else to kiss you," Josh smiled. "And I still never, ever want anyone to kiss you except me."

"Neither do I," I found myself blinking fast, to drive the tears away.

"Can you call to let us know you arrived safely?" Josh's mom asked as she walked toward the swing.

"I'm not sure, Mom," Josh said softly. "We land in Kuwait and go into Iraq in Humvees."

She dropped her head, and her lips were trembling.

"If I can call you, I promise I will," Josh said. Then he stood and embraced his mother. "It's ok," he said softly. "Try not to worry."

There were lots more tears at midnight, when Josh and I left for my apartment. His mother and dad, my parents, his sister and grandparents—all of them cried as they hugged Josh goodbye.

"Wow," he said as we got in the car to leave. "That was hard to do."

I reached across the seat and placed my hand on Josh's. There were no words for how I felt at that moment. I curled my fingers over his and held on tight.

For the rest of the night, we cuddled together quietly on the couch. We talked only about light subjects. We watched the sun come up, and then we silently got in the car and drove to the airport. By the time we got there, my body was actually trembling. My teeth chattered like I was freezing cold. Inside, I felt panicked. I was sure that all this time, trying so hard to stay strong for Josh's sake . . . all of it was going to go downhill. I was going to completely unravel, fall apart, get hysterical. I was dizzy from holding my breath and swallowing tears.

I felt Josh's eyes on me as we walked hand in hand through the airport. Suddenly, he stopped walking and turned to face me.

"Tell me, Kate," he said.

"Tell you what?" I barely whispered. "Tell you that I love you? You know that. Tell you that I don't want you to go?" I started to cry. The tears were hot, spilling into my hair and down my cheeks.

"Tell me what else you're thinking," Josh said.

"Nothing," I said, with my head down, so he couldn't read my face.

"Kate. . ."

All the months of dread and secret terror rose up and gushed in the form of uncontrollable sobs. "I'm so afraid for you," I cried as I buried my face against Josh's uniform. "I'm afraid for you to go there, Josh. I don't want you to carry a gun. I don't want you to aim a gun . . . I don't want any of this."

He held me tight, and I could feel his breath against my cheek and his hands in my hair.

"I'm sorry to put you through this," Josh whispered. "I really am."

"Please promise you'll come back," I sobbed now, without being able to breathe. My head was throbbing. My eyes burned. My heart was breaking in my chest.

"I'll do everything in my power to come home, Kate," Josh said. "You think I have any other goal but that one?"

His attempt at a joke fell on my hurting heart without a response.

"I'll write to you," I said as I tried to regain some composure. "And I'll send you plenty of pictures and newspapers, and whatever else you need. Okay?"

"I know you will," he ran his hand along the side of my face, tilted my face toward him and kissed me lightly on the lips.

"I love you, Kate. I've got to go," Then he turned and quickly walked away from me. Because I know Josh so well, I knew that was the only way he could leave. He refused to fall apart in front of me. I stood by the massive glass window and waited for the airplane to taxi and officially take my heart all the way across the world to Iraq.

Six days later, I received a short email that he had arrived safely. He promised to call soon. So my entire life immediately began to revolve around my cell phone. Our friends and family waited impatiently and stayed in constant contact with each other, hoping for hope that Josh was safe. Because of security issues, none of us knew where Josh was. So when I watched CNN and saw a bombing in Baghdad, I became weak in the knees with fear that Josh was there and that he was injured.

"I try to comfort Josh's mom," I said to my friend, Lisa. "I try to reassure everyone, but I have this terrible, nagging fear."

"Of course you do," Lisa said. "Josh's in a far away place, surrounded by war. It's only natural that you would fear for his safety, Kate."

"No," I said slowly. "It's more than that, Lisa. It's almost like a premonition."

"Don't say that," she snapped.

"I haven't told anyone else," I said as tears began to blind me. "But somehow, I feel it in my bones, Lisa. Something bad is going to happen."

"No," she said flatly. "You must push those thoughts out of

your mind. We're planning your wedding, Kate. We're finding the perfect honeymoon spot. We're not going to think about anything that isn't positive."

"Yes," I finally nodded, although my heart still felt the same. It was almost like my mind and my emotions were preparing for a loss, a crisis, a pain that was bigger than me.

Two months after Josh was sent to Iraq, my nightmare was realized.

Just before dawn, Josh's father was knocking on my apartment door. As I scrambled out of bed, grabbed my robe and opened the door, I knew that our lives would never be the same. I could hardly stand as I leaned against the doorframe for support.

"Katie Did," Josh's father, Thomas, has called me that sweet nickname since I was a little girl. But never has he said it in a trembling voice, with tears rushing over his rugged face.

"Tell me," I whispered. I pressed my lips together and willed my heart to keep beating.

"Josh has been injured," Thomas said.

I heard shreds of phrases such as "road side bomb . . . " "medvacked to Germany ... " "not sure the extent of the injuries . . ."

"But he's alive," I said in a small voice that wasn't mine. "He's still alive." I grabbed the door frame, fearful that I would slide down the wall like a rag doll. My legs were shaking uncontrollably. "What now?" I managed, trying hard to clear my head so I could listen and think.

"Pack a bag," Thomas said. "The Marines are flying Josh from Iraq to Germany. When he's stabilized, he will be transported to the Naval Hospital in Bethesda, Maryland."

I nodded. And Josh's father stared at me for a long moment. I had never noticed until this moment, that Josh's jaw line was exactly like his dad's. I never paid attention until this moment, to the fact that his shoulders were the same and his eye color was the same. I swallowed hard, wishing I could somehow get my heart to slow down.

"Did you hear me, Kate?" Thomas asked. "Are you okay? Should I wait for you to pack or can you drive yourself to our house?"

"I'm okay," I lied. "I'll be there in less than an hour."

"We can't actually leave for at least a day," Thomas said. "But we'll all wait together by the phone. The Marines are supposed to call with updates."

"Yes," I said, trying to make my lips move and sound half way intelligent.

"Well then, I'll see you in a while," Thomas said. "Just pray for him, Katie."

Thomas covered his face with his hands and sobbed. I reached out to him, patted his shoulder. I could not bring myself to embrace him, I was afraid if Thomas' pain touched mine, I would shatter into a million pieces.

"Josh needs us," I whispered. "We have to be strong."

Thomas nodded and sniffed and sighed heavily. "I've got to get home," he said in a low voice. "We'll wait for you there."

I closed the door, walked numbly to the bathroom, turned on the shower and collapsed on the shower floor in hysterical tears.

I don't think I've ever prayed that way in my lifetime. I don't think I've ever envisioned Josh before, as a broken man. I prayed for strength and for wisdom. I prayed most for Josh's survival. I have no idea how long I sat on the shower floor, sobbing and praying.

"I can't live the rest of my life without him," I whispered when I finally stepped out of the shower, still trembling. "I will do everything I can do to keep Josh alive."

Within twenty-four hours, Josh's parents, grandparents, siblings, and I gathered in silence. On the airplane, third row from the front, I sipped a cup of bad coffee. None of us knew what to expect. *What in the world does "extensive injuries" mean? Would Josh still have all of his appendages? Would he be blind or maybe paralyzed? Was this real?*

All of it was immediately very real to me as we walked through a crowded ward filled with bandaged soldiers. Some of them had lost legs or arms. Some of them spoke in slurred sentences. All of the situation became real to me when we were directed toward the bed in the corner by the only window. Half of Josh's face was bandaged. His left arm was covered with a thick bandage. His left leg was slightly elevated from the mattress and covered with bandages. His eyes were closed. His face was a ghostly white.

"My baby," Josh's mother began to sob. She fell to her knees beside the bed. She tenderly ran her fingertips along the side of Josh's shoulder and buried her face in the sheets.

"Mary, honey," Thomas tried to soothe her. But it was obvious that he too was overcome by the realization that his only son really was under all those bandages.

Trembling, I walked around to the other side of the bed and rested my cheek against the coolness of Josh's skin. My heart jumped, just at the touch of his face to mine.

"I love you," I whispered. "We will make it through this, Josh. You do the fighting. And we'll be your cheerleaders."

We held vigil at Josh's bedside for hours that turned into days. We rarely ate. None of us changed clothes. We didn't talk very often. We just sat there, willing Josh every good feeling and every positive thought that we could possibly muster.

Around noon on the fourth day, Josh's eyes fluttered and he groaned.

"You're safe, Son," Thomas said quickly as he cupped Josh's shoulder.

"We love you, honey," Mary said. "You're going to be ok."

I couldn't speak at all. I made eye contact with Josh and every single moment between us, from elementary school to this moment, buzzed through my mind with so much love that I was frozen in place. There was no way I could speak. I was drowning in hope, love, and fear.

Within a few days, Josh was struggling to sit up in the bed. He was reaching for me and smiling that sweet, crooked smile.

"I'm so weak," he muttered, disgusted by the fact that his dad had to help him rearrange the pillows.

"Give it time, Son," Thomas said. "Let your body heal."

When the doctor sat down with all of us, including Josh, he explained that jagged pieces of shrapnel had torn through the muscles and tissues of Josh's arm and leg.

"You may never regain full use of your arm," the doctor said gently.

"And you will need to work very, very hard, to ever walk again without a cane."

We listened with stunned faces and heavy hearts.

When the doctor left, Josh's parents excused themselves. They said they wanted to take showers and change clothes at the motel. But I could see on their faces that they both needed time away from their son, to fall apart, to grieve, to scream and cry their pain for him.

I stared at my hands, unable to think of what I could ever say to Josh that would sound encouraging. That's when I noticed that his body was shaking with tears. It was an action that had no sound. It was like Josh was crying from the inside, from the bottom of his soul.

Still, I couldn't make words come from my chest. So I quietly and carefully crawled into the bed with him. I curled my body around his and placed my face against his beating heart.

"I will love you through this," I whispered as the tears came. "We all will, Josh. We will love you through all of it. We will be with you, every single step of the way. I promise."

"I don't want to be a burden to you, Kate," he said. "From the way it looks, I can't even use the left side of my body."

"I don't care," I said as I pressed my lips to the side of his neck. "I don't care about anything except loving you."

As the days went by, Josh's hospital room was plastered by greeting cards from home. Entire classrooms of children wrote sweet, messy notes wishing their hometown hero good wishes.

Weeks later, after lots of physical therapy and several painful surgeries, Josh accompanied us on the flight back home.

His father helped him to his feet and we waited for the flight attendant to get a wheelchair.

"I want to walk off the plane," Josh suddenly said.

"But Honey. . . ." Mary started to argue.

Thomas patted her arm with a quiet message, "Let him try."

We held our breath as Josh hobbled off the plane, leaning on the cane. Most of the residents of our town were there, crowded close, shouting Josh's name and waving American flags. Tears streamed down their faces as they welcomed Josh home. My heart swelled with pride. Neither of us had come home as the same people we were when we left. Josh was truly a man now, a deep thinking, and deep feeling man with a long road of recovery ahead of him.

I was different, too. I was no longer a ditzy, nursing student with my head in the clouds. I was a woman, with the man I loved beside me, and I didn't care what was required to help Josh survive. Those elaborate wedding plans now seemed childish. My life with Josh wasn't at all about planning the big event. It was about staying close to him, breathing in his scent, silently willing him hope and patience.

A few steps into the crowd, Josh gingerly sat down in the wheelchair. With a defeated look on his face, he looked at me and tried to grin.

"That was awesome," I said. "I had no idea you could walk that far. Hang on, though, because your Dad is pushing the chair to the car."

We smiled at each other and my chest loosened a little bit. I had discovered that I had to celebrate the small steps, and try to make light of everything about the wheelchair, the cane, and the therapy.

Two days after Josh was home, he started to avoid me. I could feel him pulling away. He refused my calls. He ignored me when I visited.

"Tell me what's going on," I finally said. "Have your feelings changed?"

"Kate, I don't want to hurt you," he said. "But I need to be alone."

"For how long?" I asked in a trembling voice.

"For a long time," Josh said with a sigh. "And I think it would be best if you just. . ."

"If I just what?" My heart was barely beating—it was throbbing with pain.

"It would be best if you just went on with your life," he said slowly.

"But you are my life," I said quickly. "What are you talking about? How can you possibly be serious? We're a team . . . we . . . we go together, Josh. We always have."

"Not anymore," he said. Then he turned the wheelchair away from me. "I think you should go now, Kate."

I stood there, feeling my entire body flush with heat.

"No," I said finally.

"Kate," Josh breathed. "Don't make this more difficult."

"Talk to me," I said slowly. "Please Josh, just talk to me."

"I have nothing more to say," he said rather flippantly. "I've changed, Kate. And I think it's better for you if we. . ."

"You don't decide for me what's good for me," I snapped. "You don't get to dump me like I'm someone you barely know and not expect some kind of fight, Josh. You know me better than that."

We sat there in silence, for some long, tense moments.

"Talk to me," I said again as tears slipped down my face.

"Talk to you about what?" he asked. "Talk to you about how it feels not to be able to button my own shirt or cut my meat by myself? Talk to you about how hard it is to get out of my bed?" As he said these things, his voice got louder and his face crumbled in pain. "Talk to you about how it feels to be afraid to go to sleep because I have such terrible nightmares?"

Josh quickly hurled the wheelchair around, crashed into the table and threw the lamp across the room.

"Which one of those things can I talk to you about, Kate? Which one do you think you can truly understand?"

I sat there, partially terrified by the anger I had never seen him display. But the other part of me knew that it was an anger mixed with incredible pain.

"I said for you to get out," Josh shouted now, and his eyes were full of tears.

His parents came running into the room and he shouted at them, too, to get out and leave him alone.

"Come on, Katie Did," Thomas said. "I think Josh needs some time alone."

"No," I said stubbornly as I folded my arms and sat back in the chair. "I am not leaving."

Thomas and Mary sheepishly ducked out of the room and we were left there alone. Josh glared at me, then stared out the window.

"What do you want from me?" he asked finally.

"I'll tell you what I want from you," I said slowly. "I want you to give me a little bit more credit."

"What are you talking about?" he asked. "Are we going to make this about you?"

"No," I shook my head. "Apparently, Josh, we're going to make it about you and your personal pity party and the fact that you apparently don't think I have what it takes to stand by you."

Immediately, I was sorry. From Josh's face, I could see that my words had apparently stung him. But in a way, I needed for him to be stunned, at least for a few more moments, so I could be heard.

"Your arm doesn't work so good right now," I said. "Big deal. I'll be your arm. And your leg is weak. So what? When you need a leg, I'll be your leg."

"I don't want to be your charity case, Kate," Josh said in a whisper. "Don't you understand that?"

"Loving you and supporting you means you're my charity case?" I looked at him for a long moment. Then I grabbed my purse and stood. "We were planning to make vows to each other. Vows about staying together, for better or worse."

"Kate, I'm sorry," Josh couldn't look at me now.

"I'll tell you, I guess I should be glad it wasn't me who returned from the war with injuries, Josh. In your world, I guess I would have needed to push you away from me before you walked away on your own."

Josh hung his head, avoiding my face.

"I'm guessing our relationship wasn't what I thought it was," I said. "Because in my world, two people who love each other don't walk away from each other just because the going gets a little bit tough. I don't want to be married to a quitter."

Silently and with trembling fingers, I removed my beloved engagement ring and left it on the table as I left the house.

Leaving Josh that way was the most painful thing I've ever done in my life. I was nearly a block away before I realized I was holding my breath. In all the years we have known each other, we had never spoken to each other in those tones. We had never raised our voices. We had never threatened each other with goodbye.

For nearly a week, I attended classes, walking across the campus like I was shell shocked. I avoided my friends, my family and my telephone. I couldn't bear to believe that Josh was really driving me out of his life. But then again, I questioned whether he truly did want to be left alone. Maybe his healing was about more than I could ever understand. Maybe it really was a journey he wanted to make alone.

Early one Saturday morning, I sat on my front porch with a cup of coffee and the unread newspaper. I was staring blindly at nothing, thinking about all the years Josh trailed me on his bike, or walked me home from school, or kissed me on this porch swing where I now sat alone.

"Hey," Josh's voice came from my far left, near the trees.

When I looked in his direction, I saw him leaning against the elm tree. He was wearing his favorite Cubs hat. He had a baseball mitt in his hand.

"Well, good morning," I tried to sound not too cheerful, not too shocked, and definitely not too excited.

"I wanted to play some ball today with the guys," Josh said as he hobbled toward me with his cane.

"Yeah?" I stood slowly, with my heart fluttering around in my chest.

"I thought I'd see if I could borrow your leg and your pitching arm," he said.

I went down the steps and met him in the yard, with tears in my eyes. "You're welcome to both," I said. "But don't bet money on my batting average."

Josh placed the ball cap on my head as he pulled me into his arms. "I love you, Kate," he said.

"Then let me be your leg and hand until you can use your own again," I said.

"Only if you'll let me have your heart," Josh said. "Forever. Okay?"

"Of course," I said. "Forever and no matter what." THE END

Ron Hogan co-founded Lady Jane's Salon, a monthly reading series dedicated to romance fiction, and has been its primary host since 2009. He's also produced literary events throughout New York City, and was one of the first people to launch a book-related website, Beatrice.com. In addition to digging through the TruLoveStories archives for great stories, he publishes a digital magazine (also called Beatrice!) of interviews with some of today's best writers.